APPENDICITIS

The man who goes into the hospital won't

be the same man who comes out, if

he makes it out.

Dr. Randy Hines II

Hines Entertainment Group
P.O. Box 106
Mableton, GA 30126

HinesEntertainment.com

Author: Dr. Randy Hines II
Illustrator: Nnika Taylor
Cover design: Damonza.com

ISBN: 9781799224129

TABLE OF CONTENTS

INTRODUCTION

AND

ACKNOWLEDGEMENTS

Thank you for purchasing my book! It really means a lot to me and I really do appreciate it. My goals for this book are to both entertain and educate you, the reader. I believe that this book has accomplished both of these tasks. If you don't read books often, that's okay. This book will engage you enough that in the end you will be happy you read it. If you read books often, try not to finish it all in one day. Y'all know how y'all do.

This book will make you think, laugh, and open up your eyes to things you've never thought about, and for some it might open old wounds or trigger old feelings. Sorry. It will surely cause you to look at life differently. I say this not as a boast, but as a warning. *Appendicitis* is full of many twists and turns that will keep you guessing. It's a rollercoaster of emotions, action-packed scenes, and a hefty dose of sarcasm. Some jokes you may get, while others you may not. It's ok if you don't get some of them. They made me laugh. There are some educational opportunities in this book, as well. I want you to learn.

From idea to pen to paper, this book has been almost a decade in the making, way longer than I anticipated or would have liked it to be. However, I am truly proud of it. I want to thank God and my parents for helping me develop into the man I am. I couldn't have written this book without the values, lessons and skills they instilled in me. These include the art of storytelling, humor, recognizing feelings and emotions, and many other character traits. Without them, this book would not be possible. I love you infinity times infinity, plus one. Also, thank you to my friends who received advance copies and read either part of it or all of it. Your honest feedback is much appreciated.

There are many individual stories in this book. I won't spoil them for you. However, these stories may relate to you, one of your family members, or one of your friends. I believe that everyone has a story and this book depicts some of the common struggles of others. I hope this book will encourage you to strike up dialogue about its themes with others, one-on-one, in a book club, or on social media. Please don't be afraid to share with others. On my website there are a list of discussion questions that you may use to supplement your discussion. You can also find merchandising products related to the book. Yes, book merchandise! We legit over here. So, don't forget to visit HinesEntertainment.com. Now, a little bit about me.

ABOUT
THE
AUTHOR

D r. Randy Hines II is a board-certified family medicine physician who was born and raised in the great city of Port Arthur, Texas. He is the only son of two wonderful parents, Randy and Jeanne Hines. After having him, they decided not to have any other children because they realized he was the perfect son for them.

While growing up, Dr. Hines was often asked by strangers if he played basketball because of his tall stature. He would often sarcastically respond no and that he was on the swimming team. This would often leave people confused and stunned. He took great delight in them being confused because it bought pure joy and laughter to his soul. Dr. Hines is an avid basketball player and enjoys listening to various types of music as well as debating music topics.

In the early 2000s, Dr. Hines attended Prairie View A&M University in Prairie View, Texas. Originally upon attending this prestigious institution, he had aspirations of obtaining a degree in Biology and working at NASA. He then realized that he watched too many sci-fi movies and that he needed to stay on Earth. It was early in his freshman year in college that he decided to pursue becoming a physician. He obtained a bachelor's degree in Biology with a minor in Chemistry and later, a master's degree in Biology. Somehow in the midst of attaining these degrees, he became a member of the Zeta Beta chapter of Kappa Alpha Psi Fraternity, Inc. After acquiring these degrees, he then matriculated into the University of Louisville School of Medicine and received his doctoral degree. He completed his residency training in Atlanta, Georgia and today practices in the suburbs of Atlanta. He attends church three out of four weekends a month because God said he needed to rest on the fourth. He hopes that you will enjoy the book as much as he has enjoyed writing it. Now, off to reading you go. Enjoy the book.

CHAPTER 1

A

SICK

BUMBLEBEE

"What's the score?" asks Allen.

"Eleven up," I yell, out of breath while dribbling the basketball.

The game was now tied. We had come all the way back from five points down to even the score. Whoever scored the next point would win the heated contest. I always had a love for comeback victories. There was something about them that made them more meaningful, more memorable, and frankly more enjoyable. My greatest comeback victory was a doubles game of ping pong against my ex's new boyfriend in college. We were down 3 to 18, playing to 21. I thought, *I'll be damned if he beats me! Anyone but this lame.* And he didn't. My teammate and I came all the way back and won the game. They didn't score another point. Victory was mine! And victory was also mine when my ex-girlfriend came to visit me that night.

"Jermaine! Come set a pick," I shout. Jermaine sprints in my direction and sets a firm pick on my defender. I drive hard to the right, pounding the basketball toward the basket. The path to the basket is wide open, more open than the HOV lane at 2 a.m. I pick up my dribble and take two long strides before jumping in the air for the game-winning layup. While in the air, the klutz of the gym, Fat Steve, jumps toward me in an attempt to block my shot.

Fat Steve is a man of tremendous girth. He's approximately 5'9" and weighs just a smidge over 300 pounds. His neck is short, and his calves are wide. He wears every piece of Nike gear one could possibly purchase at a sporting goods store. A yellow Nike headband on his head. Yellow Nike wrist bands on each arm. Yellow Nike volleyball knee pads on his arthritic knees. White Nike T-shirt.

Navy blue Nike shorts. Black Nike shoes. Fat Steve is a walking advertisement for how not to dress when playing basketball.

He's notorious for "accidentally" injuring players. Partly because of his size, but also because of his hustling nature. Fat Steve plays as though he's a walk-on trying to earn a scholarship. Three weeks ago, he dove on someone trying to get a loose basketball. Damn near took the guy's head off. The guy almost fought Fat Steve after he got up with a bloody brow. It took two of us to hold the guy back. Fat Steve apologized profusely, but the guy didn't want to hear it, he just wanted blood for blood. I haven't seen him play here since.

In the air, I glance at Steve and then back at the wooden basketball backboard. I lay the ball smoothly off the backboard and simultaneously I'm clobbered by Fat Steve. We both crash to the floor and I hit my head. I lie underneath 300 pounds of a mediocre basketball player, seeing stars and wondering if I made the game-winning shot. My teammates roll him off me.

"Did I make it?" I ask after I'm able to see daylight again.

"Of course!" Jermaine informs me as he pulls me up off the floor. I clap my hands loudly in celebration.

My teammates proceed to give me sweaty half hugs and damp high fives in celebration. I've loved playing with these guys since moving to Louisville. These were my new friends. We played basketball early in the morning once a week in a small run-down recreational gym. This was my stress relief. Everyone has one. Some people have food, some people have alcohol, and others have cigarettes. Basketball is mine. Nothing distracts me from life's troubles more than basketball.

"Good shot, Daniel. I can't believe you hit that shot. You lucky I didn't have my good Nikes on. I surely would have thrown that in the stands," says Fat Steve followed by a jovial laugh. We all sit on the metal stands changing out of our sweaty clothes. "Did you play basketball in college?"

"Thrown my stuff in the stands Fat Steve? Yeah, right. And no, I didn't play in school. I wasn't smart enough to make good grades and play basketball at the same time. Not with my major. So, I gave up on my hoop dreams in high school."

"Where are you from again?" asks Steve.

"Port Arthur, Texas, and I went to school at Texas Southern University."

"Oh yeah, you from P.A., home of UGK. One of the greatest rap groups of all time. Pimp C had the best verse on that song Big Pimpin' they did with Jay-Z. Somebody told me that when they say 'big pimpin' in P.A.T.' on the hook they were talking about Port Arthur, Texas. I was always like, 'who in the world is Pat?'"

"Yep that's true. We've had a lot of famous people come out of our city. Janis Joplin, Jamaal Charles, Jimmy Johnson, and of course, me."

Everyone laughs.

"What's so funny?"

"Man, you a fool. You're not famous. I bet y'all country as hell down there in P.A. Y'all probably wear cowboy hats and boots. I bet your mascot was like a crawfish or a picture of a cow being tipped over."

"No, it wasn't a cow. It was a bumblebee." I snap back, which is followed by exuberant laughter by the other basketball players. I can't help but laugh, as well. It was a country mascot. I wouldn't dare tell him that we yelled "sting 'em" at opponents. That would only add fuel to his country bumpkin argument. I begin putting on my hoodie and sweats while thinking of a witty comeback.

"See. I was right! A country ass mascot."

"Man, forget you, Fat Steve. I loved my country high school mascot. It struck fear in the heart of opponents far and wide. I don't have time to argue with you all day about mascots. I have to head home. I haven't been feeling well since I woke up. I was a little queasy earlier and threw up. However, I still came through to play and performed well under pressure. Unlike your dad under your mom last night."

"Ooohhhhh," scream all the players. One of the players throws a towel in the air as he laughs. Allen, our basketball court, jester rolls on the ground laughing. You could have sworn that joke lit him on fire. Fat Steve doesn't say a word. He just puts his head down in defeat. I lightly jog out of the gym on a high note to the front door.

I open the front door and feel the arctic winter air slice across my bare face. It is the middle of December, and we are experiencing a winter like no other. Well, no other for a Texan like me. I'm not used to 12-degree wind chill and wearing eight layers of clothes. On some days, I feel like Randy from a Christmas story, with the many layers of clothes I have on to keep warm.

I get outside and gingerly begin to take steps toward my 2004 black Honda Accord. I say my steps aloud with the hopes that this will help prevent me from slipping on the icy path. Left foot. Right foot. Left foot. Right foot. Leeeeefffftttt fooooootttt. My left foot starts to slip in my black high-tops. *Hold it together, Daniel.* My feet begin to skate back and forth, kicking up ice like Nancy Kerrigan. *Oh, why me!? Why me!?* I regain my balance. That was close. I continue cautiously walking to my car and eventually make it. A big, airy sigh of relief exits my mouth as I collapse onto the car's roof. I slide into my car and turn the heat on broil. Lil Boosie blasts through the speakers as I begin to warm up.

"Mmmmhhh," I groan as I grab my right side. It is throbbing with pain. *I must have pulled a muscle trying to stop myself from falling,* I think. As I turn down the ratchet music and begin to back out of my parking space, my phone begins to ring. "WIFEY" pops up in bold capital letters on the screen. The internal mental debate then ensues. To answer or not to answer.

I mean, I love talking to my Sweet Cakes, but I just want a quick little break from talking to her. Honestly, a break from talking to anyone. I just want some me time. I've learned in marriage that you rarely get this and that this time is very precious. Wifey is always around. I go to sleep, she's there. I wake up, she's there. I use the bathroom and unfortunately, she's also there. There's nothing like getting a moment alone.

However, I've also learned that marriage is about sacrifice. I must sacrifice myself for the betterment of the marriage. That's the only way we're going to make it through together. Despite my selfishness, I love hearing the voice of my Sweet Cakes. The voice of the angel I fell in love with four summers ago.

We met at a swanky Kentucky Derby party in the Galleria area of Houston, Texas. I had never been to the Kentucky Derby, but I always had been intrigued by the fanfare for the event. This party attempted to emulate the event while the race played on various big screens in the restaurant. The event was packed and very upscale. Gentlemen dressed in fine tailored blazers and slacks. Women dressed in colorful dresses and hats with brims bigger than Saturn's rings. There were cutouts of horses plastered on the walls and cocktails named after each horse in the race. This party attempted to embody every bit of the spectacle along with an open bar and appetizers. Since I couldn't make it to the event in Kentucky, this by far was the closest thing to wet my whistle.

It was at the appetizer table where I literally ran into this beautiful brown-skinned beauty with a booty. Her mouth was full of meatballs and her small plate was loaded with barbecue chicken wings and cheese. All of these items instantly spilled on to my cream-colored blazer as she turned away from the table.

"I'm so sorry," she apologized as she attempted to wipe the barbecue stains off my jacket. However, this only made the stain worse. It smeared even further.

"Now you have to buy me a drink," I told her.

"But the drinks are free," she said while continuing to smear the stain on my jacket.

"Well that should make it even easier for you," I sarcastically stated back.

She got me that drink and we talked for the rest of the night. Partly because I couldn't approach any other women with a huge barbecue stain on my blazer. But more so because I didn't want to talk to anyone else. She was the most beautiful woman at the party. Men and women alike turned their heads when she walked. Men looked to check out her curves in her sexy red dress, while women looked with envy to see if her purse matched her shoes. Her purse matched her shoes. It always did. She exemplified grace and elegance, but she also had a teaspoon of sarcasm, which I found to be totally sexy. That day, I knew I had found the love of my life. The love of my life who I would answer the phone for after the fifth ring.

"Hey, Sweet Cakes."

"Hey, my love. What are you doing?"

"Just got done playing my last game, and I'm about to head back home. "

"How'd you do?"

"Won three and lost one. I hit the game winning shot for the last game. They can't hold me, son!"

"You tell 'em babe. They can't hold you. Just like you couldn't hold your food down this morning. I heard you throwing up."

"You heard that? Yeah, my stomach was a little upset this morning. It must have been something I ate."

"Well the only thing you ate this morning was the breakfast I cooked you. I hope it wasn't that."

"No, Sweet Cakes, it wasn't that. That breakfast was great. Thanks for making it for me." Actually, it may have been that. The breakfast was horrible. The full-hearted attempt at eggs and toast was a disaster. The eggs were so runny they could have won a gold medal in the Olympics. The toast was bright yellow on one side and Wesley Snipes black on the other side. She tried to keep the Wesley side face down, but I saw it after picking it up to bite it. "How's your toast babe?" she asked. "Fit for a vampire slayer," I replied. We both laughed, but for totally different reasons.

"Well, do you feel better?"

"Yes, I feel a little better. Still a little queasy, but now my right side and hip hurt. I think I pulled a muscle after I almost slipped and fell walking to my car."

"Hmph. Now does your hip hurt or does it hurt right above your hip? Press on your hip bone and tell me if it hurts."

I pressed on what I thought was my hip bone and the pain didn't worsen.

"Nope. No pain."

"Now, does your pain hurt right above that area?"

"Yeah. I guess. I hope you're not trying to go all Dr. Gregory House and diagnose me. I hate when you try to diagnose me. Please stop. I just pulled a muscle and that's it."

"I'm sorry, babe, but this is what I do. I'm a doctor, and sometimes I can't turn it off. Just like you can't turn off your engineer brain when you see electrical stuff. So, you talked to me about your symptoms and you opened the door. So, I moseyed on through."

"You must have not read the sign outside the door. It said whites only. I don't trust you Negro doctors."

"I hate you and your face. Do you know how hard it is for a black doctor? Let alone a female black doctor."

"Yes, Sweet Cakes I know. You tell me melanin medicine stories at least once a week. Subliminal racism stories, menstrual cycle chronicles, and discussions of how to keep your hair nice while on the go. Those are our weekly conversations. So yes, I know."

"And don't you forget it! It's hard being a black. And even harder being a black physician sometimes. What's our saying baby?"

"Melanin all day every day," I grumble.

"Yes, melanin all day every day. I can't take this black off. Nor do I want to, but sometimes it does pose a challenge."

"In case you forgot I'm black too! I'm black mixed with education. So, I know how it is. Now, what are you diagnosing me with Dr. House?"

"Well on my differential is gastritis, Crohn's disease, appendicitis, kidney stone, and just for fun, ruptured ovarian cyst."

"Ruptured ovarian cyst? Aren't ovaries in women? Last time I checked, I didn't have ovaries so we can cross that off the list. You also forgot to say muscle strain, which is what I have. This is not an episode of House with some complicated diagnosis. It's a muscle … aaaahhhh," I groan as my side starts to hurt again.

"It's not a muscle strain, honey. I'd consider that if you were moving and having pain. However, currently you're having pain at rest. Also, this morning you were nauseated and threw up. If I were a betting woman, I'd put my money on appendicitis. You need to go to the hospital. Immediately."

I could hear it in the tone of her voice that she was concerned for me. Instead of a suggestion, she said I needed to go. Immediately. As much as we laughed and joked together, she did have a serious side that saw the light when necessary. This was one of those times. I respected her judgment and insight into the crazy world of medicine.

Friends and family members call, text, or send Facebook messages asking medical questions that she always has an answer for. *No, it's nothing major, but make sure you go to the doctor. Yeah, that's serious; make sure you get that checked out immediately. Just take some Benadryl, and the rash will go away.* These were some of the various responses I would hear her telling them. Now, it's my time to receive the advice, and put my trust in my wife.

"Okay. I'll go get checked out. Just for you. What hospital should I go to?"

"Just go to the new University Hospital. I'll text one of the doctors I know in the ER to let them know you're coming. You shouldn't have to wait long to be seen. That's one of the perks of having a wife in medicine."

"Is it too late to go back?"

"To go back where?"

"To my old girlfriend. She's not a doctor. She wouldn't make me go to no stupid hospital."

"Yeah, you can go back to her. Right after you get evaluated at the hospital."

"Okay, Sweet cakes. I'll take the back roads since the highway is probably still icy."

"Okay. Text me when you get there. Love you."

"Love you more."

-

CHAPTER 2

THE POINT

of

NO RETURN

As I enter the emergency department waiting room, a security guard promptly instructs me to remove all metal objects from my pockets. It baffles me that hospitals need metal detectors. I know they're needed for safety, but who would think to bring a knife or loaded gun into a hospital? Who are they going to shoot? A dying patient? A nurse? A doctor? That wouldn't make any sense at all. Nevertheless, I proceed to take everything out of my pockets and put it in a tray. In the tray goes a wallet with 21 dollars, a black Galaxy phone with a partially cracked screen, and a Batman keychain holding a large assortment of keys that could rival any janitor's set.

I've always admired Batman but did so even more after watching the movie *Batman Begins*. He overcame so many obstacles in that movie. He lost both of his parents, traveled overseas for superhero training, ordered weapons that didn't work, and his house burned down. That's a lot for one man to triumph over, even in one fictitious movie. Yet, despite all these hurdles, he found a way to accomplish his goal of protecting Gotham from corruption. Hence, Batman serves as an inspiration for me. Whenever I work, I take on the mindset of Batman and don't let anything or anyone stop me from reaching my goals. I even tell myself that I am Batman for encouragement, although I know that couldn't happen. Not because he's not real, but because "the man" wouldn't allow that to happen.

I walk through the metal detector.

"OK. You're good," says the hefty sized security guard.

"Thanks Officer Winslow," I mumble back while picking up my items. I hope he didn't notice my sly *Family Matters* jab. I walk toward a seat in the half-empty waiting area. There are about five people sitting in the waiting area. The local morning news is playing on the old television hanging on the wall. A middle-aged man sips smoking-hot coffee and stares at me as I look around. A large black Rottweiler sits at his feet. The Rottweiler perks up as I look in their direction. The dog's name tag, Bo, dangles from his neck. I hope Bo knows that he better sit his ass down. I'll hit him with a two-piece jab right on his black nose if he jumps at me. Bap! Bap! His owner pets him on top of his head to calm him down.

"Daniel. Daniel James," calls a voice.

"Yes."

"Hi. I'm Richard. Your wife texted me and told me you were on your way. Come on back."

"Wow. That was fast. Say, can he bring that dog in here?"

"Apparently so. He says he's a military veteran and that's his emotional support dog," he responds in a soft voice.

Richard is a strikingly handsome Caucasian young man. He stands about six feet tall with a muscular build. His gray T-shirt is one size too small and serves to accentuate his muscular frame. There's no doubt that he goes to the gym every day, including holidays. I can bet most assuredly that underneath his work station there is a plastic jug full of water that he must finish before leaving work. As I firmly shake Richard's hand to signify my manhood, his big blue eyes catch me and place me in a hypnotic trance. Undoubtedly, this gel-filled blonde-haired man is the Dr. McDreamy of the hospital. I bet he gets all the girls here. Well, all the girls except for mine.

"Thanks, man. I appreciate it. This will be an easy case for you, anyway," I whisper back.

"I hope so. I don't need anything to be wrong with you. Your wife put a lot of pressure on me already. She told me to make sure you're okay or that she'll find a way to make me work an extra week of night shifts. We worked night shifts together a few times and she knows I hate them. So, let's hope this is as easy as you say it's going to be. For your sake and mine. Let's get you triaged, and then we'll get you to one of the ER rooms."

Richard scans his badge over the sensor on a metal door. The latch unlocks, and the door opens into the front of the emergency room area. He directs me into a small room. A woman spins around in her squeaky office chair as I enter.

"Hi. I'm Alex. I'll be taking your vitals."

"I'm Daniel. Nice to meet you." Alex gestures for me to sit down.

I sit down in a blue plastic chair and Alex straps a black blood pressure cuff around my arm. Gradually she begins pumping up the cuff. Slowly, the python grip of the cuff ensues. With big eyes we both eagerly stare at the blood pressure gauge. I have no idea what the numbers mean, but I figured I'd watch as well. I mean, it's my blood pressure. She lets the air out of the cuff and begins to pump up the cuff again.

"Is everything okay?" I ask.

"Yes. I always like to check it twice for accuracy." Alex rechecks my blood pressure.

"What did you get?" I question.

"149 over 92."

"Is that good or bad?"

"It's a little high. Do you have a history of high blood pressure or are you in pain?"

"No high blood pressure, but I am in a little bit of pain."

Alex grabs my wrist and feels for my pulse. She stares at her digital watch for a few seconds.

"Heart rate 88. Can you open your mouth for me?"

"Yeah, but that's gonna cost you extra," I reply facetiously. Richard chuckles outside the door.

"Well, lucky for you I got paid today. So, I can afford it. Now open your mouth for me, please." I open my mouth, and Alex puts in a white digital thermometer.

"Temperature 100. Do you feel feverish?"

"Not right now, but I was on fire earlier while playing basketball. Get it, on fire?"

Alex rolls her eyes so far back into her head that she looks demon possessed. She hands me a stack of hospital papers and points toward the door. I take the papers and walk outside the room to meet Richard.

"You're quite the funny guy," says Richard.

"Yeah, I am sometimes. However, whenever I'm nervous or anxious I make more jokes. I think it's my coping mechanism."

"Well don't get nervous or anxious. Everything is going to be ok. I'm going to take great care of you. Let me show you to your room," Richard informs me.

We begin walking down the chilly, bright hallway. It's fairly quiet. No patients strung out in the hallway. No one yelling out in agony. No doctors running around frantically like the ones on *Grey's Anatomy* or *Scrubs.* No J.D. and Turk around causing mischief. Just peace and quiet.

"Quiet this morning," I say to Richard.

"Yep. It usually is around this time of day. Our goal is to try to get all the people who came in overnight out of the ER. We either admit them or send them home if they don't need to stay. That way, I and the other morning shift doctors don't have a crazy load of patients waiting for us when we come in. So, the doctors who worked the night shift did a good job. There's not that many people here now. There's usually a morning rush of sick people who come in later. It's still kind of early and they probably haven't woken up yet. Trust me, when they wake up, they'll be here. Here with that same cough or vaginal discharge that they've had for a month and now want to get checked out for. Let me give you a quick tour before I bring you to your room."

"That would be nice. It would give me some cool points with the wife. I could tell her later. Oh, I saw this and that. Richard let me shock a patient. It was really fun in the ER. I can't wait to go back!"

Richard starts to laugh. "If you tell her that, I'm surely going to get more night shifts." Richard begins to point out the different sections of the ER as we begin walking.

"Okay, in that back section over there is our drunk tank area. All the patients who come in drunk or high on drugs go in that area. I think we have three people over there right now sleeping off their high. We'll assess them a little later and then send them home, if they feel better. They often come in with some scrapes and bruises from falling. We usually let medical students practice suturing on them."

"That's cold, man."

"Hey, it's the honest truth. Think about it, everyone has a first patient they do a procedure on. Even brain surgeons have to have a first patient to operate on. Everyone has to start somewhere. So, we let the med students learn on the drunk people. They can take their time while they're knocked out and not feel pressured."

"I guess."

"Now, back there is our trauma area. That's where all the big shit goes down. Gunshots, car accident victims, stabbings. You name it. That's where the real action is. Whenever a trauma comes in, the head nurse yells 'Code Superman' on the PA system."

"Why 'Code Superman'?"

"This signals everyone to fly to the trauma area and save lives, like Superman."

"That's cheesy, man."

"Yes, very cheesy. It started before I got here. Honestly, I would have picked Batman. He's way cooler and anyone can be Batman. Not everyone can be Superman. Am I right?"

"Yeah, sure." I respond while looking away.

"Upstairs, we have all the different patient rooms. ICU, labor and delivery, surgery, et cetera, et cetera. The cafeteria is located in the basement floor below us. They shut down in the next hour or so to transition from breakfast to lunch. And here's your room. Lucky number 20."

We enter the small room composed of clear sliding doors. The walls are painted a lazy gray with no accent colors. At the center of the room is a medium sized hospital bed with white sheets that I hope are freshly clean. An outdated television is mounted to the wall. A rerun episode of *The Fresh Prince of Bel-Air* plays on mute. Carlton is stealing the basketball from Will. Richard slides the clear doors closed behind us.

"I'm going to ask you a few questions to get the ball rolling on working you up."

"I know the drill," I state as I plop down on the bed. "The wife has given me the rundown on all the usual questions you guys usually ask. I'll tell you all you need to know."

"Well, go-ahead, Mr. Know-It-All. Give it a shot."

"My stomach started hurting this morning. I threw up two times. I think it may have been the eggs and toast Lisa cooked me. That shit was nasty. I went to play basketball after that. I felt better playing, but my right side started hurting afterward. It's a sharp pain at the right lower part of my stomach. It doesn't spread anywhere. On a pain scale, it's about a 5 out of 10. I haven't taken anything to make it go away, and nothing makes it worse. It's just constant. I haven't had a fever, chills, chest pain, or shortness of breath. I think I may have pulled a muscle. However, my wife thinks I may have appendicitis or a ruptured ovarian cyst."

I continue staring at Richard as he chuckles with his hand covering his mouth.

"How am I doing so far?"

"Actually, you're doing great. Continue."

"Okay. Ummm. My past medical history consists only of seizures. My last was five years ago and I've been off my medication for two years. I haven't had any surgeries before. I currently don't take any meds. I'm allergic to latex, but no medications. The only family history I have is high blood pressure in my father. I don't smoke or drink. And the only thing I get high on is Jesus. Anything else?"

"Nope. That's about it. I think you covered it all. Your wife taught you well. You don't know how much that helps out when people come in knowing their information. It makes it so much easier to help them. Now I'm going to do a physical exam on you."

Richard takes the fire engine red stethoscope off his neck and listens to my heart for a few seconds. He then lifts up my hoodie and places the stethoscope on my back. It's ice cold.

"Take a few deep breaths for me in and out of your mouth."

I breathe in and out deeply, as though I'm trying to blow out trick birthday candles.

"Alright lay back for me. I'm going listen to and feel on your stomach."

I lay back and immediately grimace. The pain is starting to intensify. *Man, I hope he doesn't find anything major wrong and I get to go home.* I hate seeing doctors. They always find something wrong, like when you bring your car to the shop. You go to the doctor's office for a cough, and they tell you that you have high blood pressure. You take your car in for an oil change, and they tell you that you need new tires. *If you don't just give me some cough syrup and change my damn oil!* I didn't ask you to search for other problems that I can't afford to fix. I can only afford one crisis at a time.

"Okay, Daniel. I'm gonna listen to your stomach and then do some pressing on it. Let me know if you have any pain." Richard once again places the cold stethoscope on me and begins to listen to multiple areas of my stomach. He stops listening and then begins to press on my abdomen. The inconspicuous medical torture continues.

"Ouch. Yeah that hurts over there," I state as he presses on the lower right side of my abdomen, where I've been experiencing pain.

"Okay. Now, I'm going to press a little harder on your abdomen in the same area. Tell me if it hurts still."

Richard presses even harder in that area. I reach up and firmly grab his wrist.

"Yeah, bro. That shit really hurts. Chill out on that area for a second if you don't mind."

"Okay. No problem. I'm just going to press on the left side now. Tell me if you feel pain on the right side when I press on the left side. I know it might not make sense, but just roll with it." Richard presses on the left lower side of my abdomen.

"Yeah, it hurts on my right side when you press my on the left. Not as much, but still hurts. "

"Rovsing's sign positive and tender in the right lower quadrant," Richard mumbles to himself.

"What does that mean? Is that good or bad? Cancer? Is it cancer. Give it to me straight, doc? How much time do I have to live?" I freak out.

"Relax, Daniel. All signs are pointing toward appendicitis right now. So, here's what we're going to do. We're going to get some blood work and imaging on you. You're going to get a CT scan of your abdomen and pelvis. So, sit tight, and I'll get the wheels in motion." Richard begins walking out of the room.

"Wait. Wait. CT scan? Is all this necessary, Richard?" He turns around and walks back in.

"Yes, it is. You have all the usual findings. You have been having pain in the right lower quadrant of your abdomen. That's where your appendix is located. You almost jumped off the table when I pressed on that area. In addition to this, you have been throwing up and have a little bit of a fever. We have to check to see if you have appendicitis and make sure your appendix hasn't ruptured.

"I'd rather be safe than sorry. So be prepared for the possibility of having surgery today or tomorrow. I know you probably didn't want to hear that, but you said give it to you straight. So, I'm giving it to you straight, like a shot of whiskey. I'm going to go put some orders in for you, and I'll check on you a bit later. Your nurse will come get your blood for lab work and someone will transport you to the CT machine. So, sit tight."

Richard gives me a slight comfort tap on my thigh and then walks out of the room. As he left, so did any chances of me leaving the hospital anytime soon.

APPENDICITIS

Now here's an educational opportunity. There are going to be more of these throughout the book. Don't freak out. I'm going to make them all really simple. Let's start off with appendicitis.

Definition: Inflammation of the appendix (1). Inflammation is a response to injured cells that results in an area that becomes red, hot, and swollen (2). Any word in medicine that has the suffix -itis means that structure has inflammation (1). For example, hepatitis means inflammation of the liver. Gastritis means inflammation of the stomach. Appendicitis is inflammation of the appendix. Got it?

Anatomy and physiology: Well, what is the appendix? The appendix is an extension/projection of an area of the large intestine (a.k.a. the colon), (1). Think of your house as your stomach and the driveway from your house as the small intestine (see picture on previous page). The driveway connects to a large road. The large road is your large intestine also known as your colon. That road also has one small side street with a dead end. That side street is your appendix. It is said that the appendix (side street) has a role in the immune system and contains good bacteria that help to digest food.

Cause: Remember that the appendix is an extension of the colon and sometimes this extension can be blocked (3). So, imagine a truck leaving the stomach we'll call it "the poop truck." Usually it goes down the driveway (small intestines) and then gets on the big road (large intestine). After that, the poop truck continues straight along the large intestines and drops off its "load" at the rectum. Unfortunately, sometimes the poop truck accidentally turns right on the side street (appendix). It sees it's a dead end and tries to make a three-point turn, but it gets stuck. It can't even back up. It's really stuck. This blockage results in increased pressure within the appendix and leads to inflammation. Thus, you develop appendicitis.

Symptoms: Nausea, vomiting, abdominal pain, and decreased appetite (4) — basically, most of the stuff Daniel has going on. Abdominal pain often starts around the belly button and then travels to the right lower part of the abdomen. These symptoms only occur in half of all patients with appendicitis.

Treatment: An appendectomy, or removal of the appendix, is the best treatment (4). Any word in medicine that has the suffix-ectomy means removal (1). Tonsillectomy, for example, means removal of tonsils. Lumpectomy means removal of a lump. Boyfriend-ectomy means removal of your boyfriend and get a real one. If appendicitis is caused by infectious bacteria and there is a collection of pus, the patient can often receive antibiotics before having surgery.

Now, you've learned a little something. Don't you feel a little bit smarter? Now, let's get back to the story. It's just getting started. Don't say I didn't warn you. Insert evil laugh.

CHAPTER 3

DIAGNOSIS

MURDER

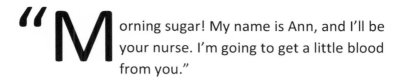

"**M**orning sugar! My name is Ann, and I'll be your nurse. I'm going to get a little blood from you."

After rummaging through the cabinets in the room for equipment, the robust nurse in light blue scrubs walks happily to my bedside and rolls up my right sleeve. Ann appears to be in her early 50s, but has the spunk of a 22-year-old. She smells like cocoa butter. I'm sure she waxes her brown skin with it nightly after she exits the shower. Ann throws down a bunch of empty test tubes by my side. Then, like a magician, she pulls a dark blue ribbon out of thin air and wraps it tightly around my arm.

"Alright, sugar, make a tight fist for me."

I grip my fist as tight as a child holding on to a piece of candy while Ann begins tapping on my arm looking for a vein.

"Isn't there a machine that you can use to find my vein?"

"Yes, there is, but I don't need that thing, sugar. I've been doing this longer than you've been alive. How old are you?"

"14 going on 15. My quinceañera is next month."

"See, just like I thought, smarty pants. Longer than you've been alive."

"Good. I don't want you poking around my arm searching for a vein. I like seasoned veterans who know what they're doing. I don't want anyone practicing on me like I'm one of those drunk people in the back."

"Who told you about that?"

"No one here. I watch *Grey's Anatomy*. That show is just like real life."

"Yeah, sure it is. Coworkers having quickies in closets. Hearts beating in a box. There are so many HIPAA violations in that show."

"So many violations," I reply, not knowing what in the world HIPAA means.

"Okay. That's it. I got all the blood I needed."

I look down on my arm only to see the blue ribbon gone and a freshly placed band aid on my arm. The three test tubes are now filled with blood.

"Wait. What just happened? When did you stick me? When did you draw the blood? When did you place the Band-Aid? Are you some sort of witch?"

"I told you I was good, and yes, I am a witch. Team Slytherin."

"Well, I'm team Gryffindor. So, we might have an issue."

"Well, we'll settle our beef later, sugar. I have to drop off your blood work. I'll be back later to check on you. Someone will be here shortly to transport you to the CT machine. You have to drink this liquid before you go. It's called contrast. It will help give a better picture on the CT. So, drink all of it," Ann hands me a cup full of liquid and a gown. "And put on this gown and wipe all that sweat off your forehead you look a Gryffin mess."

"Thanks. I was starting to feel a little warm. It must be from still having this stupid hoodie on. See you later, Ann." Ann exits the room and slides the glass door closed.

I take a sip of the contrast and touch my forehead. It is drenched with sweat. I take off my hoodie and begin putting on my gown. I should have taken off this stupid hoodie long ago, but I'm still not used to the cold weather. I am cold all the time. It hasn't been easy for this Southern boy to get accustomed to Kentucky's winter climate. However, I didn't hesitate to move up here for my love's job. Hell, I would have moved to Mars if I had to. I just wanted to be with her and make her happy.

Moving with Lisa back to her hometown of Louisville, aka the Derby City, brought her heart so much joy. While dating, she would tell me various stories about the fun times she had growing up here. From her first kiss during the country's biggest fireworks display known as Thunder over Louisville, to her countless arguments against fans of her rival University of Kentucky. She had countless stories of her life in Kentucky. In my heart of hearts, I knew that we would have to move here once she graduated medical school. It was only right. She loves her hometown, and this is where she wanted to be. However, if I had my wish, we'd be in Atlanta. The ATL.

I've traveled there a couple of times on vacation, and I freaking love it there. They have an abundance of restaurants, representing various ethnicities. Korean. Jamaican. Greek. Soul food. The assortment of museums there are a sight to see. The High Museum of Art in Midtown Atlanta is my favorite. It always has unique exhibits on display. In addition to this, I love Atlanta's music scene. The music there always has me dancing and bobbing my head. The fun and excitement of the city is limitless. I would absolutely love for us to live in Atlanta, even if we don't know a single person there. Which we don't.

We would be living in the land of strangers. Luckily, we're both good at adjusting to new situations and making friends. As an adopted child with two wonderful parents, I am pretty good at making new friends. I had to find a way to socialize and not feel lonely. Thank God my parents put me in basketball and karate, which provided an easy source of friends, who would eventually turn into family. Consequently, I never felt like I needed a brother or sister. I had my "framily."

I asked my mom once if she ever wished she could have children. She responded, "It wasn't in God's plan honey. And if I did have them, I may have missed out on the blessing of having you. I'm so thankful for you. You are mine through God's plan. No matter what anyone says." I loved her for that answer. My parents never made me feel like I was adopted. They made me feel loved. Sometimes overly loved. I could probably sell my extra love on eBay and get good money for it, but I wouldn't. I'd hoard all that extra love for myself. It's a joy to be over-loved rather than under-loved. Some people aren't loved at all.

Sweet Cakes was equally as loved by her family, and her family is huge — two brothers, 10 aunts and uncles, and more than 20 first cousins. She knew each one of them by name and branch on the family tree. I, on the other hand, would be lucky if I recognized them at the next family gathering. They all loved her. Friends and family members alike loved having engaging conversations with her. She could go from talking about the latest political news to arguing about who was the greatest singer of all time. Her personality is so infectious. People connect with her, and she connects with people. That's what probably makes her a great doctor — her ability to connect with people. And we have a great connection

Since, our first date we have been inseparable. On it I told her "you're mine until you find someone better. And trust me you won't find anyone better." She laughed, but I was dead serious. I don't know if at that point she thought I was her husband, but I knew that she was my wife. I didn't want anyone else to have her and no one else did since that date. We always reminisce and laugh about me telling her that on our first date. Sometimes, you have to speak stuff into existence.

A few months later we were living together or as old people call it "shacking up." We didn't want to, but it just seemed like the optimal situation. We were always at each other's house and hanging out together. After, crunching some numbers and having a conversation we figured it would just be best. We didn't tell our parents for fear of judgement. Even though we were *grown* we still valued their opinion of us. Living together bought us closer.

We got to learn each other's tendencies and insecurities on a whole new level. I know she likes to sleep with a box fan on and she knows I get scared when it thunders. She holds me and caresses my hair without judgement when it rains hard. It comforts my soul. We know each other like the back of our hands. If I come back in another lifetime, I hope that I can find her again. Just so I could love her twice. I miss her. I wish she was here with me now to comfort me.

"Mr. James?" says a young sad voice wheeling in a wheelchair.

"Yes?"

"Hi, I'm Todd from transportation. I'm going to be wheeling you down to CT. Can you confirm your name and birthday for me?"

"Daniel James. 07/02/83."

"Thanks. Alright, hop in this wheelchair for me, and I'm going to wheel you down to CT."

Todd is a thin young white man, approximately five feet, ten inches tall and one hundred pounds soaking wet. He has weak posture and his body frame hunches forward like an old grandpa. The repetitious action of leaning forward to push people in wheelchairs has most likely contoured his body to be in a forward position. The puffiness around his eyes signifies that he's been either working all night or is still waking up to start working. The blue-collar life is starting to take a toll on him at such a young age. He's not fit for this life. He should have gone to college.

"Can I leave my stuff here?"

"No, I'll put your valuables in this plastic bag. It'll be in the back of your wheelchair. There are a lot of sticky fingers around here. So many people are in and out of rooms here. I don't want your stuff to get stolen, so we'll take it with us."

I hand Todd my valuables. My keys, phone, wedding ring, and wallet. Todd secures them into a plastic bag and neatly tucks them in a pouch behind the wheelchair. I carefully step down from the bed and begin shuffling toward the forest green wheelchair with the 20-inch rims. I plop down in the chair.

"Time to drive, Ms. Daisy. To the CT machine, Toddrick!" I exclaim.

"It's Todd. Just Todd. And, yes sir." Todd pushes the wheelchair.

I could hear it in the tone of his voice that he didn't like being called Toddrick or the Ms. Daisy reference, but I don't care. I'm going to enjoy this opportunity to have a young white man wheeling me around. This doesn't happen too often. Hell, it hasn't ever happened to me. So, I'm going to soak all of this up for what it's worth. Today, I will gladly be Ms. Daisy.

"Now you make sure you go the speed limit, Toddrick. We can't get any speeding tickets. Okay?"

"Yes, Mr. James."

As Todd wheels me in the creaky wheelchair down the hallway, I can see there are more people starting to trickle into the emergency department. To my left, a woman lies on a stretcher with a brace wrapped around her neck. A bloody bandage is affixed to her forehead. She moans in pain. Behind her is a man on another stretcher with some sort of breathing apparatus on his face. He breathes heavily and keeps his hand firmly attached to the apparatus. White smoke seeps through the mask with each breath he takes. To my right, I hear hurling and peer into the room as I roll by. I glance in and see a young lady pouring all of her guts into a blue vomit bag that is already half full. Richard was right. I guess all of the sick people are starting to wake up. I pray that whatever is going on with me doesn't keep me trapped in here with them. The emergency room is a smorgasbord of people and germs. And I don't plan on getting acquainted with either one of them, if I can help it.

"Roll down the windows for me, Toddrick. I want to wave at the kiddos. Hello kiddos! Come by later; I made some brownies," I jokingly state at the fictitious children.

"Are you okay, Mr. James?" questions Todd.

"Why, yes I am, Toddrick. Never been … aaahhhhh," I groan as my side begins to hurt again.

"Never been better, huh, Ms. Daisy?"

"Uh huh. Turn the radio up, please. I don't want to hear myself groan."

After entering the CT room, Todd and the radiology technician help me out of my wheelchair and onto the machine's table. As they strap me in, I begin to feel more pain in my side. I regret not asking my nurse for some pain medication before I left.

"Okay, this should only take about 15 minutes," states the white female technician. "I'll put some headphones on you, and you can listen to music during the procedure. Would you like me to put it on the local rap station?"

"No, actually, could you put it on the country station? I love Toby Keith and Carrie Underwood. Her voice just touches my soul," I replied back. The technician stares at me in amazement as though I had just pulled a rabbit out a hat.

"Are you serious?" she asks.

"I dug my key into the side of his pretty little souped-up four-wheel drive | Carved my name into his leather seats | I took a Louisville slugger to both headlights | I slashed a hole in all four tires.
Maybe next time he'll think before he cheats!" I bellow out the Carrie Underwood lyrics. "Shall I continue singing, or are you going to put it on the country station? I can go all day."

"The country station it is, Mr. James. I'm so sorry. We'll get the imaging started."

The tech puts the loosely fitting headphones on my head while Todd checks the straps one last time. They then leave the room, and I'm left all alone on the table strapped in like Frankenstein's monster. "Boot Scootin' Boogie" blares through my headphones. Not one of my favorite country songs, but it'll ease my anxiety while I'm in this confined space.

I wouldn't say that I'm claustrophobic. I'll just say I'm semi-claustrophobic. A closed room with a huge, noisy machine like this doesn't bother me that much. However, crowded elevators really ramp up my anxiety. They make me feel like a lone sock cramped in a sock drawer. Everyone is so close. Strangers accidentally touching you as they get on. People talking loudly on their phones about subjects no one cares about. *Yeah, girl, I had so much fun last week. I lost my shoe and my virginity. One of those I can't get back. He he he. Don't tell mom.* Ma'am, no one cares about your conversation, and based upon your outfit, your mom probably knows you're not a virgin anymore.

"Hey, Daniel," says the startling voice looming over me.

"Oh, Richard you scared me. I was just daydreaming and listening to my country music. Is it over with already?" Richard begins to unstrap me from the table.

"Yeah. I was in the back watching you get imaged. It looks like you have appendicitis. You're going to need surgery. Luckily for you, you're one of our VIP patients, and we can knock this out fast. So, I'm going to need you to get on this bed over here and we're going to bring you up to the operating floor for surgery. I've already contacted the surgery team. They have an open surgery room available, but we have to bring you up there right now."

"Wait. Wait. Surgery? I don't even feel all that bad. Just a little nauseous and some stomach pain." Once I'm finally unstrapped, I sit up.

"Well that's all because of the appendicitis."

"Can't you just give me some medicine and send me home? What do you guys call it? Outpatient? Can't this be treated as outpatient?" I ask.

Richard grabs a chair from the hallway and slides it in front of me. It skids loudly on the floor. He plunks down, puts his hand on my knee, and looks directly into my eyes.

"Look, Daniel. I know this is a lot to happen unexpectedly. Trust me, I get it. You came in thinking it was something simple and now you're having a surgery. Quite the start to the morning. However, you need to have this surgery."

"Will I get to call Lisa before I go upstairs?"

"No time right now. We gotta get you upstairs pronto. I don't want anyone to take your surgery room. I'll call her for you and give her an update. But, right now I need you to sign this surgery consent form and hop on this bed."

I pause for a second to take everything in. Surgery. Wow. I've managed somehow to avoid it my 28 years of life, but now there's no denying it. Today, it will be my turn to go under the knife. I grab the ball point pen and long white consent form out of Richard's hand. I shakily scribble my signature next to the giant X. The X that doesn't mark the spot of treasure, but my impending surgical doom.

"I'm scared, Richard."

"That's understandable for your first surgery, but it's a fairly routine surgery. We have a great surgery team here, and you will be taken care of. Now, let's get you upstairs."

"One last question. Is this the surgery where I get ice cream at the end?"

"No that's a tonsillectomy," responds Richard followed by a chuckle.

"Well I'm getting ice cream at the end anyway. Rocky road."

"Ice cream does sounds like a good plan, Daniel. Now, let me introduce you to Charles. He's one of the surgeons. He, along with one of the nurses, is going to wheel you upstairs to the surgery floor."

Charles assists me over to the bed and latches the guardrails in place after I get in. The loud sound of the guardrails locking into place awakens me to the reality of the situation. *Am I really about to go under the knife? Am I really being wheeled to the elevator for surgery? For surgery?* The little comfort that Richard provided was nice, but it didn't help much. I bet he uses that same pickup line on all of his patients. *Oh, it's a routine surgery. You'll be okay. It doesn't even hurt the first time.* Yeah right.

As the nurse pushes me into the wide elevator, Charles presses the number 8. All the way to the top floor of the hospital we go. As the door slams shut, I close my eyes to relax myself and try to find some peace and comfort.

"First time having surgery?" asks Charles.

"Yes." I quickly reply as I try to travel back to Peaceville.

"Oh, it's not that bad. This is a simple routine surgery. We just put you to sleep. Then, we'll cut you here, here, and here," he states as he touches my abdomen. "Then, we'll take out your appendix. Easy peasy. Unless something goes wrong. Then, we'll have to filet you all the way open."

Well, it looks like someone has infiltrated Peaceville. Sound the alarm! An intruder has knocked down the metal bar gates with LEAVE ME ALONE displayed on the front. Clearly, this guy is not good at reading body language. My eyes are tightly closed, I'm clutching the white sheets in my hands, and my teeth are clenched as though I'm having surgery right now. I absolutely hate needles and now this guy wants to cut me wide open. Cut me open! That's not normal. My skin is designed to keep my insides wrapped up like a mummy, but now this guy wants to unwrap the mummy. This pharaoh is not pleased.

It kills me how carefree everyone is taking this surgery. Just a routine procedure. What is routine for them sure as hell is not routine for me. They may be accustomed to doing the surgery, but I am surely not accustomed to having surgery. I'm about to be put to sleep and cut open. *Will I wake up? Will I wake up the same? What happens if I don't wake up? Will they cut out the right thing? How many appendices do I have? What happens if I have two appendices and they take out the wrong one? Will they have to cut me open again? I know I'll surely die from that surgery. Then, who will take care of Sweet Cakes? Will she remarry? She better not go back to her ex. I'll haunt her ass for the rest of her life if she does that. I would be the most irritating ghost of all time. I'd probably flip the toilet paper the opposite direction, hide the TV remote, or put the thawed meat back in the freezer. Guess who's not having chicken for dinner? Cheating Sweet Cakes and her new husband, that's who.*

Wait. Hold up. What am I doing? Am I really freaking out here? I am. I'll be okay. Just breathe, Daniel. Keep it together. Go back to Peaceville. Where the weather is a nice 75 degrees and you're lying in a field of bluebonnets eating green grapes. Yes, Peaceville. The land of sunshine, happiness, and serenity.

As the elevator reaches the top floor, the door opens and the nurse pushes me out. I'm more relaxed and calm now, as they roll me toward the operating room. No longer am I clutching the covers like I'm Charlie Brown's friend Linus. My eyes are wide open as we pass the other operating rooms and I read the room numbers. *Room 1. Room 2. Room 3. Room 4.* We make a sharp left turn and enter room 5.

"Okay, Daniel. These lovely people in here are going to get you prepped for surgery. I'm going to go scrub in. My attending Dr. Baker will also be scrubbing in. The next time you see me will be in the recovery room, and your appendix will be out. You'll be okay," encourages Charles.

"Thanks, Charles." Charles and the nurse who rolled me in exit the room.

"Mr. James, I'm your anesthesiologist, Dr. Holloway," states the muffled voice of a woman who has replaced Charles in my line of sight. She towers over me like a Martian over its abductee, ready to dissect and possibly probe me. A light blue mask covers her mouth and light blue cap covers her head. "I'm going to be the one putting you to sleep. Are you allergic to any medications?"

"No. Just latex."

"Okay, good. That's one less thing I have to worry about. I'm going to be giving you some medication to help you go to sleep. I call this my 'knockout juice,'" she states while tapping a hanging bag of liquid medicine. "I'm going to put an IV in you, and then we'll begin sedating you. Normally my nurse would do that, but it's just me. Just me. Where is everyone?" she questions under her breath.

Dr. Holloway puts an IV in my arm and then hooks it up to the IV bag.

"Okay, Daniel. I'm going to start the medication. I want you to count backward from one hundred, and you will gradually fall asleep," says Dr. Holloway.

"100, 99, 98, 97," I count aloud.

"That's it. You're doing good."

"Hey. Are you Dr. Holloway?" an out-of-sight manly voice inquires from the door entrance.

"Yes, I am. Why? Who is asking?" she replies back.

"96, 95, 94, 93."

"Do you work with Dr. Morrison?" the voice questions.

"Why yes I do from time to time. What can I help you with?"

"92, 91, 90, 89," I continue counting and let out a sigh.

"Do you remember a patient by the name of Marilyn Smith?"

"I'm sorry. I don't remember her. I have worked with so many patients."

"88, 87, 86, 85. I'm getting sleepy."

"It's okay, Daniel. Just go to sleep. Once again sir. May I help you? Who are you?" she sternly yells to the pestering man.

"To cut a long story short, she was my wife, and you helped with her surgery. But since you don't remember her. Let me show you something that will help you remember her."

The door loudly swings open and bangs against the wall. Two loud shots ring out from a gun. Dr. Holloway falls flatly on top of me. I attempt to push her off, but I'm too weak from the medicine that is coursing through my veins. What in the world is going on? The assailant walks over to me and lingers over me. All I can see is a shadowy figure above me. My eyes are so tired and heavy.

"Well you said that you were sleepy. Let me help you out a little," he calmly states as he twists the knob up on my medication.

I reach up to grab him, but my arms are pinned by Dr. Holloway. More medicine begins to course through me. My eyelids are so heavy. I can't fight off the sleepiness. Leaving Peaceville. Next stop Dreamland.

CHAPTER 4

LIONS, TIGERS AND CHAOS, OH MY!

awake in confusion and with the weight of an elephant on my chest. Harkening screams echo in the distance.

What's going on here? Where am I? Wait, am I still at the hospital? Have I had my surgery yet? I attempt to move my right arm, but I feel it pinned down. *What is on my chest?* I lift my head up to see what is weighing me down. As I peer over my torso I see a body laying over me. My eyes then pan to the left and see the wide-open eyes of Dr. Holloway. My adrenaline kicks in and I push her off of me. I jump off the table and land on the floor. One could have sworn that I had just seen a giant tarantula.

What in God's name is going on here? Is she really dead? This can't be real. I must still be under sedation or dreaming. Somehow Dreamville has turned into Nightmare Land.

"Wake up, Daniel! Maybe if I slap myself, I'll wake up," I state out loud to myself. I look down at my right hand to muster up enough courage to slap myself only to see that my entire arm and hand is covered in bright red blood. Immediately, I run over to the sink and start gagging.

Frantically, I turn on the warm water and attempt to wash the cold blood stains off my arm. I hysterically press the liquid soap dispenser located adjacent to the sink and recommence scrubbing. My gown is also tainted with blood. Sigh. *This is real. A little too real. Who was he? Why did he shoot Dr. Holloway? Who was she to him? Where did he go? And where are those chaotic screams coming from?* I begin to rinse off the soap suds, which have now turned red on my arm. Blood-mixed water drips from my arms.

"You guys have thirty seconds left to get out of here," yells a grungy loud voice from outside the operating room.

Thirty seconds? Thirty seconds until what happens? Well I don't know want to find out. Let me get the fuck out of here. There is something big about to go on here and I don't want to be a part of it, at all. This is one party that I would gladly decline an invitation to. No, I'm sorry, Mr. Madman, I'm going to be busy today and can't make your murderous rampage. However, before leaving, I have to close Dr. Holloway's eyes and say a quick prayer for her.

As I turn away from the sink, I see Dr. Holloway lying on her back in a pool of blood surrounding her torso. Her lifeless eyes remain open. She didn't have a chance. She deserved better than that. No one deserves to be slaughtered like an animal. That's not right. No matter what she did she didn't deserve to die like that.

With a quick closing of her eyelids and a sign of the cross over the body, the "Daniel's rite of passage" ritual has been sealed. I quickly run to the door and grab the handle only for my hand to slip. I try to grab the handle again and my hand slips once more. *Damn it!* My hands are still wet from washing them off.

Hurriedly, I wipe my hands on my bloody gown and try my hand again on the door handle only for it to slip again. *Dang it!* Now it's covered in blood, too. All I wanna do is get out of this room. With the speed similar to a cheetah going after its prey, I run to grab a towel on the shelf by the sink. Ferociously, I wipe my hands off until they're as dry as sandpaper.

I run back to the door and grasp the handle with all my might. This time my hand sticks to it like Spiderman to a wall. I pull the door open and cautiously take a step onto the freezing, hard floor in the hallway.

"Times up!" shouts the voice from the hallway. "Everyone left in here line up in the hallway."

Swiftly, I remove my foot from the hallway as though it were dipped into a scolding hot bubble bath. I pray to God he didn't see my pale, size-12 foot stick out of the room. That surely would be the end of me. *Now, what do I do? How in the world do I get out of here? Where is my north star to freedom?*

As I look across the hallway, my north star appears in bright lights. E-X-I-T shines in bright orange capital letters like the Krispy Kreme hot sign. That must be the exit for the stairway.

"Alright. All I have to do is run across the hallway, open up the door as quietly as a mouse, and go down the stairway to reach the land of the free and home of the sane," I say to myself. I check the hallway to make sure it's clear for my escape. Like an old wise tortoise, I slowly stick my head out around the corner to see if the coast is clear.

I gaze down the hallway and see the backside of a tall slender white man with brunette hair standing in the hallway. He has on light blue scrub pants and a long white doctor's coat with a black strap crisscrossing his back. He directs hospital employees in the hallway. The Glock 22 in his right hand encourages them to move fast and follow his directions.

"Hurry up! Everyone line up. I don't have all day. Single file line," he yells to the scared-faced hospital staff. "You guys had 22 minutes to get out of here. Hurry up." The look of sheer terror on their faces could easily rival that of any young, blonde girl in a horror movie. However, this isn't a movie. This is real life. Not reality TV "real life." This is active shooter, Columbine and Virginia Tech, real life.

However, I still have a chance to make it out of here alive, if I can just make it to the exit door. The coast appears to be clear, while the mad man's back is turned. Here goes nothing. Quietly, I run across the tan linoleum floor to the exit door and push the handle. *Click clack!* sounds the door. It's locked.

"Who's back there!?" shouts the shooter.

"It's me. The last one here. I was just checking the door for you. Wanted to make sure that it was locked." I pull on the door. "Yep. It's good and locked. I guess I'll make my way down to you now."

As the shooter turns around, I can see that the strap around his shoulder is holding an AK-47, which swings wildly upon him turning. Now, I can see his full face. He's a six-foot-tall, muscular white man with a cleanly shaven, dark goatee. The blue eyes of the forty-something year old man are cold, calculating, and determined. His athletic build is hidden under his white coat and black V-neck T-shirt. The hems of his scrub pants are tucked inside his scuffed, tightly laced black combat boots.

"Come on. Make your way down here," he motions with his handgun. I trot down toward him and make my way to the area as instructed. Sitting on the ground with their backs to the wall are about fifteen staff members, men and women dressed in surgery attire. They sit with their legs crossed and faces filled with fear.

"Sorry about that. Nothing personal just business," The gunman says. "Is that Dr. Holloway's blood on you?"

"Yeah it is. I'll be okay. Blood isn't that bad. I'd rather it be someone else's blood than mine. The goal is to keep it inside you. Ya know? Ha. Ha," I reply with a nervous laugh.

"Yeah. You'll live, Daniel."

"I hope so. Wait. How do you know my name?"

"I read your chart. Do you want to make it out of here alive, Daniel?"

"Well, matter of fact, yes I do."

"Well I have a mission for you, Daniel. I would say 'if you choose to accept it,' but this isn't *Mission Impossible.* There is no option. You have no choice. Do this mission and you'll make it out alive. Got it?"

"Got it," I eek out followed by a big gulp.

The lone gunman reaches down on the ground next to one of the overly terrified nurses and picks up an empty black JanSport backpack and tosses it to me.

"There's a black shirt in the bag and some scrub pants. Take all of your clothes off and put them on. Hurry up."

"Here, in front of everyone? I don't want anyone to see me naked."

The deranged man squints his eyes in pure disgust. His brow wrinkles giving him a Benjamin Button appearance. He then turns to the hostages huddled on the ground and points at them with the AK-47 strapped around his chest. They all gasp and huddle closer trying to protect each other.

"Who in here has seen a penis before? Raise your hand up high. Who has knowingly seen a penis before? Be it your own penis or someone else's penis," he asks.

Everyone in the mixed-gender group extends a hand toward the heavens.

"I've seen a couple. And I'm not afraid to say it," remarks the flamboyant male nurse at the end of the row.

"See, Daniel, everyone has seen a penis. So, nothing to be ashamed of. Now hurry up and change," he repeats in a stern voice.

Hurriedly, I take the small black shirt and light blue scrub plants out of the backpack. I reach around to the backside of my gown and untie it. My gown drops to the floor. I bare all of my beautiful brown skin for the world to see. A random breeze passes over me. *Who opened a window?* My back is cold. My butt is cold. My nuts are cold. My penis is shriveled and curved to the left. I wish I could say that I was in the pool, but I wasn't. If there's any pool that I'm in now, it's the pool of shame. *Someone throw me a life raft, please.* I'm drowning in shame and embarrassment. I finish getting dressed.

"That wasn't so bad. Was it?" says the gunman.

"Yes, it was." I emphatically reply. "I hate to feel vulnerable and open like that."

"You'll be okay. Now, listen up. Give me your full attention. Here is your mission. I'm going to only say it once. So, you need to pay attention. You can't ask any questions. If you follow all of my instructions, you'll make it out of here. Take these two pills."

Slowly he opens his hand and exposes two oblong shaped yellow pills. Hesitantly, I take them from him and hold them in the flickering light above me.

"What are these?" I question.

"Obviously, you don't know how to follow directions." Immediately he turns around to one of the women sitting down on the floor and pistol whips her with the Glock. She screams and clasps her hands tightly around her mouth. Blood begins to trickle between her tightly woven fingers.

"Whoa. Whoa! You didn't have to do that. I'll take the pills." I toss the pills back in my mouth like a shot of vodka and swallow.

"Good. Now, I told you that you can't ask any questions. The actions that you make or don't make today will have a huge effect on others. So, follow the rules accordingly and do as I say. Open the middle pouch of the backpack and remove the item in there."

Hands shaking, I hastily open the pouch to find a short metal rod. It's a bright green colored baton used in track relays with the word **HONESTY** engraved in big block white letters on one side.

"Here is your mission, Daniel. That is one of many batons that you will collect on your journey out of the hospital. You will collect one from each floor from a specific person. This person will be similarly dressed like you and fairly recognizable. Got it thus far?"

"Yes."

"Now, each baton will have its own unique word inscribed on it like the one you have in your hand now. This word relates to each person you receive a baton from. You will need to find out how this word relates to this person. If you make it to the end you'll get the explanation of the baton that you possess currently. Still with me?"

"Yes."

"You will be able to save one person from each floor to take with you, and you can only take the elevator. You can only use the front or the back elevators. No stairs. I repeat, no stairs. They're locked. Each floor must be done in consecutive order. Don't skip a floor or try to escape without finishing your mission or there will be consequences. Whoever you save, you must share with them the stories that you have learned on your mission. Like a baton in track and field, you will continue to pass the messages you've learned to each person you save."

"Oh, that's just beautiful and creative child," chimed the flamboyant nurse. Dr. Holloway's killer cuts his eyes toward the outspoken nurse. He then reaches down and picks up a red container by his feet. He begins walking and dousing liquid on the staff seated on the floor. He starts with the male nurse who randomly spoke out of turn. The stench of the liquid travels up my nose. It smells like gasoline. The staff members keep their heads down and tremble as he pours it on top of them.

"Now, if you do what I say you'll make it out of here alive. Like Daniel in the Bible, you must have faith. However, if your faith is lacking in what I have told you, the lions pouncing around the hospital will surely eat you up. There are many lions around here, Daniel, and they're chomping at the bit. Ready to devour you at the first sign of fear. There will be many trials and tribulations on your mission. You will be challenged mentally, physically, and emotionally. But you must remain strong in all aspects. The pills I gave you were Percocet pills. They should help you with the pain you were having."

"Thanks."

"Now, in the interest of making things easy, I have picked your first person to save and take with you."

The mad man stops pouring gasoline just before reaching a man in a janitor uniform. He motions with his handgun, for the Hispanic male in the janitor's uniform, to rise from his seated position.

"This is Enrique. He's one of the janitors here. Who better to help you navigate the hospital than him? He knows it from top to bottom. Unfortunately, he speaks little English. But I'm sure you'll figure out how to communicate with each other."

"Yo, hablo español un poquito." I calmly state to him.

"Bueno," replies Enrique with his eyes facing the floor.

"Looks like you two are friends already. A regular Lamont and Julio friendship. Junkyard buddies. Now, time's a-wasting. You two should get on down to the elevator."

"What are you going to do with the rest of these people here?" I ask. "I'm sure there are still patients up here."

The gunman turns around calmly toward the nurse who kept making comments and shoots him in the leg. I put my hands on my head in shock.

"Aaaaahhh. You shot me!" he screams in anguish. "Damn it, Daniel! Stop asking freaking questions." He grabs his leg and begins applying pressure.

"I'm sorry! I'm sorry! It's just second nature. This is all so nerve-racking. Just give me a second to gather myself."

I put on my newly acquired backpack and pull its straps tightly around my shoulders. I pace back and forth, processing all that I've just been told. *Mission. Messages. Batons.* I have no idea what is going on here. What did I just get myself into? Why did he choose me? Is there any way I can get out of this? I can't ask for him to pick anyone else because he'll hurt someone else. Unfortunately, this is my burden to bear.

"It's time for you and Enrique to leave and get on the elevator," says the unnamed assailant.

Enrique and I begin the slow trek down the hallway toward the large silver elevator. I press the down arrow and the doors open immediately, as though the elevator had been waiting on me to start my journey. I get onto the elevator and look down the hallway at the group of fearful hostages and at the gunman. *What will happen to them?*

"Good luck to you, Daniel," he states.

"Thanks. I didn't catch your name," I say as I press the button for the next floor. The assailant pulls a match out of his pocket and strikes it on his gun. It burns brightly in the air.

"Just call me Maestro," he yells back as the doors start to close. He flicks the match at the staff on the floor. Desperately, they start running. Two of them catch on fire. The sound of gunshots ensues as the doors close.

CHAPTER 5

OVER 99 BILLION

SERVED

The elevator doors open on the seventh floor. Enrique and I step out of the elevator into the dimly lit hallway. The elevator doors slam loudly behind us, and I survey the area for safety. I take a squat on the ground and gather my bearings. What in the world just happened? The shock of what I just saw has sunk in. I had just seen someone get lit on fire and another person shot. My hands begin to shake. *What have I gotten myself into? This isn't how I predicted this hospital experience to go.*

I was supposed to come into the hospital get diagnosed with a muscle strain then go home. Simple. Not be dragged into some hospital takeover. How did I manage to get roped into this? Why didn't he choose one of the nurses or someone else? Why me!? Why am I the one who must carry out this task? I don't know, but at least I have someone with me. Too bad he can't speak English. I run my fingers through my hair and scratch my scalp in anguish. I survey my surroundings.

Stacked around the elevator doors are piles of random items. Miniature packets of graham crackers, orange juice boxes, bed sheets, and an assortment of pills blanket the floor. As I stare at the various items, a man in dingy clothes runs up and tosses more graham crackers onto the pile.

"Freebies," he states with big bright eyes before running back off down the hallway in the direction of another man running toward him. They high five each other as they pass by.

The next gentleman in a hole filled shirt and stained black jeans runs towards the pile with an arm full of various pill bottles and packets. The fortissimo sound of rattling pills increases as he reaches the pile. One of the bottles crashes to the floor. He sidekicks it toward the pile with his dirty white New Balance shoes. He reaches the pile and opens his arms. The pills begin to pour down to the ground like rain from a nimbus cloud. He looks at me and gives me a head nod. I nod in return. He runs back into the abyss of the hallway to gather more items I assume. I pick up one of the graham cracker packets and standup. I'm hungry.

"Ready?" I ask Enrique after stuffing a piece of golden graham cracker into my mouth.

"Que?" he questions back.

"Listo?" I ask in Spanish with a mouth full of cracker.

"Sí."

I stuff a few more crackers in my back pocket for the road, and we start to stroll down the dark corridor. Some of the ceiling lights have been busted. It appears that we are on a regular hospital floor. Just a whole bunch of patient rooms. Cries for help mixed with the sounds of hospital monitor beeps reverberate from the rooms.

"Help! Is anyone there?" a patient loudly questions from one room.

"Nuuuurrsseeeee!!!! Where is everyone?" exclaims another.

"Someone come turn this damn beeping off," demands another patient.

So many cries. So many people in need. *Who do I help? Better yet, can I help them?* I don't know. There is no way that I can help them all. Where is the staff on this floor? Where are the nurses and doctors? I hope they didn't desert their patients stranded on this boat of disaster. *Did they jump ship like it was the Titanic? Are they paddling away from the hospital in a little lifeboat waving bye with an orange vest on?* I hope not. Like a captain, they're supposed to go down with the ship while the band plays, not abandon it. *Where is the loyalty? Where is the commitment? Where is the honor? So far, the hospital staff is totally nonexistent.*

"Help! Someone, help me!

Instantly, I run to the cry for help with Enrique trailing behind in my dust.

"I can't feel my legs," the voice continues. "I'm dying!"

That doesn't sound good. *Could they be having a stroke? Did they fall out of the bed? Did someone shoot them?* As I make my way to the room, the first man I encountered runs past me with a handful of apple juice boxes toward the elevator. He doesn't seem to care about the yelling going on around him.

Upon entering the room, I'm instantly punched in the nostrils with a pungent odor that could rival any carnival Porta Potty. Sitting hunched over on a bedside commode is a man over 500 pounds, sweating profusely. Beads of sweat dot his forehead. He clutches a half roll of used toilet paper in his right hand. The hospital gown he's wearing is stained orange on his chest. The stain is most likely remnants of yesterday's dinner.

"Help me get off of this toilet. My legs fell asleep while I was dropping off some kids in the pool."

I put my shirt collar over my nose and respond, "Help you get off the toilet? You mean, help you get off the toilet, please."

"Yeah, please. You and Hector behind you. Get me off this stinking toilet."

"His name isn't Hector. It's Enrique."

"Tomato los to-ma-tos. Same difference. Get me off of here."

I look back at Enrique. His eyes are as big as two china dinner plates. By the look on his face he is none too eager to help the morbidly obese man off the toilet. Hell, neither am I. Enrique puts his hand over his nose to filter the horrid smell.

"If we get you to the edge of the bed can you roll yourself onto it?"

"Yes. Now, vamanos muchachos."

Enrique proceeds to grab young Jabba the Hut's right arm and I grab the left. With all our might we strain to lift him up. The toilet water begins to splash and swish side to side in the commode. I glance down and see a huge wet piece of feces the size of a baby's arm. *Christ, please don't let any of that nasty water get on me.* We help him off the toilet and begin to take shuffling steps toward the queen size bed. We drop him butt first onto the edge of the bed and watch him roll back. He tucks himself tightly into the covers like a human burrito. The half-eaten dinner roll on his tray suddenly catches his eye. He grabs it and begins snacking on it.

"Gracias, Carlos. And what's your name?" he asks looking at me while smacking on the roll.

"My name is Daniel, and for the second time, his name is Enrique."

"What's shaking guys? There was a whole bunch of commotion outside my room earlier. Woke me up from nap on the toilet. Then, it got all quiet. I've been yelling for a few minutes for help and no one has come. I think I've heard other people yelling, too. Finally, you guys came, but, you're obviously not nurses. I can tell that by your clothes and nurses are only women. Right?"

"Um, yeah. Well, I don't know how to say it, but the hospital has been taken over."

"Taken over? Yeah, right. What's really going on. Is there a fire drill going on or something?"

"No, really. There is a real-life shooter in the hospital. There may be others."

"You don't say," he states chewing with a mouth full of roll. "So how are we going to get me out of here?"

"How are we going to get you out of here? We aren't the rescue squad. What's your name?"

"Kenneth."

"Well, Kenny no offense to you, but how?"

"How what?"

"How are we going to get you out of here? You needed help getting your fat butt off the toilet. How in the world are we going to carry you out of the hospital?"

"Oh, it's simple. You don't have to carry me. All you have do is go down to the medical supply closet at end of the hallway on the right. In there is a big wheelchair that you can wheel me out of here in. See, simple and easy. And, I resent you calling me fat. I'm not fat. I'm big boned."

"No, dinosaurs have big bones Ken. You're not a Kenasaurus. You're just Kenny. How did you get so big anyway? What are you forty-three, forty-four years old?"

"Actually, twenty-six."

"Wow. Really, Kenasaurus." I look at Enrique who looks puzzled by the conversation that we're having in English in front of him.

"Él es veinte y seis anos." I state to Enrique. His eyes open wide, as though I'd asked him to pick Ken up again.

"I've always had trouble with my weight since I was a teenager. I'd do well for a short time and then fall off the wagon. At one point, I lost over a hundred pounds, but then I gained it all back. I eat for many different reasons. Pleasure. Depression. Boredom. Companionship. It varies from day to day. Emotion to emotion. My eating habits really took a turn for the worse after my parents divorced. That brought me down mentally and my weight up physically. I put all my pain and sadness into food. It makes me feel so much better. You know the way some people turn to drugs when they get down?"

"Yeah," I reply.

"Well I turn to food. Food is my drug. It's how I get high. When I bite into a cheeseburger or a fresh slice of hot pepperoni pizza, I feel the endorphins flowing through my arteries. It takes me away from life's problems. Food doesn't judge you. Food doesn't ask you why you don't have a girlfriend. Or why do you breathe so hard? Or tell you that everyone's parents get divorced. Food isn't judgmental at all. It's the perfect friend. It satisfies my emotional needs, doesn't talk, and takes me to a place of happiness. Unfortunately, this food friendship has gotten out of control and has affected my health. I have diabetes and that's what put me in the hospital. I ran out of my insulin for a few days and my sugar got high. So, that's how I ended up here."

"What's your favorite food to get high on?" I question.

"Oh, McDonald's, for sure. I absolutely love their affordable food. Especially their apple pies. They are de-li-cious. I could eat those all day. I have at least two for breakfast and two for dinner. The first two for breakfast for my fruit of the day. The second two are dessert for dinner."

"Come on, Kenasaurus. Apple pies don't count as your fruit for the day. I know you have a lot of life problems going on, but you've got to find a better outlet to deal with your stress. I wish we had time for a Dr. Phil moment, but we don't. We've gotta get out of here."

"Yeah, *we* do. Emphasis on the word 'we.' You're gonna come back and get me, right?"

"Sure, Ken. The wheelchair is in the supply closet down the hallway on the right."

"Right! Thanks, man. And can you bring me a couple of graham cracker packets too? They have a box of them in the closet."

"Don't worry, Ken. I got you right now," I reach in my back pocket for the crackers I picked up earlier and toss them into Kenny's stubby hands. Enrique and I exit the room.

Slowly and quietly, I close the door behind us. I look Enrique straight in the eyes, point at the door, and shake my head slowly side to side. There is no way in hell that we'll be able to get Ken out of the hospital. Especially, if I have to go floor by floor per Maestro's instructions. I get to take one person per floor on this journey and for easy travel's sake, Kenasaurus won't be that one person.

"Hey, guys. What's going on here?" says a tight shirt-wearing young man walking up to Enrique and me.

"Have you been sleeping under a tree?" I ask.

"Well sort of. I've been sleeping, but not under a tree. I was in my room waiting for my sister to come pick me up. My nurse had just given me my paper to go home, and I fell asleep. I've been so tired since I've been here. You get absolutely no sleep here in this hell hole. Nurses in and out, taking your blood pressure. Monitor alarms going off. People coming in giving me breathing treatments. You get sleep while you can, and I was sleeping like a rock while I could."

"Breathing treatments, for what? As big as you are nothing should be wrong with you."

"I had a bad asthma attack yesterday, and they kept me overnight. My asthma gets bad in the winter. The cold air really gets to me. They had to give me a couple of breathing treatments and some steroids to help open up my lungs."

"As buff as you are, you don't need anymore steroids," I reply.

"So, what's going on? Where is everyone?"

"Stooooppppp!!!! Don't hit her!" yells a distant voice.

"That's what is going on. If you want to make it out of here alive you have to follow me. I'm pretty sure more answers lie in the direction of those screams."

"What do you mean?"

"What's your name?"

"Van, but everyone calls me Rip because of my muscles," he boisterously states with a quick pop of his pec muscles. Rip, who stands taller than six feet, is just like his nickname describes. He is ripped from head to toe. His muscles are jacked. His biceps are the size of two bowling balls and his shoulders are broader than the Grand Canyon. His spiked blond hair only adds to the gym rat persona he gives off. He would surely give Paul Bunyon a run for his money.

"OK, Rip Van Weights. I'll explain as we walk. Time is ticking."

As we stride down the hallway, I give Rip the rundown of what has occurred so far and what I know. The twenty-something white man listens attentively as I give him the details of the mission Maestro has bestowed on me. Unlike me, Rip doesn't ask any questions and just soaks it all in, everything from my description of Dr. Holloway's shooting to the explanation of the baton and backpack. He listens intently as we head toward the screams. I also inform him that he is the one person that I will be saving on this floor. A look of relief ripples down his face as he hears the good news. I need a guy like Rip. He's big and in tip-top shape. I won't have to worry much about him. He can protect himself and me at the same time. Unbeknownst to Rip, he is my newly appointed bodyguard. No one is setting me on fire with him around.

Our walk culminates at the main desk area of the floor. There are large desktop computers on the counters in the front and in the back. I assume that this is where nurses and doctors congregate to do their hospital work. On the floor of this area is a hoard of distraught people. Sitting on the floor cross-legged are a few nurses, a couple of patients, and a group of casually dressed women huddling in one corner. One of the women appears to be bleeding from her right leg.

"Welcome, Daniel. We've been waiting on you. I'm Ron," utters a man sitting on top of one the counters. Adjacent to him is a tall man standing behind a wheelchair. They're both dressed exactly like me in light blue scrub pants and black T-shirt. These are the guys I'm looking for.

"Hello, Ron. What happened to her?" I say while pointing at the lady in tan dress slacks with blood oozing from her leg. It's fairly evident that she gets all her style tips from Murphy Brown.

"Oh, that's Candice. What happened to her? The system happened to her, that's what happened to her. Mac, push the wheelchair around." Ron carefully jumps from the countertop to one of his feet. The other foot he keeps bent off the ground. This leg of this foot is caged in some metal contraption with rusted pins penetrating it. The skin around the pins is dark red and his leg appears swollen. He flops down into the wheelchair. Mac pushes him in the black wheelchair towards me.

"The system?" I ask.

"Yes, the system happened to her. Just like me, she has fallen victim to this corrupt American medical system. America. I used to believe in her. I used to believe in the land of freedom, hope, and opportunity. The stars and the stripes. The place that everyone hates, but everyone wants to come. Why is that?"

"Well, it's like you said. It's the land of hope and opportunity. You can live out your dreams here. You can be anything you want to be, from a movie star to a doctor to an entrepreneur. The opportunities are limitless," I reply.

"Exactly right, Danny boy. Limitless. Limitless ways to reach your goals and to provide financial stability. Not only for yourself, but your family, as well. If you have one. Correct?"

"Right!"

"Now, Daniel. How do we reach those dreams? How do we reach for the stars? What is our rocket ship to greatness?"

"Well, I guess you could say hard work, dedication, and getting an education. Those are some of the ways that come to mind."

"Good answers. Your friends you brought with you have any answers?"

"Pumping iron? That's how I reach my goals," Rip declares, then flexes and kisses his enormous biceps. The entire room looks at him with confusion.

"Good suggestion, Hulk, but I'm going to go with Daniel's answers. Yes, Daniel. All those things and more. I did all of those things and America's system failed me."

"What do you mean?" I question.

"What do I mean? I followed the American dream blueprint. I attempted to do things the right way. The American way. First, I graduated from high school. It wasn't easy, but I did it. Step number one completed. Step two, I went to college. Not because I wanted to, but because that's what America says you're supposed to do in order to make it. Travel the safest road. However, I quickly found out that road wasn't for me. School isn't for everyone. College just didn't fit me. I couldn't stay focused in class. The classes weren't interesting and didn't speak to me. I'd rather get some money in my pocket than sit in class all day listening to someone lecture me to death. I'm more of a blue-collar person. I like to get my hands dirty and put in an honest day's work. So, I went and got a job. A job that some people may look down on, but a job I enjoyed. A job at McDonald's. You like McDonald's, Daniel?"

"Oh yeah I love McDonald's. Shoot, I just met one of your biggest customers down the hallway. He absolutely loves McDonald's, as well. Loves it to death."

"Everyone loves McDonald's. I didn't think I would like working there. It was just a temporary job. Something until I figured out what I really wanted to do with my life, but I ended up liking it. I started off as a low-level crew member, making fries. Then, moved to the grill making burgers. I would carry those heavy boxes of burger patties from the cold freezer daily. The 4:1 meat boxes were always the heaviest. However, I enjoyed cooking them on the grill. The grease from that grill use to pop my skin like a mother does a bad child. But I loved it. I made the best burgers in town. Even my managers could tell that my burgers tasted better than other crew members."

"Is that right, Ron?"

"Yep. My managers loved my food. They loved my food so much that they promoted me to floor manager. I just totally skipped crew trainer and went straight to floor manager. All I had to do was take a test and I aced it. I became the youngest manager in Jefferson County. Things were coming together."

"Sounds like it. You got a job and money coming in," I interject.

"Not a lot of money, but money nonetheless. I had all the things I wanted. A job and money in my pocket. My next step was to become a store manager. I wasn't going to rush to make it happen, but that was the next goal. Then, life happened."

"What happened?" I ask.

"My girlfriend got pregnant. So, the plan to move up to store manager had to be ramped up. There was no way I could support us on my $11-an-hour salary as a floor manager. I heard that there was going to be a new store opening in St. Mathew's Mall and they were looking for a potential store manager. With that information, I began to network up the corporate ladder to put my name in the loop. I met with everyone. The general manager. The sales department. The marketing department. Anyone and everyone I could to show them my passion for the golden arches. I showed them my sales during my time slots as a manager which were higher than any time during the day. In addition to that, I provided letters of recommendation from co-workers above and below me attesting to my work ethic. I practically had the job in the palm of my hand. I could feel it in my grasp. Then, like clockwork winter rolled in."

"What does winter have to do with anything? I don't follow," asks Rip.

"The winter storm last year. Don't you remember it? It was horrible. That storm wiped out power in over 10 counties. It was a doozy. I made sure I woke up earlier than usual to make it on time to open the store during the days of the storm. One of the principles I live by is: 'To be early is to be on time, to be on time is to be late, to be late is unacceptable.' Therefore, I made it my business to make sure that I was early and on time every day. One early morning during the storm I was walking to my car to go to work. It snowed about three feet the previous night and my stupid self fell walking to my car. I was kicking up ice everywhere trying to break my fall, but I couldn't save myself. I even heard someone laughing at me as I crashed to the hard pavement, but I couldn't see where their snickers were coming from. After I fell, I picked up my leg up only to see it wiggling like a piece of spaghetti."

"Oh, shit! That's nasty." I reply.

"Sure was. Under my work pants I could see that the bone was sticking out. Somehow, I still managed to drive myself to the hospital. To this very hospital. They brought me in and said I'd have a *simple* surgery to repair the bone. They would stick some pins in my leg and I would be out in two weeks tops. Well that was a lie. A week turned in to ten days. Ten days turned into an infection. An infection turned into repeat surgery. Repeat surgery turned into a month. A month turned into no Christmas at home."

"Wow. That's tough, bro," chimes in Rip.

"Yeah, but that's just the beginning. Do you think they kept my job? Nope. They replaced me at my old job and gave my new job away. The job I had been hoping, praying, and wishing for. They say when one door closes another one opens. Well, all my doors were closed and nothing was open. I was in a hallway full of locked doors. My daughter was even born while I was in the hospital. I couldn't even be there to see my firstborn enter the world. This weighed heavily on my conscience. Eventually my girlfriend brought her to see me, but I couldn't bear looking either one of them in the eyes."

"Why?" I ask.

"The precious look in my daughter's pretty brown eyes and her chunky cheeks made tears roll down my face. Not tears of joy, but tears of sadness. The sadness of not being able to provide for her and her mother. My girlfriend looked at me like 'What are you going to do to help. You're the man.' And her eyes were right! It's the man's job to be the provider and protector for his family. And I couldn't be the man they needed. You could have cut my balls off that day. I wasn't a man. I was a lowly patient. I was Mr. Ronald Kroc in room 713. That room right over there." Ron points at a room across the way.

"I was a patient stuck lying in the bed trying to get healthy. I knew when I got out that I didn't have a skill or trade to fall back on. I mean my skill was flipping burgers. That's not a skill. I tried to do it the American Blue-Collar Way. Work a hard-honest job, but then life punched me with a gut check."

"Well that's just life," I interpose. "Life is full of ups and downs. Life knocks you down and you get back up. That's also part of the American Way. We are fighters!"

"That is most definitely true, Danny boy. I totally agree. I sulked in my bed for weeks on end, but then came to the realization it wasn't going to help my situation. Feeling sad for myself wasn't going to benefit me in any way. I just needed to dust myself off and develop a new game plan to help myself and more importantly my family. Enter Candice my social worker," Ron points at the woman whose leg is bleeding. "Toward the end part of my stay, I reached out to Candice to help me with my situation. I lost my job. I lost my apartment. I have a growing family. And now I have an enormous medical bill waiting in the wings. I just needed some assistance and guidance along the way to get me back on my feet.

So, I asked Candice. Sweet Christian Candice who parades around with her gold crucifix chain and holier-than-thou attitude for help. I explained to her my story. How I grinded and worked hard. How my job fell through and now I will need some help finding new work and a place to live. I needed help with paying for pain medication. I vowed to pay the hospital back because I hate owing money and the bill was my responsibility. But I just needed some temporary help just to get on my feet. Do you know what she said? Do you know how she coldly responded?"

"'I would love to help'?" I guessed.

"No. She said not my problem." Ron grabs a metal crutch lying on the counter and with the top end strikes Candice in her injured leg three times. I wince as she screams in agony. Enrique and I rush forward to try to help her and stop Ron. Mac pulls a handgun from behind the wheelchair and points it at us.

"Not so fast," he slowly states.

"'Not my problem!' Not your problem? It's your job to help fix my problems. You literally get paid to fix people's life problems," Ron yells in Candice's face. "This angered me to my core. In my time of need, I had no one to help me. No one to turn to. The same American system I trusted to help me up is the same American system that kept me down. Every day after physical therapy I sat in the hallway watching life pass me by. Day shift leaving. Night shift coming on. Candice walking through the hallway laughing and joking with her coworkers. Fake-ass child of God."

"I'm overworked. I tried to help. I tried my best!" yells Candice.

"You didn't help squat, Candice. The only help you provided was finding a shelter. Where was your compassion, Candice? What happened to loving your neighbor like you love yourself, Candice? I've been homeless and broke for almost a year. A freakin' year! My girl won't let me live with her unless I have a job. 'No jobless man in her house,' she tells me. Well, I can't get one of those because no one wants to hire me with these rusty pins still in my injured leg. I know I need to get them out, but I never went back to the doctor after I left the hospital. I'm afraid to go back to the doctor.

I'm afraid of the bill I may get. I'm afraid of them telling me I need to have another *simple* surgery. I'm afraid of potentially being trapped in this hospital again. It's a vicious cycle that I go through in my head daily. So, I choose to walk around with these pins in my leg rather than potentially face those things. Now, I'm pretty sure that my leg is infected. I probably caught a bug at one of the dirty homeless shelters. I met Big Mac over there one day at one of them. Show them your arm Mac."

Mac shows his swollen right arm. It's red and twice the size of his left arm. The fire engine red color extends from his elbow down to his hands. You can tell he is in pain by the way he grimaces as he rotates his arm from side to side.

"Mac got wasted a few weeks ago. Drunk a little too much of that fine Kentucky bourbon and took a tumble. He got a pretty nice gash on his arm. He came to this hospital and got some stitches put in," explains Ron.

"I barely remember what happened," Mac chimes in. "I was super drunk. I woke up and someone was stitching my arm. Woke up again and someone was walking me around holding me up. Woke up one more time, and I was back in the shelter. It was like magic."

"Then, three days later his arm started turning red and swelling. He went back to the ER. They wrote him a prescription for some antibiotics and pain meds to take. He told him he couldn't afford them. You know what they told him before they sent him on his merry little way?"

"Not my problem," I responded quickly.

"Not. My. Problem!" Ron responds, punctuating each word with a jab to Candice's leg. "But you know what's Candice's problem now?"

"Her leg?" I guessed.

"No, that knot on her head."

I look at Candice and don't see a knot on her head. "What knot on her head?"

Ron takes his crutch and swings for the fences at Candice's head like it was a baseball on a tee. She slumps to the floor. Her coworker crawls over and holds Candice head in her lap. She's knocked out cold.

"That knot right there. You see it now?" says Ron.

"Ah, come on, bro. That's not right. Get it, *knot* right?" says Rip while nudging my arm.

"Yeah, that was unwarranted," I add while rolling my eyes at Rip.

"Unwarranted, but necessary. Sometimes you have to beat the point into someone's head until they get it. Looks like she got the point. Right on her forehead," Ron responds.

The first man that I saw running when I came out of the elevator now walks into our area. "We're almost done grabbing supplies," he says.

"That's Barry. The friend he's running around with here is Cam. We call them Beebop and Rocksteady. Can't find one without the other. I met them at the shelter as well. They're helping me ransack the place for items. Drugs, food, medical supplies, and whatever else we can find. Stuff the system normally won't give us common folks. Like this wheelchair. I don't have to walk around with these crutches anymore." Ron then reaches around into his back pocket and tosses me a green baton. I catch it and flip it over to read the word inscribed on it: *COMPASSION*.

"You get the message, Danny boy?"

"Yeah. All you wanted was a little bit of compassion in your time of trouble. You wanted to be helped in your time of need and treated like a person. You worked hard to do it the right way, but didn't get the help or compassion you felt like you deserved from the system."

"Not only deserved but was entitled to!" Rip yells while pounding his chest. "Everyone the system touches! The millions, or better yet, billions of people it has served. They should be treated not just as patients, but more so as people. As human beings. Or children of God, if you believe in that mumbo jumbo stuff like sleeping Candice over there.

"It appears that you get my message, Daniel. I appreciate you understanding where I'm coming from. Now time for you to mosey on along. You've got more floors to visit. I'm going to assume you picked up Muscles over there as your personal protector. Wise choice, I guess."

"Yeah, I did. What are you going to do with Candice and everyone else here? And where is the rest of the staff? The doctors and the nurses."

"They're around here. You'll eventually find them. However, Candice and I are just going to have a little more fun," Ron says with a smirk on his face while patting his crutch in the palm of his hand. He bends down over Candice and whispers towards her ear. "Don't go into the light yet, Carol Ann. We're just getting started. Now this is your last warning to get out of here, Daniel." Mac motions with his gun for us to start walking.

"Escort them to the elevator, Mac. I want to make sure we don't have any trouble with them."

"Alright, we're out of here, Ron," I reply while stuffing my backpack with the newly acquired baton. Enrique, Rip, and I turn around quickly and walk back to the elevators. Mac hovers over us like a chaperone at a high school dance as we walk. He keeps the gun pointed at us from behind.

"Are we really going to just leave all those people there?" whispers Rip as we walk.

"Yes, we are. We can't help them right now," I whisper back. "You know how a flight attendant says put on your mask first then you can help your neighbor put on theirs? Well, we're putting on our masks first by getting out of here. We can only help them once we get out of here. If we don't do as they say, we may never be able to help them. Got it?"

"Got it," says Rip in agreement.

As we reach the elevator doors the pile of various items originally by the door has now doubled. I reach down and grab two handfuls of crackers and a couple juices. I toss them in my backpack. Mac squints his eyes and cocks his gun.

"It's going to be a long day for us, Big Mac. We may need this stuff for later. Have a little *compassion* for us," I state while looking him in his glossy eyes. He lowers his weapon.

"Get on the elevator, Daniel," his deep voice instructs. We get on the elevator. I press the sixth floor button and the doors slowly close. I yell out to Mac.

"What's on the next floor?"

"The psych ward," Mac eerily responds.

DIABETES

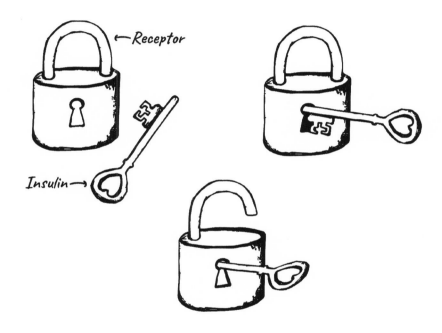

Definition: Diabetes is a group of metabolic disorders sharing the common underlying feature of hyperglycemia (3). Basically, it's a disease that causes one's blood sugar to be too high. That's why some people call it "The Sugar." A diabetic's blood sugar might be too high because the body has problems making insulin, the insulin is not working properly, or both. Read on for more about insulin.

Anatomy and physiology: Insulin is a protein produced by the pancreas that acts to lower sugar levels (1). The pancreas is a gland located in the abdominal area. Think of insulin as a key (see figure). When a person eats something with sugar, the sugar eventually ends up in the bloodstream. Then, the body says "hey, there's some sugar inside me. I need to lower my sugar level, or this is going to cause problems." So, the pancreas starts making keys aka insulin to lower sugar levels. The keys work with receptors on the cells. Think of the receptor as a lock. Once the key fits into the lock and turns, the cell opens up and sugar goes in, thus, decreasing the sugar level. The sugar is used by the cell to make energy.

Classification: There are two types of diabetes — Type I and Type II.
Type I: The loss of ability to produce insulin most likely by autoimmune destruction (the body attacking itself), (4). Basically, the body is not producing enough keys. This is the most common subtype diagnosed in children under 20 years old (5). It accounts for approximately 4% of the entire diabetic population (5).
Type II: A combination of peripheral resistance to insulin and an inadequate secretory response of the pancreas cells (3). Basically, the body is not producing enough keys and the few keys it does produce don't work as well at the locks, thus, the sugar level is going to be high.

Complications: A sugar level too high is very problematic. Uncontrolled diabetes can lead to a wide array of complications. This can include strokes, high blood pressure, eye complications including blindness, kidney failure, heart attacks, nerve problems, and infections (3).

Treatment: This consists of giving a person more keys (a.k.a. insulin), making the keys work better, decreasing the amount of sugar the body absorbs, or getting rid of the sugar in the bloodstream faster. Also, diet and exercise can help to improve one's sugar level (4).

CHAPTER 6

HAIL MARY

T he elevator doors open to a brightly lit hallway. Approximately, ten feet from the elevator is a large steel door with a glass window in the center. I and my companions on this mission exit the elevator and head toward the steel door.

"Are we really going to go in there? That's where all the crazy people are. Let's just get back in the elevator and go downstairs," Rip says in a scared, high-pitched voice.

"Yes, we are going in there. We can't deviate from what I was told to do. I'm afraid of what will happen if we do. That guy Maestro is a maniac. I saw him shoot one doctor. After that, he shot someone else because of me, then he lit a group of people on fire. So, yeah, for now, we'll continue to stay the course. If things get too crazy, then we'll try to break out of here."

"Define too crazy," Rip questions.

"I'll let you know when we reach it," I respond.

We arrive at the large door, and I peer through the dirty one-foot by one-foot glass window. I wipe it off with my forearm to get a little better view inside the room. Inside, multiple people run back and forth in hysteria. I presume they are patients based upon the gowns that some of them have on. Others have their gowns off. At the back of the room is an unorganized pile of approximately ten round tables and twenty chairs. It appears as though the patients put them back there to give themselves more room to run around freely. I continue to survey the room. Sitting on a desktop a few feet opposite of the door is a figure who appears to be wearing the same garb as I am. The figure swings their feet, watching the patients run around back and forth.

"Abra la puerta por favor, Enrique," I instruct. Enrique scans his badge on the electronic lock and the door unlatches.

"Bienvenido a la casa de locos," says Enrique.

"Gracias," I respond not knowing what the hell he just said. We enter the psychiatric area, and I'm immediately greeted by a sweaty gentleman who throws his arm around my shoulder. He reeks of body odor. Perspiration dots his forehead.

"Hey, we need another player. We're playing football," he says, out of breath. He huffs and puffs with each sentence. "We just lost a player, Chris. He's the guy over there in the corner wrestling the chair. He just walked off the field and started wrestling it. He thinks it's a bear. I'm Stewart, by the way." I look over to the corner and see a bald middle-aged male in a heated wrestling battle with a plastic blue chair. Surprisingly, somehow the chair appears to be winning. Grizzly chair – 1. Chris – 0.

"No, I'm not interested in playing," I respond and wave him off.

"Ah, come on. It's the last play for all the marbles. And trust me, some of these guys really need some marbles. They've lost all of them."

"No, I'm good, Stewart. I don't have time for any games right now," I repeat more firmly. Instantaneously, a loud thunderous slam in the background occurs. Everyone glances in the direction of the sound. Chris even stops wrestling the chair.

It appears that the sound originated from the person sitting on the desk earlier. She is a beautiful, thin, long-haired Asian woman with the most perfect posture. Next to her is the small handgun she had slammed on the counter.

"Play!" she loudly demands.

"You heard her, Daniel. Play!" says Rip before pushing me toward the group of guys. I stare at her angrily, as I slowly take my backpack off. I jog onto the makeshift field with my new teammate. Stewart gathers the team in a huddle.

"Come on guys, huddle up. She said play. This is for everyone's marbles."

 What's the play?" I question my team.

We all huddle around Stewart. I look into the eyes of my co-ed teammates. I can tell that some of the lights are on and some are off in their heads. There's not a lick of talent besides me in this circle. We are a long way away from being Super Bowl Champions.

"Okay, it's shirts versus skins. We're the shirts. This is the last play. If we score, we win. I want everyone to go long and I'll throw it to whoever is open. Got it?" explains Stewart our appointed quarterback. Everyone looks confused. We're definitely going to lose. Stewart breaks the huddle.

I walk to the line of scrimmage and take my position at wide receiver on the far-right side. The other players on my team take their respective positions, as well. The shirtless team, also co-ed, takes it position on defense. It isn't until now that I realize that there are women with no shirts or bras, on the shirtless team. Luckily, the shirtless team has decided to keep their underwear on. This is the craziest pickup game of football I have ever played. The end zone appears to be marked off with chairs and the out of bounds area behind it is littered with the extra chairs and tables. I hope I don't fall into them.

I reach my starting position on the line and look for my defender. A massive beast of a man walks slowly from the opposite end of the pseudo football field and lines up directly in front of me. He is exactly the size of an NFL linebacker. He even has a white helmet on his head, but I don't think it's for football. The helmet is covered with dents and its strap is pulled tightly around his chin. Drool slowly drips from his lips down his bare chest and travels to the waistband of his boxers. He wipes the drool from his mouth with his forearm as he gets closer to me. A big string of slimy spit connects his lip to his forearm.

"What's wrong with him? Is he going to kill me?" I ask my teammate lined up next to me.

"I want Polynesian sauce and upsize my waffle fries please," she responds. Clearly, we aren't in the same place right now. Stewart prepares to hike the ball.

"Down. Set. Hut!" he yells. Instantly, my teammate next to me starts running in the wrong direction. I shake my head in disgust as she runs opposite of the play. Her defender chases her. I look ahead at my defender. He's locked in on me, ready to tear my head off at the slightest move. *How do I get around him?*

Swiftly, I reach forward and pull down his boxers. They fall to the floor and expose his genitals. I take off running at full speed toward the end zone. A loud roar ensues behind me, as I run. I look back to see my defender, whose face looks eerily similar to a white

Ving Rhames, charging at me from behind. His feet stomp loudly like a giant T-rex chasing its prey, aka me.

"Hey, I'm open!" I scream at the top of my lungs as I run free. Stewart looks my way and sees me with my hand raised, running toward the end zone. He cocks back and throws a small brown object high in the air in my direction. I jump toward the sky with my arms fully extended to catch the game winning touchdown pass. *How did they get a football in here, anyway? There shouldn't be any sporting equipment in here. Let alone in the psych ward.*

As the oblong object spirals, slowly in my direction I begin to notice that it isn't a football. There aren't any white laces. No leather covering. It's just an odd brown object flung my way. The object continues to spiral clockwise and inches closer to me. *What is this thing?* As it gets closer, I'm finally able to see it in plain sight. I was right. Indeed, it is not a football. It is a flying turd. Yes, a flying turd. I thought I'd never see the day of a flying turd, but that day has arrived.

What have I gotten myself into? The super turd bowl apparently. Straightaway, I put my hands down, but it's too late. This flaming fecal football is headed straight for my face with no change in direction in sight. The cold and wet fecal ball strikes me dead on the left cheek and splatters on the floor. My last bit of dignity falls afterward. My dinosaur of an opponent tackles me in to the collection of tables and chairs behind the end zone as I miss the pass.

"Oh!" yells the collective of the room in observance of my utter destruction.

I'm now buried under all the room's furniture. I push my helmeted defender off me and attempt to climb out of the assortment of chairs and tables. They pull me back into them like a Chuck E. Cheese playpen full of plastic balls. Rip and Enrique pull me back to civilization. Rip is laughing hysterically.

"Ah, man. You were supposed to catch that. You were wide open!" Stewart screams at me.

"I'm sorry that I didn't catch that shit. Literally, that shit." I respond angrily.

"Whatever, man. Yo, Donald make us another football."

I look over at a corner in the back of the room. An older white man with red hair squats with his pants to his ankles. Dropping from his bottom in a swirling pattern is soft serve fecal matter. He reaches between his legs and begins to mold it as if he is making a sculpture. This isn't his first rodeo making fecal football. He has perfected the art.

"I'm not playing the next game. You guys got it."

I walk over angrily to the young lady sitting on the counter that demanded I play football. As I get closer she grabs the gun on top of the table.

"You don't need that gun. I'm not going to hurt you. I'm just hot that you had me out there playing football with shit. Thanks, Coach Crazy."

She hops off the countertop and looks me in the eyes, "The name is Coach Mary. And don't call me crazy ever again." This statement is followed by a casual push of the gun on my forehead. I would say that I was afraid, but I'm not. I'm actually turned on.

Hail Mary, full of grace, the beauty is with thee. Never have I been so attracted to an Asian woman since the Yellow Power Ranger or Connie Chung. I love me some Connie Chung. She could report the news to me anytime. Tell me about the unrest in the Middle East, Connie, and I'll tell you about the unrest you put in my heart.

The fresh smell of Mary's sweet perfume flows through my nasal passages to my pleasure center. Her long black, wavy hair falls down her back like Rapunzel sitting on her window sill. Mary is tall and slender like a Victoria Secret's model. Her dark, alien-green eyes pierce my soul, which only adds to her mystique. Her feistiness has somehow aroused me. I may call her crazy again later just, so she can jack me up. For now, Mary has me wrapped around her little finger, but I won't let her know that. Can't let her know I'm crushing on her. Plus, I'm married anyway.

"Yes, Coach Mary. I won't call you crazy again. I'm just trying to figure out what's going on here."

"Well, Daniel. You're on the psych floor of the hospital. All of the quote-unquote *normal* people who were in here already left. These are the people who remained. Some of them chose to stay because they have nowhere else to go. Some of them walked out and came back in. Some don't even know how to leave. Even though the door was wide open earlier. Some of the people here started to get bored and restless. So, Stewart over there had the bright idea of starting up a football game. Don't ask me why they chose to get Don to shit out a football. They could have easily just used a balled up piece of paper. Let me give you and your guys a tour of the place."

I wave to Rip and Enrique to come over. They walk across the football field and meet us at the desk. Rip is still laughing at me. Mary starts the tour.

"This is the common area. The tables and chairs are usually set up and dispersed throughout the room. We are normally eating in here, watching TV, playing games, or just hanging out."

"Are all the crazy people in here at the same time?" asks Rip.

"What do you mean by crazy people?" responds Mary.

"Well, you know, crazy people. The ones talking to people who aren't there. The ones beating their heads on the wall. The ones drooling like a faucet. You know. Crazy people."

"Yes. Some of those people are here, but not everyone who is in here fits your definition of crazy. Some are actually *normal* with mental problems."

"Ah, come on now, Mary. Everyone who comes in here is crazy out of their minds. They all walk around with straitjackets, talking to themselves or zoned out like a zombie. They all probably stay in one of those white padded rooms, yelling their brains out all day. Like *aaaahhhh*! Right Daniel?" Rip nudges me while laughing. This guy really has no filter or sense of awareness.

"Uh, I don't know about all of them. But maybe a good bit of them," I answer.

"Since you guys know so much about the housing situation here, let's go check out the rooms."

As we walk out of the room, the remaining patients gear up for another game of fecal football. Mary takes us around the corner to a hallway full of rooms. Rooms on each side of the hallway face one other. Each room has a steel door with a small window and slots for food trays. Mary stops at the first door, takes a metal key out her pocket, and unlocks it. She leads us inside.

"This is the room that you all are probably familiar with from TV. The white padded room with nothing in it. Psychiatric purgatory."

"Yeah! This is the exact room that I had in my head. I bet these walls are pillow top mattress soft for all the people who bang their heads on them," Rip imagines aloud. He rams his empty head into the wall. Enrique and I shake our heads in embarrassment.

"Yes, this is where the people with very serious psychiatric conditions are held. Some people can't control their thoughts or actions and need to be put in here. They may be high on drugs, schizophrenic, or have some other mental health condition which doesn't allow them to act what you guys call 'normal'," Mary explains.

"Na, they're just plain crazy. Loco en la cabeza. Did I say that right, Enrique?" asks Rip.

"Si, senor," replies Enrique.

"Well, let me show you another room, Rip. I think that you'll love this one."

We exit the padded room and walk back into the hallway. I trail behind the group peering into the other room's windows as Mary leads us to another. All the rooms are empty. There are additional padded rooms like the one Mary showed us, but surprisingly there are some ordinary rooms, as well. Mary opens the door for another room, five doors down from where we were.

"Man, this room is nice!" Rip exclaims. "Shoot, it's almost better than mine."

I make my way to the room to check out the décor. A cozy twin-size bed covered with a green blanket is located near the wall of one side of the rectangular room. Directly across from the bed is a wooden desk with a metal chair tucked underneath. On top of the desk, is a blank sheet of paper and a yellow flower pen next to it. A brightly lit table lamp on a nightstand shines on a small orange copy of the New Testament of the Bible. An old box TV hangs in the upper corner of the room. If this room is better than Rip's his room, he must live in a prison cell. An oddly placed metal hook hangs from the ceiling in the center of the room.

"See, big guy. All the rooms aren't what you had in mind. There are some normal rooms. With beds. Desks. Some even have TVs, as you can see," states Mary. She puts the gun she's been holding down on the desk.

"I bet people in here hear people talking through the TVs," says Rip. He walks behind the hanging television and pretends his voice is coming from it. "Kill! Kill! Kill!" he jokes, followed by a jovial laugh that seemed to come from the depths of his soul.

"You think you know everything like the doctors who work in here, huh, big guy?"

"Well not as much as the doctors, but I do like the sound of Dr. Rip. Has a nice ring to it."

"Well, Dr. Rip. Let's role play. Why don't you go outside the room and peek in like you're one of the doctors? Put your big, muscular head to the window and peek in like you're a doctor checking on one of your crazy patients," instructs Mary.

"Hey, I'm down for role playing! I'll play doctor. I wish I had one of those long, white doctor coats, so I could really play the part. Let me go outside of the room."

"Yeah, go outside the room," agreed Mary. "As a matter of fact, all of you go outside the room. I'll play the role of one of the *crazy* patients lying in bed. You guys play the role of the medical staff."

Mary shoos us out of the room back into the hallway. I look back to see her hastily pull the door closed. Her forearm is covered with numerous horizontal scars. We begin to crowd the door window and gaze into the room. Mary puts her gun on the desk then climbs into the bed and covers herself up.

"Does this look like a crazy patient?" she asks us loudly.

"No." Rip and I respond collectively. Enrique also continues to look through the window. Confusion is painted on his face and mine as well. What is she doing?

Mary throws the covers to the side, puts her naked feet on the ground, and walks over to the desk. She scoots back the metal chair. It screeches on the floor before she takes a seat in it. She hops forward in the chair and inches herself closer to the desk. She picks up the flower pen and begins scribbling on the paper.

"Does this look like a crazy patient?" she asks again as she writes.

"No," we respond again.

Mary finishes writing on the paper and gets up from her chair. She turns back around to the bed and lifts the mattress. From under the mattress she pulls a long white rope with a large noose at one of its ends. The mattress slams back down onto the metal frame. Mary grabs the chair from under the desk and puts it under the metal hook hanging from the ceiling. She stands on the chair and begins tying the rope around the hook.

"Hey! What are you about to do?" I yell out in a puzzled voice. Mary ignores me and continues tying a knot around the hook. With every tie of the knot around the hook my toes curl up more and more. I pull on the door handle. It's locked.

"Open the door, Mary!" I demand. She ignores me and continues tying while mumbling to herself. The incoherent mumbles intertwine with the sounds of me pulling on the door handle.

"Open this door right now, Mary!" I demand once more. She finishes tying the knot and puts the noose around her neck. She turns around and faces us. Her green eyes have turned stop-sign red. The makeup around her eyes has turned black like a raccoon. Tears flow down her round cheeks like raindrops on a window pane. Her nose runs. She wipes it on her forearm.

"Do I look like a crazy patient now?" she questions.

"Yep. Sure do," answers Rip.

"Well, I guess you found what you were looking for," Mary responds, with her voice cracking. She kicks the chair from beneath her feet. The noose constricts around her neck like a python. Her feet dangle helplessly in the air.

"Oh, shit!" Rip shouts in amazement. "That chick is really crazy. She just hung herself!"

I pull on the door with all my might. It doesn't open. "Hold on, Mary! I'm coming." I turn to Enrique who is in a state of total shock staring at the door. "Keys!" I yell to him. He doesn't move. He continues to stare at the door in pure, unfiltered, total shock. I punch him in the chest. "Keys. Enrique."

"Que?" he answers.

"Damn. What's the word for keys?" I think out loud. I respond with hand gestures. "Um el jango jingo. Um el thango to open el dooro. Um llavar? Um, llaves. That's it. Llaves! Llaves, Enrique." Thank God, I paid attention in Mrs. Consuela's Spanish 101 class. If I hadn't, I'd be playing charades with Enrique forever. Enrique slowly reaches in his pocket and pulls out an assortment of keys.

"Which one is it?" I ask Enrique. He continues to stare through the window in shock as Mary dangles from her rope. The circular motion of her torso begins to rotate less and less.

"You better hurry. She's not going to make it much longer," Rip encourages.

"Say, if your ass not gonna help me, can you just shut up?"

"Temper, temper. Mr. Dre. Mr. NWA. Mr. AK coming through with a handful of keys y'all better make way. See how I just flipped that Eminem line? Man, I crack myself up! Eminem is the greatest."

"Rip. Shut the fuck up! I don't have time for you and your antics. A woman is dying in there and you're freestyling rap lyrics. Rap lyrics! Do you not realize the severity of this situation? You're not being helpful. Not being helpful at all right now. Plus, Eminem is overrated anyways." I try to open the door with the first key. No luck.

"Man forget that girl. I don't know her crazy ass. Why should I care if she hangs herself?"

"You should care," I respond.

"Why should I?"

"Because."

"Because what? Because, you say so. Once again, I don't know her. If she wants to hang herself let her hang herself. Whatever is making her hang herself has made her crazy enough to hang herself. Maybe by her dying it will bring her some peace. So, who are we to stop her? Some people just want to die. She may find the peace she wants in death. And what do you mean Eminem is overrated? Overrated?! You've got to be kidding me. Who is in your top five?"

I don't care what Rip says. Some people just want to die? That makes no sense. I understand we all go through things in life, but nothing should ever make you want to kill yourself. Just get some counseling or something. What problem would be solved by killing yourself? I've got to save her. I continue to try and open the door.

"Whatever man. Even if she wants to hang herself, we should still try to save her. That's what a decent human would do.

Not just let someone die even if they wanted to. And I don't have time to discuss my top five rappers. Trying to save someone here." I try the next key. No luck.

"Well, who is your number one then?" Rip questions me again while poking me in my back. "You can at least tell me that."

I stop trying to open the door. With squinted eyes, I look at Rip in frustration. "Look you big dope, if you're not going to help me leave me alone."

"Ah, come on. Play along?"

I try the next key and the door unlocks. I look back at Rip, "Your mom. Your mom is my number one. How's that for an answer?" I run into the room toward Mary's pale lifeless body hanging from the ceiling.

"Stupid fake ass lookin' Arnold Schwarzenegger asking me about rappers and shit. I'm trying to save a life." I mumble to myself. I squat down and try to lift Mary up off the hook, but to no avail. I readjust and try to lift her off again with all my might. Once again, no luck. She continues to hang.

"Hey, Daniel. The paper that she wrote on reads *'I just want to be heard. I just want to be loved'*. Well I guess we heard her. I don't love her, but I definitely heard her psycho ass. Heard her loud and crystal clear."

What does she mean she *wants to be heard*? *Wants to be loved*? *Who wouldn't listen to her? Who wouldn't love her?* Just looking at her, I couldn't imagine why anyone wouldn't. Clearly there is something more going on in her head. The old saying "don't judge a book by its cover" has never been so fitting. Most men would gladly listen to her, if they only judged her by her cover. It glistens in the light like a brand-new book at Barnes & Noble. Her impeccably straight spine supports her cheerleader captain frame perfectly. However, that's the outside of the book. *What is going on inside of this book? If you read her pages what will you find?*

Would you find beautifully laced words of poetry? Flawlessly framed stanzas and thought-provoking sonnets that would put the great Emily Dickinson to shame? Or would you find stick-figure drawings with their eyes scratched out in black ink like a horror movie? What lies in the pages of Mary's book? I don't know. It's certainly more than what meets the eye. However, what I do know is that this book is not hanging from a shelf, but from a noose draped around her neck and her head folded down like a dog-eared page.

"Can you help me out here, Rip?"

"Move your scrawny butt to the side."

Rip brushes me to the side and with his brute strength easily lifts Mary off the hook. Nonchalantly, he tosses her face first onto the squeaking metal bed. The back side of her black shirt flips up showing her lower back tattoo. A tattoo of the Waffle House sign in bright yellow and black ink covers her backside. Quickly I flip Mary over and remove the tightly wound noose from around her neck. The dark red ligature marks and pattern around her neck are reminiscent of a holiday candy cane. She isn't breathing. Immediately, I start CPR. Finally, I get to use the skill Sweet Cakes taught me.

I remember her teaching me to press the breasts and then give the breaths. Breasts to breaths she would say to me. She always made things simple for me. I would jokingly respond and say, "so, fondle then kiss. Got it." She never thought that joke was funny. I miss her. I miss her so much. I've got to make it out of here alive for her. She's my world. She's my moon and my stars. I glance outside the door while doing compressions and see Enrique's brown eyes stare at me in shock.

"Do you know what you're doing there?" Rip asks.

"Yes, I know what I'm doing." I respond as I huff and puff while doing chest compressions. This isn't as easy as it looks on TV. I give two breaths and resume compressions. "One, two, three, four," I mumble to myself, counting compressions.

"I guess, man. Well I don't appreciate you talking about my mother. That's not cool man. I don't play like that. You don't really know me or my mother."

"Well, I'm sorry, Rip, but you were getting under my skin. You're trying to talk to me about rappers while a woman is hanging, about to die. Now, I'm doing chest compressions and you want to address a 'yo momma' joke. You really need to work on your timing, bro. I think between us two I'm on the only one who senses the severity of this situation. Enrique is over there frozen out of his mind. I know he gets it." I give Mary two breaths. She gasps and begins to move. Enrique runs in the room.

"Whatever, man. Just don't talk about my mom again."

Mary coughs, groans, and slowly begins to open her eyes. "Where am I? What happened?"

"You're at the hospital. You just tried to hang yourself. I did CPR, and got you back."

"So, I'm not dead or in heaven?"

"No. You're still here on earth."

Mary reaches for the rope again. I move it away.

"Damn. I just can't die. No matter how many times I've tried to kill myself, I just can't." Mary bangs her fist on the bed. "I always manage to come back somehow. I swear I have more lives than Catwoman. I'm going to the Aokigahara forest next time. Then, for sure I'd be dead."

"Why did you try to kill yourself?" I question.

"Because of life. Because of love. Because of people like him," she states while pointing at Rip.

"People like me? What did I do?" Rip responds in a shocked voice.

"You're so judgmental. You just think that everyone in here is coo-coo crazy. And that is so far from the truth. A lot of the people who are in here are not crazy. They are just *normal* people with normal problems. Stuff a lot of people go through but are too scared to talk about."

"How do you know?" Rip asks.

"I know because I am one of them, you big dope. I am one of those normal people. I have been in here so many times that I've lost count. I've been in here for depression. I've been in here for suicide. I've been in here for faking like I'm suicidal just so I can have someone to talk to. Someone to *hear me*. *To listen* to what's going on in my head. To get my thoughts out and give me some guidance. However, it all ends the same."

"How is that?" I ask.

"With some shrink giving me drugs. Drugs with God knows what in them. Causing all kinds of side effects. Had me walking around here like a damn zombie. All zoned out. Talking slow. Moving slow. Thinking slow. All those doctors want to do is drug you up. They don't want to talk to you to figure out what's truly going on in your head. And you know what? You know what's truly crazy?"

"You trying to hang yourself?" interjects Rip.

"Rip, can you just shut up?" I yell at the top of my lungs in utter frustration.

Mary slowly sits up, swings her long legs over the bed, and places her feet on the floor. She stands up, readjusts her shirt, and tightens up her scrub pants. She puts her hair in a ponytail, then takes the flower pen from the desk and pushes it into the knot in her hair. Suddenly, she grabs the gun on the desk and rushes ferociously toward Rip. She grabs him firmly by the genitals and places the gun to his temple. Enrique and I stare in complete shock at the quick turn of events.

"Call me crazy, again. Call me crazy one more mother fuckin' time. And I'll show you crazy. I'll rip your balls off and feed them to you. It's the season of giving, and I'm in the mood of giving you balls in your mouth. Do you want your jingle balls in your mouth?" Mary asks as she grips his balls tighter. I clench my own for self-protection.

"No, ma'am," Rip answers in a high-pitched voice.

"You sure? You sure you don't want to shit out your own small testosterone filled balls?"

"*Aaahhh*. No, Mary," Rip whispers in angst.

"You better put some respect on my name," she demands while squeezing again.

"No, Ms. Mary!"

"Well, don't ever call me crazy again," she demands before releasing his balls. "Or I'll turn you into a squirrel and have you swallowing nuts. Now, where was I?" Mary questions in a happy voice after releasing Rip.

"Um, you were talking about the doctors," I remind her.

"Oh yeah. The doctors. I like you, Daniel. You listen. I like that. The doctors don't listen at all. The crazy thing I was referring to, before I was so rudely interrupted by miniature golf balls over there, was that I feel like I can relate more to the other patients than the doctors."

"How so?" I question.

"Only they genuinely get me. Only they understand true mental warfare. Sometimes the greatest war is the war right between your ears. I go through mental battles daily. I fight demons inside that no one knows about. No one, but me. I silently fight those demons while the world passes me by. I battle with my depression. I battle with relationships. I battle with eating. I battle with my looks. I see blemishes that no one else probably even notices. Battle after battle after battle. There's a daily civil war going on in my head. I'm a walking battlefield. I am the north. And I am the south. I am the soldier. And I am the civilian casualty. I am the war and the war is me. And there are only certain people who can relate to my war and the battles that take place daily in my head. People who have been down in the trenches. Who have sloshed through the proverbial mental mud. Those who have dodged the shots of suicide. Those who have dived away from the bombs of depression. Frankly, only they can understand me.

"Not those stupid doctors. They haven't been through anything in their lives. They sit there in their chair taking notes, trying to get in your head. Nose all up in the air, acting all high and mighty. Acting like they can understand you. Constantly looking at their watch."

Mary pulls the chair out from the desk and sits in it. She grabs the flower pen in her hair and paper from the desk and mimics a doctor taking notes.

"'How does that make you feel, Mary? Well, did you take your medicine? Did you use those breathing techniques?' No, I didn't take my meds, and no I didn't fuckin' breathe slowly! That shit never works for me. They would know that if they ever listened to me. But they don't. They just give me meds and send me on my Mary little way. They know how to treat problems, but they don't how to treat the person. You get me, Daniel?"

"Yeah, I get you. If you're in the foxhole, you want to be able to look to your left and right and see guys you can trust. Someone with a little grit on their face. With some scars on their hands. People who look like they've been through some things. Someone who has been through the ups and downs of life. You relate more to those type of people."

"Right! I'm really starting to like you, Daniel. You get me. I've been in those trenches. I've battled with and still battle with depression. There've been days where I could literally feel the weight of the world on my shoulders. I could feel gravity pulling my soul to the ground. There have been days where I've just laid in the bed all day in darkness. Just lying in bed with my thoughts and total silence." Mary looks at Rip. "Big guy, have you ever laid in total silence? Turned off the TV, shutdown your laptop, put away your phone, closed the blinds, and just sat in total silence?"

"No," he mumbles while hunched over still clutching his family jewels. I must admit myself that I have not laid in total silence with my thoughts either. I'm afraid if I do that, I may hear the truth about myself.

"Well, it's quiet. Almost as quiet as you have been since I almost castrated you. Silence is scary. It's just you and your thoughts. I have laid in the bed for hours with my racing thoughts. Thoughts about myself, my family, current relationships, past relationships, and the world in general. Those thoughts can drive a person mad or further into the depths of depression, making you not want to be around anyone. Not even yourself.

"And there's only one way not to be around yourself. You kill yourself. That easily stops the thoughts. There have been many days, like today, that I've tried to kill myself. I've overdosed on pills. I've cut my wrists. I even left the car running in the garage one time. But for some ungodly reason I'm still alive."

"God must have you here for a reason. He must really love you. You're one of his special angels," I respond.

"God doesn't love me. No one loves me."

"How do you figure?"

"No one has *ever* told me they loved me. Not my mom. Not my dad. Not my siblings. Not any of my boyfriends. I mean *no one*. Do you know hard it is going through life feeling like no one loves you? Even God. If God loved me why would he surround me with unloving people?

"Why would he trap me in this tormented mind? Why would he have allowed the things that have happened to me in life? Why would he put me in this horrible body? I hate my body. I wish my stomach was flatter. I wish I didn't have these stretch marks. And I wish my nose was thinner and my hair was longer. Men call me beautiful all the time, but I don't see it. I don't see it at all. I see an ugly monster. Molded by the misguided hands of God."

It both amazes and confuses me how much she focuses on her imperfections. I don't know why some women do that. I see her as the upper echelon of beauty, but she doesn't. She focuses on the blemishes of her body's canvas. It's one thing that I may not ever understand as a man. I wake up, brush my hair, throw on a semi-wrinkled shirt and tie, and go about my day. Surprisingly, someone will tell me I look nice with my effortless outfit.

Women on the other hand wake up early to do their hair and makeup, pick out an outfit, pick out accessories and a purse to match their outfit, as well. All to look presentable to the world that may not recognize all the effort they put forth for it. The struggle of being a woman in today's judgmental society. If only they could be more appreciative of their natural beauty, but the world doesn't breed that type of environment. It doesn't allow it. The world must change.

"First of all, I don't know what in the world you're talking about. You're beautiful in my eyes. Stunningly beautiful. Don't you agree, Rip?"

"Yeah. Balls of beauty," he responds in anguish.

"Second, I love you."

"What?"

I squat down in front of her and look into her bright green eyes. "I said, 'I love you.' As a firm believer in God, I'm supposed to love my neighbor as I love myself. And you, Mary, are my neighbor. Therefore, I love you like I love myself, and I do love myself. I don't know if that works vice versa because you don't love yourself. So that would mean you probably don't love me. Whatever. But I love you. If no one has ever told you that you're loved, let it be me to tell you that you are loved. Mary, you are loved."

I find it heartbreaking that Mary has never experienced true love. I have never met someone who has never experienced love in their life. There are certain people who would expect to love you. Your mom. Your dad. Your spouse. They are *supposed* to love you, but I guess that's not necessarily true all the time. Sometimes the people in your life who are supposed to love you don't. Or maybe they do and just don't show it.

Mary begins to cry again. Black tears run down her face once more. She lifts up the mattress and pulls from underneath it a green baton. She hands it to me. It spells **LISTEN**. "Thank you, Daniel. Thank you for loving me and listening to me. I just wanted to be heard. I just wanted to be loved. And you have done them both. That's all I wanted from anyone. And I thank you."

"You know what I'm going to do, Mary? I'm going to save you. You're the person I want to save on this floor."

"Really, Daniel?"

"Yes. It's obvious that the big man upstairs isn't through with you yet. There's more in store for you. I want you to make it out of here alive to reach your potential. Your potential is so far in the distance that you can't see it right now, but I believe that you will reach it."

"Thanks, Daniel. I really needed to hear that," Mary wipes her tears with the barrel of the gun. "I don't hear that enough. All I hear is 'Mary, you're crazy.' I'm not crazy."

"You're right. You're not. I'll never call you crazy. Let's get out of here. Can you leave the gun?"

"Yeah. We can leave the gun. I don't even know if it works anyway." Mary pulls the trigger and the gun fires into the ceiling. Cement debris and dusts falls from the ceiling on to my head.

"It looks like it works," Mary says with a laugh. She stands up and skips toward the door. "Come on guys let's go explore the rest of the hospital."

I dust myself off and we all follow Mary out the door back, down the hallway. We pass back through the common area where the fecal bowl continues. Mary stands at the door blowing bubbles with her blue gum and looking at her split ends. My side is starting to hurt again.

"Come on guys. We don't have all day. Let's go. I'm sure Maestro has more in store for us," Mary says in a jovial voice.

As Enrique, a gingerly walking Rip, Mary, and I get on the elevator, I worry about Mary's last statement. *What else is in store for us on this journey?* I don't know if I'm more afraid for myself or the others left in the hospital. The unknown disturbs me. It's unsettling. Mary presses the button for the next floor.

"To the labor and delivery floor! Who's ready to catch a baby? Whooaaa!!!!" yells Mary.

SUICIDE

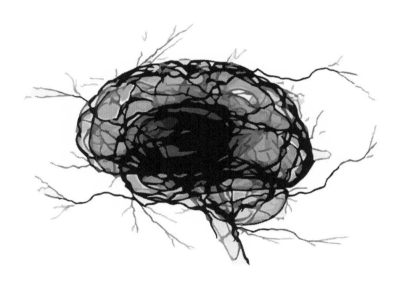

Definition: Suicide is the intentional taking of one's own life (1).
Statistics (Accurate as of 2018), (6)

1. Suicide is the 10th leading cause of death in the United States.

2. On average there are 129 suicides a day.

3. Middle-aged white men have the highest rate of suicide.

4. Men commit suicide 3.54 times more often than women.

5. Firearms account for more than half of all suicides, followed by suffocation.

6. Suicide rates based on ethnicity (2016): 1. White 2. Native American 3. Asian Pacific Islander 4. Black

7. The highest suicide rates based on age (2016): 1) 45-54 2) 85 and older 3) 55-64

Factors that contribute to suicide: There are many different reasons that people choose to commit suicide. Some of the most common reasons include: relationship problems, substance abuse, physical health problems, mental health problems, job issues, and money troubles. Individuals who suffer from anxiety and depression are at increased risk of committing suicide. Sadly, many reasons people commit suicide are unknown. (7)

I remember when you told me the time you tried to kill yourself. Just took a handful of pills and a few sips of alcohol. You said that if you didn't wake up you just didn't wake up. I believe that you wanted to wake up but was content with if you didn't. I'm glad you woke up. Someone reading this has attempted to commit or is thinking about committing suicide. Life is hard. I want you to know that you are loved and heard. Get the help you need before it's too late. Please don't hurt yourself. I know it can be scary talking to someone but make the leap. You can call the National Suicide Prevention Lifeline at 1-800-273-TALK (8255) or simply text TALK to 741741 to get help. (6)

CHAPTER 7

BASURA

"**O**h, God! Get this baby out of me! *Aaaaahhhhhh*," shouts a female voice as the elevator doors open to the fifth floor. Her voice is so loud that we can hear it through the closed doors of the hospital's maternity wing.

"Looks like someone is about to have a baby. I hope it's a girl. All boys are stupid. Except for you, Daniel, because you love me," says Mary. She winks and flashes a big smile at me. I flash an awkward, halfhearted smile in return. Enrique swipes his badge on the door and we enter.

We walk down the hallway toward the screams. Mary prances ahead of us like a little child in a school yard. Rip, Enrique, and I walk slowly behind her as if we're headed to the death chamber. But it's a different kind of chamber we're headed to. It's the delivery chamber. Someone sounds like they're about to deliver a baby. The motherly instinct in Mary gravitates toward the room in eager anticipation. The male instinct in us gravitates towards the empty room playing the Dan Le Batard show on ESPN. *I agree, Dan, they don't get the show.* Mary reaches the room and waves for us to hurry up. We finally reach the room.

"Ooooohhhhh shit!" yells the panting pregnant woman. "Get this baby out of me!"

The skinny, red haired woman tightly clutches the side rail of her bed. Her legs are spread wide in front of the doctor standing directly in front her. A nurse at the head of the bed holds the pregnant woman's hand and wipes her forehead. The brunette doctor turns around to us wearing a mask and bloody gloves.

"Hey, can one of you guys help me out here?" says the calm woman through her light blue mask. We all look at each other hoping that someone would volunteer to step up to the plate. No one steps up.

"You, black shirt, hold up one leg," says the doctor looking at me. "You, Muscles, hold up the other leg. Grab her by the bottom of her thigh and pull toward her head. Keep her knees bent. This will make it easier for her to push the baby. Now, hurry up! I can't deliver this baby by myself."

With the pace of a sloth, Rip and I walk over to the bedside. Rip grabs the right thigh with one arm and pulls is back as instructed. I, with all my might, lift the left thigh with both of my arms and pull back. I look weak compared to Rip.

"Okay. Come on now. I can see the head. Just breathe. Push when you feel the next contraction," instructs the doctor. Rip looks down between the pregnant woman's open legs.

"Did you get a good look at my pussy you perv?" she inquires.

"Actually, I did. There's a lot of hair going on down there. Yours and the babies, but I think I can tell the difference. Your hair is a little less curly." Immediately, the laboring woman reaches up and wrings Rip's collar. She pulls him in close. Their foreheads press against each other.

"Look funny man. Just help lift my leg up and quit being such a perv. This isn't a peep show. If you want that, you have to pay."

"Has the window closed to pay, already? If not, I have cash."

"Oh, you think you're so funny. If I wasn't trying to push out this baby I would. Ooooohhhh, shit! Here comes another contraction." She lets me go and grasps the bedrails.

"Okay, guys, hold her legs up. And you mom, push! Push with all your might!"

She pushes with the strength of a thousand oxen. The bed creaks as she grabs tightly onto the plastic rails. The pale head of the baby pops out. The baby's face points toward me and it's covered with slime. Not the cutest baby, but definitely not the ugliest. It's going to need a good bath after all of this.

"Keep pushing! It's almost out!" the doctor commands. The mother continues to push and moan. Finally, the baby pops out.

"It's a girl!" shouts the doctor. The nurse walks around from the head of the bed and the doctor hands her the baby. The doctor clamps the umbilical cord and hands the scissors to Rip.

"Well, don't mind if I do. I've always wanted to do this, but with my bare hands" Rip cuts the cord. "Next time, I'm just going to rip it in half. That's what I'm going to do with my own kids. Barbaric style." The nurse walks away with the baby.

"Congratulations on your beautiful baby girl. Did you know what you were having?" I question the new mom.

"No, I didn't."

"Oh, you wanted it to be a surprise?"

"No. I just never went to the doctor to find out. I haven't been to the doctor my whole pregnancy. My water broke earlier today, and I just came on in."

"Um, okay. That's strange. Well, did you have any potential names picked out."

"No. None at all. How about you pick out a name?"

"No. No. You can't put that kind of pressure on me. It's your child. You pick the name."

"No, I insist. You pick the name. It would be my pleasure."

"I don't know what name to give her. What name do you give such a quiet baby? Not even crying. I thought that most babies cry after they are born. At least that's what happens on TV."

"She's not breathing," the nurse says calmly. She starts compressions with her fingers.

"What do you mean she isn't breathing?" asks Rip.

"Like I said, the baby isn't breathing. I'm doing CPR."

"Alright let's bring the baby down to the NICU stat! There's not much blood coming out of the mom's vagina. She should be okay," says the doctor. "Muscles, I want you to stay here and keep rubbing her stomach right here." The doctor grabs Rip's hand and places it on the lower part of the mom's abdomen. "I want you to keep rubbing here. This will help the uterus firm and decrease the bleeding. Can you do that?"

"Yea, I can do that. No problem."

"Good. Now don't be surprised if the placenta falls out. It's kind of looks like an alien Frisbee. It'll be attached to the umbilical cord that's coming out of her vagina. You're not squeamish, are you?"

"No! Do you see how big I am? Nothing grosses me out."

"Good. I'm counting on you. There are a lot of crazy people roaming the hospital right now. I've heard some shooting and saw some of the doctors dragged out of here. The terrorists were nice enough to let me stay, but I don't know if they'll be back. So, you're going to be responsible for protecting her. We'll come back to check on you guys. Now, the rest of you come with me. Amy, put her in the basket and let's roll her back to the NICU."

"OK, Tina," the nurse responds back.

Amy gives the unresponsive baby two breaths in her mouth and then places her in a rolling crib. The baby is pale, beginning to turn light blue, and lies motionless. This doesn't look good. This doesn't look good at all. Amy wheels her through the door and down the hallway. Dr. Tina continues the chest compressions as Amy pushes the crib. Mary, Enrique, and I trail behind. Rip stays back with the baby's mother.

"Come on little baby! You gotta make it!" Mary encourages while Tina continues compressions.

We make one turn down one hallway and then another turn down another before reaching a sliding glass door. Tina places her badge on the scanner and the door slides open. We enter what I suppose is the NICU. In the NICU there are multiple babies in incubators. The children's families are standing at each child's bedside. One of the fathers rushes toward us as we come in.

"A nurse rushed us all in here. Then, she locked us in. Why are we being held in here? We've heard screams outside. What's going on?" he asks.

"Out of the way, sir," demands Tina. Amy wheels the nameless baby girl to an empty incubator and Tina places her in it. Tina then continues CPR while Amy places an oxygen bag mask on the baby and then hooks her up to a monitor. Something about witnessing CPR being performed on an infant has changed everyone's demeanor. The look of anger that was initially on everyone's face as we entered has been replaced by looks of concern.

Just a few minutes earlier, I was doing CPR on Mary, and now I'm watching it being performed. Now, I can see why Enrique looked at me with so much shock and moved slowly when I asked him for the keys. It's tough being on the opposite end watching someone try to save a life and there's nothing you can do to help. Absolutely nothing. Mary grabs my hand as we watch Amy and Tina perform CPR. The palm of her hand is soft and warm. We interlock fingers. She squeezes tightly.

"Come on! Don't you die on me," says Tina. Amy gives two breaths with the oxygen bag mask. I glance around the room and notice that somehow, we have all unknowingly gravitated closer to the child. One woman cries quietly on the chest of her husband's flannel shirt. He calmly strokes the back of her brown hair while he bites his lip to fight back tears. Suddenly, a monitor starts to beep.

"We have a heartbeat! She's breathing now," shouts Tina. The entire room let's out a collective sigh of relief. A couple of people start to clap. The baby starts to cry. I've never been so happy to hear a baby cry in my entire life. Tina looks at me.

"You. Go check on Muscles and mom. Tell her that we saved her baby's precious life. Here's my key card so you can get out and back in. Hurry up and get back. I'm going to need your help."

I let go of Mary's hand and snatch the key card from Tina and dash away. I scan the card at the door we entered in. It opens, and I take off running. Down the hallway, I go running shoeless toward the delivery room. My backpack jostles from side to side on my back with each step I take. I can't wait to see the look of happiness on the mother's face when I tell her that they were able to save her baby's life. I couldn't imagine being in her position and seeing her baby like that. The baby girl, who's been in her womb for nine months. The baby she's been talking to, nurturing, and waiting on to come into the world. And when she finally comes in to the world she's unresponsive and whisked away from her. That must be heartbreaking. She must be so worried and distraught right now. I finally reach the room. Her bed is empty. Rip is passed out slouched on the ground. I run over and kneel beside him. I slap him across the face.

"Wake up, Rip! Wake yo ass up!" I demand while gritting my teeth. Rip's eyes begin to slowly open. "What happened? Where is she? Where is the mom?"

"She said she had to go," he groggily responds.

"Had to go? Go where?"

"I don't know, man. She just said that she had to go. That nasty placenta thing fell out of her, and then I just felt all woozy. I just remember her saying 'I gotta go' as I passed out. She couldn't have left that long ago." I look on the floor by the empty bed and see the out-of-this-world looking placenta. It's dark blue color, wet surface, and engorging blood vessels only adds to its alien mystique. I can see why Rip fainted after seeing it fall out of her. A bloody trail leads out the door and into the hallway.

"Come on man. We have to go find her." I help Rip up to his feet. We take off down the hallway, following the bloody trail.

Where did she run off to? Why did she say she I have to go? Would she actually leave her child here? Not just a child, but a newborn baby. No one in their right mind would abandon their baby here, especially amid all this chaos. Maybe she said she had to go because she was worried about her baby and wanted to find her.

We reach the front door where we originally entered. A hospital ID band lays on the floor next to the door. I pick it up and read the name: Amelia Airheart. I look through the window of the door and see that the bloody trail has ended at the elevator doors. She's left. I pound my fist on the metal door.

"Fuck! What is going on here?" I scream and throw my hands up in the air.

"My bad, bro. Sorry I didn't stop her from leaving," Rip says with a soft pat on my back.

"It's okay man. It's not your fault. I just don't understand why she would leave. Where did she go? Let's head back to the others."

Rip and I walk back to the NICU. Rip looks defeated and embarrassed that he was not able to carry out his responsibility. I am equally disappointed in him. It was his fault that she was able to leave. He had one job which was to just watch her. On the other hand, I have a feeling that no matter the circumstance, she would have still found a way to leave. If Rip hadn't passed out, she probably would have sweet talked him into wheeling her out of the hospital and into a taxi. He probably would have even paid the fare.

We reach the NICU. I scan the key card again and we enter. Upon entering the room, I sense that the atmosphere has changed.

"Welcome back, Daniel. We've been waiting on you to return," Dr. Tina says.

"Yeah, we hurried back as fast as we could. We couldn't find the mom. She left. Wait. How do you know my name?" I question. I scan the room. Tina and Amy are now dressed in the same outfit as me. Tina sits in a rocking chair, moving to and fro ever so slowly with a baby clutched in arms. Amy stands behind her staring at the baby with a gun at her side.

Enrique and Mary quietly stand off to the side of them. Each of the parents I saw earlier stands again by what I assume is their child's incubator. Their heads face down. Some of the parents are sniffing and crying. Each incubator is now wrapped in a white trash bag with a small hole towards the head of each child.

I sigh and guess, "Maestro?"

"Bingo!" responds Amy.

"Tell us what you see in here Daniel," says Tina.

"I see distraught parents and sick babies. And I see incubators that are now wrapped in white plastic bags. Looks like they may be trash bags. That's what I see."

"Take a peek into one of the incubators. Tell me what you see."

I squeeze by the parents of one child and take a closer look into the incubator through the hole cut out in the trash bag. I report my findings.

"I see a small infant sleeping under some kind of blue light. I'm going to assume he is a boy because of the blue socks he's wearing and the blue light. His eyes are covered with a blindfold."

"Now look at another baby."

I make my way over to another incubator. Standing alone by herself is the child's mother. She sobs heavily into the palms of her hands. I whisper to her, "Stay strong."

"I see a small infant. A very small infant. Probably, could barely fit into the palm of my hand. It's shaking a lot and looks very jittery. Like its freezing cold."

"It, is a girl. It has a name. Her name is Michelle," mutters the mom under her breath.

"I'm sorry," I whisper back in a soft voice.

"You know what I see Daniel. I see flowers. Precious delicate flowers slowly sprouting throughout the room. Some flowers taking slower to blossom because they are a little sick. While other flowers in here are growing at just the right rate. I used to have my own precious delicate flower, Daniel. Zach was his name. Oh, how I miss my precious Zach." Tina stands up out of her chair and hands the baby she is holding to Amy. Tina begins to walk between the incubators.

"Oh, my little Zach. The baby of the family. We already had two girls, but my husband wanted to try one more time to have a boy. He loved our two girls, but desperately wanted a son. His own little mini me. Someone he could play catch with. Someone he could work on cars with. Someone who everyone would recognize as his son just by looking at him.

"I was oh so happy to give him that son. I will never forget the look on his face as we cut the cake at our gender reveal party. Never have I seen someone so excited to get a blue slice of cake. 'We did it!' he said. 'No, you did it. I told you we just needed to try new positions to get a boy,' I replied.

"A few years later the pitter patter of Zach's little steps resonated throughout the house daily. He would come running around the corner with the biggest smile on his chunky cheeks. He loved for me to pinch those cheeks," Tina wipes a tear from her own chunky cheek.

"Tina, what happened to Zach?" I question.

"Well, if you must know, my husband killed him!" The somber mood in the room takes an even more somber tone. Everyone in the room ears perk up and give Tina their full attention.

"Killed him? What do you mean he killed him?" I probe.

"I mean exactly what I said, Daniel. He killed him. How ironic a person in charge of saving other's lives couldn't even save his own son's life. Despite what you may think Daniel, I am a real doctor. I am a board-certified obstetrician and gynecologist here at this hospital. I catch babies and look at vaginas all day. I enjoy catching babies more than looking at vaginas, but hey it's part of the job. In my opinion, there is no greater feeling in the world than helping bring life into it. For nine months, give or take a few weeks, I'm with a family throughout their entire journey. From them finding out that they are pregnant. To the delight on their face when they find out whether they are having a boy or a girl. To the delivery. I am with them."

"I'm sure you've worked with a lot of families," says Rip.

"Why, yes. Yes, I have Muscles. I've worked with hundreds of families. A lot of good families. I see married families. I see single mothers. I see couples who are surprised to be pregnant. I see people who have been struggling to have a child. I see hordes of good people, but I also see an equal amount of bad people."

"Who do you define as bad people?" I ask.

"Do you think that every person or family that gets pregnant is fit to have children? Working in this field has really made me think not everyone should have the right to have children. Women strung out on drugs. Spouses who show up to doctor's appointments drunk or high. Parents on their phone during the entire visit. Mothers who don't have any prenatal care and just show up to the hospital when their water breaks, like the mother you met today. Those are the bad people."

"She just showed up today?" I ask.

"Yep. The only reason I know this is because this isn't her first time doing this. This is either her second or third time. I helped deliver her first baby. A beautiful healthy baby boy a few years ago. She left the hospital in the middle of the night. Said that she was going for a smoke break and never returned. Just deserted her baby. I heard that a similar woman came in and did the same thing last year. I never got confirmation that it was her, but I suspect it was her based on the description I got. She uses a different name every time she comes. The first time it was Jane Doe, but she spelled it J-A-I-N-E D-O. She's not the brightest crayon in the box. I think she's homeless and sleeps with men for money. I didn't happen to catch her name this time."

"It was Amelia. Amelia Airheart." I respond.

"And just like Amelia jetted out of here and is lost forever. How fitting of a name. Maybe she's brighter than I thought. See Daniel people like her, and others treat their children like trash." Michelle's baby begins to cry loudly. "See there goes one of those trash babies right there."

"Don't call my baby trash!" yells Michelle's mother.

"I will call your baby how you treat her. Like trash. T-R-A-S-H. Trash. You see, I know about you, Ms. Amber. Date of birth 06/22/83 from Glasgow, Kentucky. You delivered 10 days ago. You came in high is a kite on cocaine that day. I bet you don't even remember who delivered your baby. Do you?!"

"No. No, I don't," she mutters with her head down.

"Doesn't even remember who delivered her baby, ladies and gentlemen." All of the eyes of the room fixate on the mother and burn a hole through her. "It was me. I was between your legs delivering your crack baby and you don't even remember me being there. Wow. I wonder if you even remember who was between her legs when you conceived the baby, but that's a question for a different day. Because today's question for you, Daniel, is which baby you're going to save?"

"Going to save?" I respond confusingly. Tina rips the white trash bag off baby Michelle's incubator.

"See, baby Michelle isn't worthy of a white trash bag. She doesn't come from a pure household. See these other families in here. They represent a good household. People who deserve to have children. They're educated. Have money. They have good jobs. Went to their doctor's appointments. The mothers took their vitamins. These are the people who should have children.

They did all they could to protect, love, and help their children. As good parents should. Although, their children are damaged goods right now they didn't treat their unborn children like trash. Unlike, Amber and Amelia. Their children get black trash bags. Because they are trash and unfit to bear children. Amelia left her child out here by herself like a trash bag on the corner on trash day. Left to fend for herself and get picked up by God knows who. And you Amber treated yourself and unborn child like trash by using crack. Couldn't even stop using for nine months. Such a shame."

Tina opens a black trash bag and lays it in an empty crib. Amy places what I know now to be Amelia's baby into the trash bag. She then walks over to Tina who is now at Michelle's incubator. Tina opens another black trash bag and unlocks the incubator. Amber grabs Tina's arm.

"Don't you lay a hand on my baby or I will fuckin' kill you," warns Amber.

"Um, Amy if she touches me again shoot her, please," Tina instructs.

"No problem," responds Amy. She shoots a warning shot by Amber's head. Amber ducks quickly. She then raises her hands in the air and takes a few steps back away from her baby. More babies start to cry because of the loud gunshot.

"See Daniel I find it highly ironic that now she wants to protect her baby. Who was protecting her baby while it was in the womb? Surely not her. Not her own mother. You couldn't stop using drugs for a couple of months?" Tina opens the incubator. She lifts up Michelle and places the black trash bag flatly under her. She places Michelle down in the trash bag. Michelle begins to cry with a high-pitched sound that could shatter a wine glass. It's a cry of pain and anguish. I pity this baby's pain. No child should suffer like this.

"I'm sorry. I'm sorry!" says Amber. "I couldn't stop. It just wasn't that easy. The cravings were crazy and going through withdrawal was even crazier. When I came down from my high I would always ball my eyes out crying as I rubbed my womb asking for my baby and God to forgive me. I would say that was the last time. Even though I knew it wasn't true and that I would probably be using again in a few days or even hours. It's not that easy to quit."

"Pitiful. Just pitiful. If a parent can't even protect their own child, who will? I did all that I could to protect and take care of Zach and that still wasn't even enough. But at least I tried. My husband and I live crazy lifestyles. I work ridiculous hours here at the hospital and my husband the same as a cardiologist at his clinic. Nevertheless, we made it work and divided the workload. Usually, I would bring the kids to school. However, one day I couldn't, and he had to bring them. He bought our two girls to school first. Then, he was to drop off Zach at daycare and head to work. However, he forgot to drop off Zach. He totally forgot about sleeping Zach in the back seat. He went straight to work and left him in the back seat. Trapped in the hot car. It wasn't until he got off work that he realized he left him. He looked in the rearview mirror as he got in the car after work and saw Zach's limp body slumped over in his car seat."

"Oh, Tina," I respond in sadness.

"He drove straight to this hospital and bought him up here to this floor. He's a freakin' cardiologist and hadn't even done CPR or anything for that matter. Stupid ass. He just freaked out and did the first thing he thought of which was to bring him to me. He found me in the break room, and carrying the limp body of our two-year-old son, he screamed 'help me!' But I couldn't it was too late. Zach was already dead."

At this moment, I am speechless. I don't know what to say. I cannot find any word or combination of words that could comfort her. Sometimes there aren't any right words. Sometimes the right words are no words.

Everyone looks at Tina with eyes of sorrow. We all have totally forgotten about her putting a baby into a trash bag. At this moment, we are back in time with Tina as she sees her dead child.

"We buried Zach and gradually tried to move on with our lives, but we couldn't. Things weren't the same. My husband was overcome with so much guilt and grief that he sunk into a deep depression. He couldn't work or focus on anything. I also fell into a deep depression, but chose to over work to distract me from what was going on at home. I hated going home to see my husband. Every time I looked at him, I saw my son. It was uncanny how much they looked alike. Looking at him instantly brings back the pain of losing my son. They say that time heals all wounds, but what they don't say is that you will have a scar. Every day that I look at my husband I see that scar. He is a constant, daily reminder of my pain from the loss of my child."

"Why couldn't you just have another child to replace Zach? Another mini me." Questions Mary from the back of the room. Tina looks back at Mary with squinted eyes. She starts to walk towards Mary.

"Make another child? Make another child to replace Zach? Obviously, you haven't had a kid before nor have been pregnant. Every woman who has had a child or been pregnant raise your hand." All the women in the room raise their hand except for Mary.

"Now every woman who has lost a child either through sickness, accident, or a miscarriage keep your hand up. Everyone else put your hand down." Half of the women in the room put their hand down. Five women, plus Amy and Tina, keep their hand up in the air.

"Now for those of you left who have lost a child put your hand down if you have ever truly gotten over the loss of that child." No one puts their hand down.

"If you don't think about that child once a month, once a week, or once a day, put your hand down." No one puts their hand down. Tina gets in front of Mary's face with her hand raised high and stares deep into her eyes. Their nose touch as though they're Eskimo kissing.

"And last question. If you think having another child would ever replace the loss of that child, put your hand down." No one puts their hand down.

"You can't replace one child with another child. A child is not like a meal that you messed up cooking and can just cook again. Starting from the womb each child is special and irreplaceable. I named my children while they were in the womb. I talked to them in the womb. Each gave me different weird cravings and did things to my body that the other child didn't do." Tina lifts her black shirt. She points to the stretch marks on her side and then pulls on the rolls of her stomach.

"Each child is special and unique. So, no. I just can't have another one to replace Zach. He's irreplaceable. Agree ladies?" All of the women in the room nod in agreement. Tina puts her hand down and walks away from an embarrassed Mary. The rest of the women with their hands raised put them down.

"Now, imagine losing your child and having to come in to deliver babies for a living. From you losing life to helping others gain life. Then, on top of that witnessing people like Amelia, Amber, and others do the things that they do to their children. It can weigh heavy on a person. These people have a responsibility to protect their children, and they have failed. They, have treated them like trash and consequently we end up here." Tina walks to the center of the room and looks at me.

"Now, Daniel you have a choice that you have to make. You must pick a child to save. One you will be able to take with you. The other one will be thrown out like the trash it has been treated as. What's your choice?" The screams of all the babies in the room begin to echo louder. Everyone stares at me. I stare at everyone.

How can I choose which child to save? Are Amber's sins greater than Amelia's or vice versa? Do the sins of the mothers really have to affect these children? No child should have to suffer for the actions of their parents. Yet, both children are suffering and will suffer more because of their mother's actions. Amelia's baby will grow up without her actual mother and likely will end up in the foster care. Michelle, on the other hand, will probably suffer from a multitude of ailments resulting from her mother's drug use. I can't pick which child to save. I won't pick.

"Tina, I am so sorry about your loss, but this won't bring Zach back. I won't pick which child lives. I don't have the heart to.

This is insane." Tina pulls two guns from behind her back out of thin air. One she points at an incubator with an infant in it and the other at the child's father who looks at her with intense rage.

"Daniel, I don't want to bring Zach back. I'm very rational; I know that can't happen. I just want people to realize the responsibility that they have in bringing life into this world. That's the message that I want you and everyone else to hear. A responsibility to provide and protect your children. Even if it means protecting them from yourself. Now, Daniel. As you can tell you're in quite the predicament. Don't pick and I'll shoot this innocent baby. Do pick and this baby lives."

Overcome with emotions and confusion, I yell, "I can't pick! I won't pick!"

Tina cocks the gun. The child's father runs toward me like a football player pursuing a tackle. Hurriedly, I back up in retreat and clumsily fall to the ground. He dives onto the ground and puts me in a chokehold from behind. I grasp at his arms to release the hold, but my resistance is futile.

"There you go! Be a responsible parent and protect your child. Fight for em'!" cheers Tina.

"If my child dies I'm going to kill you myself," he whispers loudly in my ear. "Now pick a kid." My legs kick and squirm ash he chokes me. I pull harder on his arm, but this only strengthens his grip around my neck. My breath begins to get short and I can feel myself passing out. This guy is about to kill me for his child. I need to make a choice or I'm going to die.

"I choose Amelia's child," I eek out in a faint voice.

He loosens the grip on my neck. "Say it louder," he demands.

"I choose Amelia's child to save!" Tina puts the gun down. The father stops choking me and throws me to the side like I'm a piece of trash. He stands up and walks back to his wife and child. His wife gives him a big hug with both arms. Mary rushes over towards me.

"Baby, are you okay?" Mary asks while wiping sweat off my forehead.

"Yeah, I'm okay," I respond as I stand up, rubbing my neck.

"Why did you choose her? Why not my baby!?" asks Amber.

"Look at your child, Amber! Look at her! She's in so much pain and suffering right now. Listen to the way she cries. Look at how she shakes so violently. Who knows what else she is going to have to go through in life. I heard on the news once that babies like those suffer numerous health conditions, both mental and physical. I don't want Michelle to suffer through life. I'm sorry, but I had to choose, or I was going to die."

"Well, die then! You didn't have to choose!" she shouts back.

"A worthy choice, Daniel. Now, time to throw away the trash." Tina walks back over to Michelle's incubator. Amber begins to fight Tina off her child. "Amy can you handle her for me. I just can't take her meddling anymore." Amy shoots Amber in the leg. She falls to the floor with a thud and starts screaming.

"Thanks, Amy. See, you're one of the few who gets me. We both work up here and both see the same things up here daily. So, you can attest to what I'm saying about the sorry people who are allowed to have children. And we both have lost children. We know each other's pain. That's what makes our bond even stronger. I thank you for your love and support with all of this."

"No problem, girl. We're in this thing together. And don't forget you owe me $20 from that bet. I told you that she would leave after delivering that baby."

"You're right. I thought she would at least stay for a little while." Tina closes the bag around Michelle and pulls the bag's strings tight before tying a knot. She picks up the bag and a muffled cry begins inside of it. Michelle flops around in the bag as Tina walks to the trash chute. Amy follows her with her gun facing everyone, ready to shoot anyone moving toward them.

"Say your goodbyes, Amber," Tina orders while opening the shoot.

"Please don't throw my baby away! I'm sorry! My baby, I'm sorry!" yells Amber from the depths of her soul.

"You treated her like trash and therefore she is trash. And what do we do with trash, Amber?"

"No! Not my baby!" Amber begins to crawl toward Tina. Her leg wound leaves a bloody trail behind her.

"Wait, Tina. Let's think this through. You don't have to do this," I beg of her and step forward. Amy points her gun at me.

"I have thought this through, and this wasn't my choice anyway. It was yours. Amy, since Amber doesn't want to answer tell her what we do with trash."

"We throw it away."

"Yes, we throw it away." Tina grabs the metal handle on the trash chute and opens its squeaky door. Casually, she drops Michelle in the trash chute and releases the handle. The shoot closes with a loud bang. The entire room gasps in horror. I am in utter shock. Amber lets out a yell that could only come from a saddened mother.

"My baby! How could you?"

"That baby had been treated like trash for a long time. Before she was even born. So, don't act like this is new Amber. I just did what needed to be done. Today, I freed you from being a burden to each other and society. So, don't you cry. You can do all the drugs you want to do now, and you don't have to worry about taking care of your child. And Michelle doesn't have to worry about being taken care of by a crackhead mother. Everyone wins," Tina says while dusting off her hands. "Plus, if you want another one later you can just make one and replace this one. Isn't that right, Mary?" Mary puts her head down in shame. Tina walks over to Amelia's baby and takes her out of the open black trash bag.

"What are you going to name her?" Tina asks me. But I don't answer. I am frozen in shock looking at the trash chute. *Did she really just throw a baby away? Did I just condemn a child to death, so I could live? This can't be real. I must be dreaming. Someone wake me up.* Tina presses the child, now swaddled in a pink blanket, against my chest.

"What are you going to call her?" she asks again. I unfreeze, look down, and embrace the baby in my arms. My eyes begin to well up.

"Hope. I'm going to name her Hope."

"Why Hope?"

"Because I hope that she has a good life. I hope that she and I make it out of here alive. I hope that Amber forgives me." Amber begins to sob louder.

"Hope. How fitting of a name. I hope for the same things you wished for and more, Daniel. You have done your job. It's time for you guys to go," says Tina.

"What will happen to the rest of everyone here?"

"They will get to stay with their children until all of this is over. You have my word that they will be okay. No one else will get hurt. Now, take Hope and the rest of your disciples and get out of here."

Enrique, Rip, Mary, sweet little Hope, and I leave the NICU and get back on the elevator. My hands begin to shake. My side starts to hurt again, and my neck is still writhing in pain from being choked. I hand Hope to Mary and a baton falls from underneath her blanket. I pick it up and read it: **RESPONSIBILITY**.

The realization of the choice I just made begins to disturb my soul. Maestro said the choices I made or didn't make would have a major impact on others, but not like this. Not like this. I did not throw the child away, but I did pick a child. I did choose. *Who was my responsibility tied to in that situation? Those children or myself in the midst of being choked to death?*

The pain in my abdomen is intensifying, and I am nauseated. I succumb to the pain, and take a knee on the elevator. Suddenly, I begin to vomit on the floor. I see the beans and rice that I ate three days ago in the vomit. *Why is that still inside me? Shouldn't that have digested by now?*

"Look at yourself, Daniel. You're throwing up and you're obviously in pain. Don't you think it's time to leave? We just saw a freaking baby get thrown away. Are things crazy enough now, Daniel? Are you ready to try and get out of here?" asks Rip.

I pick my head up and gaze my eyes upon Rip with a mouth full of vomit residue and respond. "Yes. Things are crazy enough now Rip. I'm ready to get out of here."

Rip presses the button on the elevator for the ground floor. The door closes and the elevator descends. I look at Enrique. Enrique looks at me.

"It wasn't supposed to be like this," he says in plain English.

PRENATAL EXPOSURE
TO DRUGS AND ALCOHOL

Marijuana: This is the most common illicit drug that women use during pregnancy. Children who are born to mothers who have smoked marijuana may potentially have a low birthweight, short gestation (born too early), and have major malformations. These malformations may include congenital heart defects, genitalia abnormalities, and brain defects. Developmental problems may also occur and can show up as early as three years old. (8)

Cocaine: Research has shown that usage of cocaine during pregnancy can lead to reduced growth of the fetus, delays in sensory-motor development, attention deficits, and other conditions. Problems with growth can last until a child is ten years old, leading to smaller weight, growth, and head circumference. Most birth defects caused by cocaine use during pregnancy are found in the brain and in the heart. Heart problems may include missing a ventricle, which is an entire section of the heart. Brain malformations may occur in the area of the brain associated with cognition and mood. (9)

Alcohol: The consumption of alcohol during pregnancy can lead to fetal alcohol syndrome (FAS). FAS is the most common non-inherited cause of intellectual disability. This form of intellectual disability can be prevented if women avoid drinking during pregnancy. FAS includes: slowing of growth prenatal and/or postnatal, facial abnormalities (ex. thin upper lip, irregularities around the eyes), central nervous system dysfunction (abnormal brain structure), and neurobehavioral disabilities (intellectual disability). (10)

Laws: One would think that for something so serious the law would be consistent across the land regarding this matter. However, laws are rarely ever that simple. The law for prenatal drug exposure varies from state to state. In some states, such as Kentucky and Louisiana, health care providers are required to test for and report prenatal drug abuse. But not all states require testing for prenatal drug exposure. In many states, prenatal drug exposure can lead to termination of parental rights. Mothers can be charged for prenatal abuse, but Tennessee is the only state that defines prenatal substance abuse as a criminal act of child abuse and neglect. (11)

CHAPTER 8

DOUBLE

TROUBLE[x]

"You can speak English?" I ask in astonishment.

"Yes. Yes, I can."

"But how? Maestro said that you couldn't speak English."

"No. He said I spoke a little English. That just meant that I didn't speak it as well as you. You're the one who defined what that meant."

I get up from my knees and wipe the vomit off my mouth. "Whatever, man. What did you mean when you said that it wasn't supposed to be this way?"

"This entire situation was not supposed to be like this."

"What? You are a part of all of this!" I grab Enrique by his collar and jack him up against the metal elevator walls. "Not supposed to be like this? What was it supposed to be like? I want answers. You hear me?! Answers!" Rip pulls me off Enrique like he was a bouncer breaking up a fight in the club.

"I'm sorry. Maestro said that he just needed my help to find the doctor who killed his wife, but he didn't say it would be all of this," Enrique answers while readjusting his clothes.

I look at Mary clutching Hope. "Did you know it was going to be all of this?"

She shrugs. "Maybe. It didn't matter to me. I planned on being dead at the end of this anyway."

Rip begins talking to himself in the corner of the elevator. "I didn't sign up for any of this. That's what I get for falling asleep. If only I would have stayed awake, I wouldn't be in this mess. Rip, you gotta do better." The doors of the elevator open to the ground floor and we walk out following the exit signs.

"I thought that we were in this together, Enrique. That you were on my team, but it turns out you're not. You're a mole!" I accuse.

"I'm sorry for leading you astray. However, I just wanted to help change the system. Make the system better. Working here in the hospital, I see so many messed up things. I just wanted to help turn things around."

"What do you mean? You got a story too? You about to hand me a baton? I can't take any more of this shit."

"No, I'm not about to hand you a baton. However, everyone has a story in here. Well, not just in here, but the world in general. It's up to you if you want to make the effort to listen to their stories."

"Well, I'm fresh out of ears today for listening. I've been through enough. It's time for me to get out of here," I respond angrily. Enrique stops walking and the rest of us continue walking ahead of him down the hallway. Enrique begins yelling angrily at me from behind.

"You haven't been through shit, you punto!" Instantly, we all stop in our tracks and turnaround.

"Nigga, what?" I respond, infuriated. Normally, I don't like saying the word "nigga" in front of mixed company unless I'm really angry. I am now livid. He just called me a punto.

"You haven't been through shit!" he yells even louder down the bright corridor. "I work here six days a week and see shit every day. And you haven't been through or seen shit at all. You ever seen a man with a gunshot wound to his head? Gushing blood and fighting for his life? You ever heard a family screaming and crying on the ground after they find out their family member died in an accident? Listened to a woman find out she had a miscarriage? I bet you haven't. Never seen or experienced close to anything of the sort. So, like I said you haven't been through jack shit."

Mary and Rip turn their heads and stare at me for a response. I look at Enrique with a blank face. My angry, wrinkled brow has now resolved. He's right. I haven't been through or seen any of that. I guess going through shit is relative to each individual. Shit varies from person to person and I'm low on the shit scale according to Enrique.

"As a custodian, I see a lot of shit here. Good shit and bad shit. I blend in like camouflage. People rarely pay me any mind, but I am very observant." He begins to yell even louder. "I'm the one cleaning all the blood up in the ER after the gunshot victim comes in leaking blood everywhere! I'm the one changing the trash bag next to the family that has been here for over a week hoping their brain-dead family member pulls through! I'm the one who hears the doctors talking bad about the patients! How they're fat or crazy. I see so much shit daily and there was nothing I could do to help. I thought I was too powerless to make change. Until, I met Maestro. He shared with me how I could help change the system."

"By doing what? Killing babies?" I ask.

"No, not that. By talking to some of the doctors and nurses here. He said that we needed to go to their meetings or offices and tell them our concerns directly. Maestro and I both wanted them to care more about the patients. Show some compassion. Act like they actually cared about people. He shared with me what happened to his wife and how he wanted to help change the system. He talked to me about other problems in health care and said that we could be the jumpstart to changing things. Like a medical revolution. He mentioned that he knew of others who felt the same way. He said we would organize a sit-in.

"He and the others he knew would storm the hospital. Then, we would sit-in the doctor's offices and operating rooms until they listened to our complaints. Seemed like a great idea. Consequently, I provided him a few key cards to access the hospital and certain areas. I believed in him and his message. But I didn't agree to all of this. This was not what I signed up for."

"What happened to his wife?" I question.

"They killed her," says Maestro as he walks around the corner from a hallway behind Enrique. The hairs on my arm stand tall as he appears. He has a dog on a chain. I realize now that Maestro is the same guy that I saw in the waiting room when I entered the hospital. The dog is Bo. He growls after recognizing me. Maestro keeps a firm pull on Bo's chain as he starts barking.

"What are you guys doing down here? I know for a fact you haven't been to every floor," he questions.

I look at Mary and Rip hoping that one of them would blurt out an answer. Abruptly, Rip and his muscular frame take off like a bolt of lightning down the hallway. He looks like a running refrigerator. I look at Mary and Enrique. In sync, we all take off running in Rip's direction. This rush of adrenaline has taken away the pain in my side. I look back at Maestro. He drops Bo's chain and he starts chasing us, dragging his chain behind him.

"Keep running, Mary! Don't drop Hope." I shout. Mary looks back and sees Bo chasing us. She screams.

We both pick up pace, trailing Rip who is following the signs that say hospital entrance. Enrique has caught up to us. There are so many twists and turns in this hallway. *Left turn. Right turn. Left turn. Right turn.* I begin to wobble with each turn. I swear there must be at least 504 turns to get to this entrance.

Rip is running as fast as he can. Loudly he huffs and puffs. In the distance, I start to hear him wheeze. We make one final turn and reach the foyer of the hospital. Rip is bent over with his hands on his knees taking rapid, deep breaths.

"I need my inhaler," he says slowly in a soft, raspy voice. He's wheezing even louder.

I turn around to look for Bo charging around the corner, but he doesn't come. It's as though he's disappeared into thin air. I look outside the glass doors and see bright, flashing police lights. In the distance, there are at least ten police cars. In front of those cars are three large armored vehicles. Suddenly, a group of officers exit the back of the vehicle in SWAT gear. In precision, they march toward the hospital and enter through the front doors. They stand between us and the doors with their weapons pointed at us. Never in my life have I been happier to see the police. I pray to God that they don't mistakenly shoot my black ass.

"Help us! He's trying to kill us. Blue lives matter! All lives matter! My life matters!" I scream at the top of my lungs.

"Show us your hands!" instructs one of the officers. In accordance, we all put our hands up in the air like we're on the downhill of a rollercoaster.

"You, with the baby, walk slowly toward us," he commands.

Slowly Mary walks toward the officers. One of the officers approaches to meet Mary halfway. Unexpectedly, the officer trips on something on the ground. A loud ticking sound begins. Everyone's head turns on a swivel, looking for the origin of the sound.

"Bomb!" yells one of the officers. Without warning, a thunderous explosion occurs. Mary flies back toward me, dropping Hope as the ceiling rains down. I fall to the ground on my back and hit my head. Smoke and debris engulf the area. I can't see anything. My ears ring louder than a Sunday church bell. *Ring! Ring! Ring!* Go my ears. My head is pounding. I writhe on the ground in pain, my hands clutching my head. I've got to get to safety. Slowly, I get up and begin to search for my comrades. *Where is everyone?* Mary was the closest to the blast. I must find her and Hope first.

"Mary! Where are you?! Mary!" I shout at the top of my voice. *Can she hear me?* Hell, I can't even hear myself, the way my ears are ringing. I wave my arms frantically through the smoke searching for her or anyone. Finally, I find a hand close to the ground and begin to pull it. It isn't attached to anything. Immediately, I drop the detached hand and wipe my hand on my pants. I feel a strong grip on the back of my shoulder. Startled, I turn around to see the outline of a figure that appears to be Enrique.

He yells loudly in to my ear, but I can't hear him. Enrique grabs my hand and leads me out of the smoke to the promise land like Moses. We clear the smoke and I see he has gathered the rest of the team in the back of the hallway away from danger. Mary sits propped up unconscious with a bloody forehead. Enrique has placed Hope in her lap. My hearing starts to return slowly. Hope's wailing up a storm. Rip is hunched over with his hands on his knees coughing and struggling to breathe. His asthma has flared up amid all the dust from the explosion.

"We have to get out of this area," Enrique yells into my ear. "It's not safe here. The roof caved in. There's no way we can go out through the front doors. We have to go back upstairs and regroup."

Forcefully, he thrusts Hope into my arms and then wraps one of Rip's colossal arms around my shoulder. Enrique then picks up Mary's unconscious body and carries her in both of his arms. We head back toward the elevator. Strangely, it takes a shorter time to get back to the elevator than when we were running from it. Enrique presses the button for the fourth floor. Hope's cries echo louder in the enclosed area of the elevator. Rip looks tired. He's running out of energy to breathe. Mary's blood pings on the metal floor as it drips from her forehead. We're all covered in white dust, looking like we cook chicken at Popeye's. A two-piece mild, dark meat and a biscuit with honey would solve all my problems right now. The doors of the elevator open on the fourth floor. Rip drops to the floor as we walk out.

"He needs an inhaler," I tell Enrique. "Is there a medicine room around here?"

"Sí," he states as he lays Mary on the ground. The ringing in my ear has ceased. I can hear him clearly now. "Go down that hallway. Take two rights, and it'll be the last door on the left. Give me Hope. I'll watch over Mary and Rip. Take my key card to get in the room. I would bet my life there is one in there. Now, hurry."

I snatch the badge out of his hand, take off my backpack, and take off running. What floor am I on now? It's quiet. Colorful animal pictures decorate the walls. I hit the first right and then hit the second right. Almost to the medicine room.

"Slow down, Daniel," says a faint voice with a heavy accent as I blaze by a room. Instantly, I stop in my tracks and make a quick about face.

"Who are you?" I ask the man standing by the door.

"Someone who has been waiting on you all day," says the man. He grabs me firmly by the back of my shirt collar with his large hand and tosses me into the room. He locks the door behind us. He's dressed in a black shirt and blue scrub pants.

I enter the room and see a woman in the same attire holding a baby over her shoulder. Her shoulder is draped by a bright pink towel. Another baby sleeps quietly in a crib by itself. Next to the crib in a bed lies a sleeping young black girl. Her head slouches to the right and her mouth is wide open like a sleeping plane passenger. She snores loudly like an old man. Her arms are strapped to the bed with restraints.

"Wake her up," says the woman holding the baby. Her accent is equally as heavy as the man's. The accents sound African. The man waves a short white stick under her nose and the woman groggily responds.

"Daniel. My name is Nana. This is my husband Tundé," says the lady holding the baby. "And that is Nicole in the bed. Pick up her chart on the food tray and read it aloud."

Not this again. Not another baby situation. Couldn't be worse timing. Rip is dying. Mary is knocked out. Hope appears to be okay but is crying up a storm. So, who knows if she is truly okay. And Enrique is alone with them all. He needs my help. They all need my help. I have to get out of here, right now.

"I'm sorry, but I really don't have time for this shit. My friend out there is dying, and I need to get him his medication before he dies." I turn around to leave. Upon turning, I'm unkindly greeted by the steel barrel of a handgun to my forehead. I turn to stone as though I'd just come face to face with Medusa. This is the third time I have had a gun pointed at me today.

Never in my wildest dreams, did I think that I would have a gun pointed at me today. If someone would have told me at the beginning of the day that I would have a gun pointed at my head, I would have responded by asking what video game I was playing. *Halo? Goldeneye? Call of Duty?* Currently, I feel the call of dookie happening in my pants now with this gun pointing at my head. Shit gets real, literally and figuratively, when a gun is pointed at you.

I stretch my hand out to the food tray while staring down the barrel. I knock over a cup of apple juice onto my hand and it splashes on the floor. Great. Now, my hand is going to smell like apple juice and be sticky the rest of the day. *Dear God, can this day get any worse? Take me now Lord. Take me and my apple juice smelling hand now.* I pick up the file.

"Read it out loud," instructs Nana.

"What's going on?" Nicole asks as she begins to wake up.

"Read, Daniel."

"Nicole Thomas is a 21-year-old G10P4 who is day 3 post vaginal delivery of fraternal twins at 36 weeks. Mother reports minimal vaginal bleeding and has no other complaints. Pain is under control."

"Stop that's enough," says Nana. "Tell me what you just read. Do you have any clue?"

"No clue at all. All I know is Nicole just had some twins and she's bleeding a little from her vajayjay. Um, congrats Nicole," I slam the chart back down on the food tray. "Can I go now?"

"No. Not yet," replies Nana. "Any thoughts on the odd combination of numbers and letters you read?"

"No. No thoughts at all. Just a bunch of medical mumbo jumbo to me."

"Well those numbers have meaning, Daniel. Those numbers represent how many times she's been pregnant and how many children she has. Nicole has been pregnant 10 times and has 4 children. Already by the age 21."

I turn and look at Nicole with wide eyes and eyebrows raised. "Damn, girl. You been getting it in. You must have that good good. Boys shooting the club left and right. No muzzle at all."

"I haven't heard any complaints yet," glorifies Nicole with a smirk.

"Yeah, but you sure have been pregnant a lot. Ten times. Girl, you're only 21. Why aren't you on birth control or using protection?" I question.

"Have you taken birth control?" she asks.

"No. I'm a guy. So, no I haven't."

"Well, shut up then. You don't know nothin' about taking it. Birth control pills make me gain weight and have me feeling all weird inside. One time, while I was on them, I started pulling my hair out, for no reason. My head looked like a soccer ball. Patches of hair here and missing patches of hair there. So, I said no more birth control for me. And sex just feels better without condoms."

"Okay, understandable. But how do you protect yourself from diseases? Like AIDS and the rest of them."

"Honestly, it's just a roll of the dice. I ask all my partners if they're 'good' right before we do the do. They say yeah and then we get it in. No one has ever said no. I know it's stupid and unsafe, but hey it's my life. This is how I choose to live it. And I've been clean *so far*."

"Don't you worry about getting pregnant too?"

"Well that answer is obvious?" Tundé butts in with his deep voice.

"Sometimes, but not that much. I've *only* been pregnant ten times and had four kids. An abortion here. A miscarriage there. It's *easy* to get pregnant and almost as easy to get unpregnant."

"You take getting pregnant so lightly. You make it seem like it's so easy," I respond with a look of frustration.

"Well it is. It's like baking a cake! Mix sperm and egg. Bake at 350 degrees. Set timer for 9 months and remove from womb. That simple. You just don't have to stick a toothpick in a baby and hope that it comes out clean."

"If it's so simple then why can't I get pregnant?" asks Nana with a look of sadness on her face.

I knew that look. I have known that look my entire life. That look of sadness. Every time someone would ask my mom why she didn't have more kids, not knowing I was adopted and that she tried to have kids, I saw that look. When one of her friends or a family member announced that they were pregnant, I saw that look. Whenever she would hold a baby, I saw that look. The look of longing to produce a child of her own. The look of questioning herself as a woman. Wondering why she couldn't have a child of her own. A child with her blood coursing through their veins. A child with her round nose or her long flowing hair. A child that everyone would know was hers when they looked at it.

But she didn't have one. She had me. A child not of her flesh and blood, but one of her mind and soul. Didn't need to be of her flesh to get that. Just needed to be around her and I loved being around her. She in turn loved being around me. Some may have called me a momma's boy, but I just thought of myself as a boy who loved his mom. A mom who treated me as though I came from her flesh and blood.

Now, I stand here in the presence of a woman who doesn't appreciate the gift of bringing life into this world. She doesn't even realize the gift that she has and that Nana, my mom, and other women covet for. The gift of bringing life into the world and being called mom. With nothing else added to it. Not foster mom. Not adopted mom. But just mom. Her lack of understanding is truly heartbreaking.

"I don't know. You gotta talk to God about that. Now, why am I strapped to this bed? Let me up," Nicole demands.

"See, I long to have the power that you have Nicole. The power to have a child. Night and day, I pray to my Lord and savior to fill my womb with a child," Nana says. Then she gets on her knees to re-enact her prayer. "Lord, if it is your will let me have a child! Just once let me feel the kicks of tiny feet in my stomach. Let me wake up feeling sick as a dog. Swell my feet, Lord, until they look like an elephant because of my child growing inside. Please, Lord! If it is your will, let this be done." Nana stands back up.

"Day and night, I have prayed for nine years to God to bless us with a child. However, it seems that my prayers have fallen on deaf ears. The Lord has seen it fit for me to remain barren. Do you know how hard it is for me, an African woman to be barren?"

"No, I don't know," responds Nicole with a snarky attitude. She proceeds to pull at her bed straps.

"It is terrible. Especially coming from our culture. I am from Ghana, and Tundé is from Nigeria."

"Is that next to Wakanda?" I ask.

"I have heard of no such country, but there are many countries and cultures in Africa. And despite our cultural differences, Tundé and I have made it work. However, not being able to have children has put a strain on our marriage. He looks at me like I'm less than a woman."

"Who is going to carry on my family name? Who is going to take care of us when we get old? We need children for our legacy!" Tundé questions Nana while beating on his chest.

"This is what I have to go through daily from him. It's not enough that I beat up myself up inside, but I also get beat up from my own husband and my family. 'When are you going to have children, Nana? Nana, are you praying? Nana, what did you do wrong in life that God won't let you have children?' I get these questions all the time from my family. My sisters always make fun of me. They ask each other in front of me, how many children does Nana have? Then, one will say 'nada,' and they all burst into laughter. Sometimes they call me Nada instead of Nana. They think it's funny, but it's not. It's hurtful.

"I'm tired of all the jokes and thoughts of insecurity that run laps through my head. I'm tired of changing the diapers of babies whose mom I'm jealous of. I'm getting old now. My hair is starting to turn gray. Body parts are starting to hurt for no reason. I'm just tired of these feelings, and today, I've reached my breaking point. Today, I will get my baby."

"What do you mean, 'today I will get my baby'?" I ask with a worried look.

"Well, originally Daniel, we came to America for infertility treatment. Sadly, that didn't work out. Thousands of dollars wasted. But by chance we happened to meet Maestro. And he gave us the greatest idea. Just go to the hospital and pick a baby. Find a baby and just take it! It seemed crazy at first, but then after we thought about it for a while it in was ingenious. You can fenagle to make a baby seem like it's yours. Especially with all that is going on here today."

"You're not going to take my baby!" screams Nicole. She yanks on her straps even harder.

"Maestro recruited us for today and gave us an opportunity. He said find someone like Nicole, just take her baby, and bring it back to Africa. Why would she care? She could just make another one. Right, Nicole?"

Nicole leans over and tries to bite off her straps.

"Mix sperm and egg. Put in womb and take it out in nine months. Easy peasy. That's what you said, Nicole. So, you won't miss us taking one of your twins." Nana proceeds to lay the baby girl next to her baby brother in the crib. I jump in between Nana and the babies in the crib.

"Wait! Wait! You're just not going to take one of her babies. This is senseless!"

"Daniel, move," Nana instructs.

"No, I'm not moving. Since their mom can't fight for them. I'll fight for them. Don't worry, Nicole. I'll protect your kids. Like they are my own. I am not moving!"

"Tundé, handle this pesky American," commands Nana. Tundé sits his gun down and takes his shirt off. His muscles are huge and he is drenching in sweat.

"Since you want to be a man and stick up for these kids, I'm going to fight you like a man," says Tundé. *Lord, now, I have to fight a Mandinka warrior for some kids that ain't even mine.* I haven't gotten into a fight in years. Quickly, I put my fists up and get in a rudimentary fighting stance. *My black ass should have gone home instead of coming to the hospital.*

Tundé charges at me like a raging bull from Pamplona. I brace for full impact, but unexpectedly he slips and falls on the floor. The spilled apple juice has saved my life! I pounce on him like a spider monkey and put him in the same headlock that I was just in a few moments ago. Now, the chokee has become the choker. Oh, the irony. My adrenaline is on full throttle. I whisper into his ear.

"Yeah, you wanna fight me like a man. Well, this is what you get. I call this the T'Challa choke special. Never heard of that, have you, Tundé?" Tundé pulls at my arm, but my grip is ultra-tight. "I learned this in my homeland of Wakanda. I bet you will remember my country now. I got vibranium pumping through my blood, Tundé. What you know about that?"

Without warning, Nana places a gun to the back of my head and cocks it. I let loose of Tundé and put my hands up. Tundé gets up, panting and clutching his neck. Daniel-1, Tundé-0.

"Tundé, grab the boy. He will carry on our legacy," says Nana.

Tundé picks up the baby from the crib. Nana pans the gun back and forth between Nicole and me.

"Daniel, let me loose. She will not take my baby!" yells Nicole.

"You can let her loose after we leave the room. Don't try to follow us," says Nana as she and Tundé moonwalk backwards out of the room. "Thanks for the baby," Nana states before firing a shot past my head. I duck. The window shatters behind me. Nana and Tundé take off running with Nicole's baby in hand. I take off running after them.

"Daniel, untie me!" screams Nicole as I exit the door. I look at her and then look at Nana and Tundé sprinting down the hallway. They have almost made it to the first turn. I turn back and look at Nicole. The look of worry glosses over her young face. Her eyes well up with tears. Despite her lack of understanding of her promiscuous ways she loves her children. She doesn't want to put another bun in her oven to replace her child. She wants the bun that she has now, and wants to save that bun. Nicole loves all of her buns.

However, I have a conundrum. There are a multitude of people who need my help right now. *Do I take off running after Nana and Tundé in hopes of saving Nicole's baby? Do I untie Nicole and let her help in chasing after them? Do I go and get Rip's medicine then try and help Nicole? Rip could die if I don't help him, but Nicole could also lose her child. There is trouble everywhere. Trouble to the nth degree. Who do I help? What do I do? What do I do*? I go back into Nicole's room.

Hurriedly, I unstrap her arms from the rails. She jumps out of the bed and takes off running down the hallway. I take off running behind her, but pause when I hear the screaming cries of Nicole's other baby as we exit the room. She forgot about her other bun! I go back in the room, swaddle her and cradle her in my arms before scampering back down the hallway. I take off and Nicole is nowhere to be seen. I run faster in hopes of catching up to her.

Upon returning back to the elevator things have drastically changed. Mary is awake now. She holds Hope, who has stopped crying, in her bosom. Rip is lying motionless on his side with his back turned toward me. Enrique is standing up watching Nicole pound on the elevator door shouting obscenities. I hand Enrique Nicole's baby girl who continues to cry.

"Hold her. I'll be right back. I still gotta get Rip's medicine."

"Don't worry about it. He's already dead. He stopped breathing a few minutes ago. He just wore out of energy. Where were you?" questions Enrique.

"No, no, no. He can't be dead." I rush over to Rip's body and flip him over. His face is pale, his finger lips are blue, and he is breathless. Rip is dead. I cradle him in my arms and tears pour from my eyes down my cheeks. "No, Rip! No! I was on my way to help you, but then. Gun. Nana. Nicole. Twins. Gun again. So much trouble. I'm so sorry, Rip. I'm so so sorry, Rip! Please forgive me. I was on my way. Please, believe me I was on my way!" Enrique puts his hand on my shoulder to comfort me.

What have I done? Rip is dead now because of the choices I made. I chose to go down to the main floor which ended up getting us blown up and making Rip have an asthma attack. I chose to untie Nicole instead of going to get his medication. I even had a second chance to go get his medicine, but I chose to go and get Nicole's child. All the choices that I have made today have led to the downfall of others. My heart can't take any more.

"It's okay. It's not your fault, Daniel. We're going to get through this," Enrique comforts me.

"Yeah, sweetie it's not your fault," Mary says in support. Nicole continues to pound on the elevator doors and attempts to pull them ajar. I wipe the tears from my eyes and rise to my feet.

"What happened to her baby? Did two people get on the elevator with a baby?" I ask.

"Yeah. They came running saying that some crazy lady and man were trying to take their baby. I helped them get on the elevator to safety. It wasn't until this lady came barreling down the hallway screaming that it was her baby that I realize that I had been … How do you say? Duped? They tossed me a baton before the elevator closed. It has '*APPRECIATION*' on it." I take the baton from Enrique and place it in my backpack. I put it back on.

Suddenly, a screeching sound comes from Nicole's direction. Nicole with all her strength and might has managed to pry open the doors of the elevator. Only a mother's love could open closed elevator doors. Nicole looks back at me.

"Watch over Sarah for me, Daniel," she says. "I have to go rescue Abraham. Mommy is coming for you, baby!"

Nicole jumps through the open elevator doors. Enrique and I bolt toward the open doors to watch her. Nicole flies wildly down the elevator shaft screaming. Her arms flail in the air. She is out of control. Her head clunks one of the metal rails on the side. Her body flips over and she lands on top of the elevator which is now a few floors down below. The back of her head hits the elevator. Blood leaks from her head.

"Nicole! Nicole! Are you okay?" I yell down do the shaft. She doesn't answer. She doesn't respond at all. She doesn't even move. I press the elevator button multiple times, but it doesn't come up.

"I've got to go down and save her," I tell Enrique and Mary as I look for a way to climb down the shaft. Enrique yanks me back away from the elevator shaft.

"She's dead, my friend. She's dead. You can't save everyone," Enrique informs me.

At that moment Sarah stops crying. I look back down the shaft and then back at Enrique. He's right.

"Enrique, what are we going to do now?" I ask.

"There's a back elevator used to take patients out of the emergency room. We can take that one, and you can find a way to get us all out of here. Alive," he states while poking the center of my chest. Enrique says this so definitively, but at this point, I'm questioning all my decision-making. *How can I lead us out of here alive?*

"Okay, Enrique. Come on Mary, let's head to the other elevator." Mary, Enrique, baby Hope, newly acquired baby Sarah, and I trek toward the other elevator. We leave Rip's dead body on the floor. I am too emotional to say a prayer over him now.

We are all quiet. Even the babies. The mood of the group is somber. We are all emotionally and physically drained. So much has happened to us in these last few moments. A bomb exploded on us. Rip has died. Nicole's baby Abraham was stolen. And Nicole killed herself trying to save him. So much has happened. *Am I to blame for all of this?*

As we get on the new elevator, a backpack rests on the floor. Enrique picks it up and opens it. Out of the bag he pulls bottled water, Tylenol, and an inhaler. The doors close and the light for the next floor illuminates on its own. It's obvious that Maestro is conducting this performance now. Sarah and Hope start to cry again. I feel the walls beginning to close in around me. I'm feeling warm all over. My breathing starts to increase rapidly while a pounding sensation begins in my chest. The muscles around my chest begin to tighten. I think I'm having a heart attack.

INFERTILITY

Definition: Infertility is the inability to become pregnant after having unprotected intercourse for twelve months. In a survey from 2006 to 2010, more than 1.5 million women in the U.S., or 6 percent of the married population, 15 to 44 years of age, reported infertility. Approximately 6.7 million women reported difficulty becoming pregnant or carrying a baby to term. In couples 15 to 44 years of age, nearly 7 million have used infertility services at some point. Fifty percent of couples who don't conceive in the first year conceive in the second year. (12)

Infertility factors: Several different factors can contribute to infertility. Factors include male abnormalities (ex. Decreased sperm), ovulation dysfunction, and problems with the female genital tract. A combination of two or more of factors is most often the primary reason of infertility. Unfortunately, a major cause for infertility is unknown. (12)

Evaluation: For men, an evaluation includes a semen analysis. Some of the things that are evaluated in the sperm sample are shape, count, volume, and motility of the sperm. For women, an initial evaluation in women consists of gathering medical history. This includes menstruation history, past pregnancies or attempts at becoming pregnant, history of pelvic infections, and other items. Blood tests check levels of certain hormones that regulate ovulation. Imaging tests can also be done to rule out abnormalities with the structure of the uterus. (12)

Treatment: For men, treatment depends on the cause of the problem. If there is a structural abnormality (ex. Penile, testicular) there would be a need for surgery. If there is a hormonal imbalance, he would have to see an endocrinologist, a physician who specializes in hormones. In vitro fertilization is also an option for men who have sperm abnormalities. Just as there are multiple causes for infertility in women, there are multiple treatments. Treatments can be as simple as weight loss or better timing of intercourse to conceive. More aggressive treatments can include hormone therapy, intrauterine insemination or in vitro fertilization. (12)

If you are having difficulty with becoming pregnant, trust that you aren't alone. I know that it can be a difficult experience. Consult your obstetrician-gynecologist or primary care physician for more information

CHAPTER 9

THAT'S NOT BRUCE WAYNE, THAT'S...

"I need to get off this elevator. I can't. I can't. I can't breathe. I'm having a heart attack," I frantically inform Enrique and Mary through my panting. The walls of the elevator appear to enclose around me further. My breaths become shallow. The elevator moves to the next floor at a tortoise's pace. Finally, it reaches the next floor. In a panic, I press the "door open" button repeatedly. It doesn't open.

"You're not having a heart attack. You're having a panic attack. Just breathe, baby," Mary encourages while rocking the crying babies.

"I can't breathe. I need to get off this elevator now, before I die," I respond while rubbing my chest for comfort. Finally, the doors open. I dart out and immediately remove my backpack and shirt. I'm bare chested now.

"Just breathe, Daniel," Mary repeats.

Mary hands Sarah and Hope to Enrique. "I get these all the time. They're terrible. Trust me, I know. It feels like you're dying, but you're not going to die. Just breathe in through your nose and exhale through your mouth. Put your hands over your head." Mary grabs my hands and places them over my head. I take deep breaths in and out slowly.

She's right. It does feel like I'm dying. I've never had this feeling before. This feeling of impending doom. If this is what it feels like to live with anxiety, I want no parts of it. The walls of the elevator seemed like a funhouse as they closed in on me. I felt death grab my hand and escort me to Six Flags Underworld. And there was absolutely nothing I could do about it. Thank God for

Mary. Right now, she's my rock and I need her. Slowly, my breathing improves.

"See. There you go. You're looking better already. It's all in your head," says Mary.

"I felt like I was dying."

"Yeah it feels like that. I have one of those once a week,"

"I can't imagine that. Thanks for helping me out."

"No problem. I gotta take care of my man."

"Um, yeah."

A gunshot rings out in the distance. Screams follow. This is the first time that we've gotten on a floor and someone is shooting already. "Well, let's go see what that's all about. Enrique, what floor are we on now?"

"This floor has offices and classrooms. The classrooms are for medical estudiantes. I mean medical students."

"Classrooms for medical students?" I question.

"Sí. We have them here. They study and learn here. The shots sound like they're coming from one of their classrooms."

"Well, lead the way, Enrique." Enrique hands the babies back to Mary. They've stopped crying. I put my shirt and backpack back on as we walk. I was really freaking out. Earlier, I barely wanted to change in front of others. Now, I almost got butt ass naked in front of everyone. All because of a panic attack. I'm really stressing out. I gotta keep it together.

I can't falter now. I must stay strong, not only for myself and my companions, but also for Sweet Cakes. I have to make it home to her, alive. I'm pretty sure she knows what's going on here by now. It's probably all over the news. She's probably stressing and pulling out her tightly woven braids right now. Or blowing up my cell phone and leaving a boatload of messages. There are probably a million times infinity plus one messages on my phone. *Daniel, where are you? Daniel, call me right now! Daniel, are you okay?* I'll have to find a phone to call and let her know I'm okay. We reach the classroom where the shots originated and stand timidly at the door.

A group of young people in short white lab coats are lined up in front of the classroom's whiteboard. Some of them have already been shot. One young lady cradles her bullet riddled arm, which bleeds through her coat. There are injured people lying on the ground. A few of them are dead already. One man on the ground has been shot in the leg. Another man applies pressure on the pale man's injured leg. The man applying pressure is also bleeding from his own hand. Three people in white coats stand shaking like they're in the arctic cold. However, this shaking isn't weather-related. It's fear. A white man dressed in a Batman mask and a white doctor's coat stands, holding a gun in front of the remaining people standing up.

"You're late, Daniel, but welcome," says a man in a black dress shirt who sits in the back of the room. The classroom is lined with long tables as desks. He sits in a middle row in the back. "I'm Dr. Patel. Come all the way in. You and your friends. Everyone can sit down at one of the tables except for you, Daniel. You remain standing." Enrique and Mary both sit down. Mary gives Hope to Enrique to share the load of holding babies.

Dr. Patel is an older man of Middle Eastern descent. His tone is sharp and straight to the point. His freshly creased white coat and his matching shirt and tie add to his professional demeanor. The evenly shaved white goatee and thick glasses hanging from the end of his nose accentuates his straight-laced manner.

"Let's get to the point. Batman here wants to get in residency. He graduated from a medical school outside of the country a few years ago. Since graduating, he has had difficulty getting into residency. He wants to be a surgeon like me, but his grades and test scores are deplorable."

"I've always had a problem with taking tests," says Batman through his mask. He does a horrible Batman voice impersonation. "Failed some tests. Passed some tests. Failed some classes and had to retake them. It was a struggle. I swear I know the stuff. I just have problems with taking tests. Not everyone is a good test taker. However, I still made it through and graduated."

"Yes, he did indeed. Daniel, do you know what you call a doctor who graduated last in medical school class?" asks Dr. Patel.

"No," I answer.

"You call him doctor."

"Well played," I respond while rolling my eyes.

"Now, Batman here, aka Dr. Wayne, has had trouble getting into residency. Residency is like on-the-job training after medical school. Consequently, he needs my help to get in. I'm one of the top movers and shakers around here and can help him get in," Dr. Patel says as he holds up a brown manila envelope.

"Right here, I've got a signed letter of acceptance to our general surgery residency program. This will help get him in, but this letter won't come easy. In order to get this letter, I've developed a test for him. I realize that some people aren't good standardized test takers, but they do know the items anyway. Therefore, I've devised this test to better accommodate him. I like to call it an 'oral accuracy test.' All he has to do is shoot the parts of the body I've named. I want to test how well he knows his anatomy. The questions have increased in intensity from the start. First, we started with the hand, and as Jack can attest, Dr. Wayne got that one right."

"You're never going to get away with this!" Jack yells while continuing to apply pressure on his fellow classmate's leg.

"Well, that sounds like a yes to me," Dr. Patel responds. "Next, was the pinna of the ear. That's the lower part of the ear, Daniel. Unfortunately, he shot Brittany in the head. No points for that question."

"I told her ass not to move. She kept moving," Batman says.

"No excuses, Dr. Wayne. I'm looking for knowledge and accuracy. Knowledge of where the structure is located, and accuracy of shooting the target. You want to be a surgeon, right?"

"Yes, sir."

"Well, surgeons have to, in a split second, know where certain structures are located. They must accurately identify which structures to cut and which to avoid. One wrong cut could lead to death. I need to see that thought process in this test. You shot her in the head and not even close to her pinna. So, no point for that question.

"The next thing I quizzed him on was the sciatic nerve which is a combination of nerves that originate in the spine and runs down the back of the leg." Dr. Patel points to the back of his hip and traces the nerve down his leg. "See how I increased the difficulty, Daniel? Just like when a surgeon cuts through the skin, there's an increase in difficulty. First, it's easy. You cut through the skin, then the fascia, then the muscle, but then you start getting into the real stuff. Nerves traversing here and arteries running parallel there. And don't forget about the organs. Gotta make sure you cut on the damaged one and avoid the healthy one. Like this test, it requires a lot of accuracy and knowledge. Sadly, Dr. Wayne shot Sydney in the arm and that's nowhere close to the sciatic nerve. That made two wrong answers in a row."

"Everyone kept screaming after I shot Brittany in the head. I just got flustered and couldn't remember the nerve's location," Batman excuses. "I got the next one correct. Left circumflex artery. I know that one like the back of my hand."

"Yeah. You got that one right. Right in the heart. I was very impressed. That put you at 50 percent. Still not passing, but closer to becoming a surgeon."

"I would say 'this is crazy,' but the threshold for what is considered crazy keeps changing around here. So, I'm just going to say 'this is madness.' Why are you doing this, Dr. Patel?" I question. "You're a doctor for Christ's sake. You're not supposed to be involved in all of this."

"I have my reasons. These kids nowadays don't respect the grind of becoming a doctor. They have it too easy. I asked one of them the other day if they knew where the hospital library was. He said, 'We have a library? I didn't even know that,'" Dr. Patel stands up and throws his hands in the air.

"He didn't even know we had a library. Back in my day the library was basically our dormitory. It was where we we'd eat, sleep, and sometimes bathe. It's where we lived our entire med school lives. You needed an answer to a question. You had to go and look it up in a book. Sydney do you know what a book is?"

I look at a young lady at the front of the class who I presume is Sydney. She stands crying and shaking while holding her bleeding arm. She doesn't answer.

"If you didn't know the answer, you had to go look it up in a book. First, you had to *find* the book. And before that, you had to look up the section and location of the book via the Dewey Decimal System. Fiction. Non-fiction. Then, you could go find the book. Things have changed so much, Daniel, since I became a doctor. Now, if you want an answer to a question you just Google it and the answer pops up in less than a second. You get a picture. You get a video. You get links to other sources that appear just as quickly. Just like that, at a snap of your finger. They've got it so much easier now."

"Well, stuff is supposed to get easier as time goes along," I counter his argument. "Technology improves things and we improve as a society."

"Yes, that may be true, but along the way in the evolution of medicine we've lost some things that make up the foundation of medicine. For example, doctors barely even touch patients anymore. They would rather order a blood test or imaging than put their hands on someone. Older doctors, like me, could tell if someone had pneumonia by just listening to the patient' tell their story and listening to their lungs. That's it! These new doctors order x-rays, get blood work, and pluck a strand of hair from your firstborn child in order to make a diagnosis. What happened to just listening to the patient and making a diagnosis based upon your physical exam? Those days appear to be over. Doctors are lazy now. I miss the old days of medicine."

"We're not lazy! We're new and improved. You guys were killing people with your drugs and radiation. We have to know ten times as much stuff as you did, old man," says the black male medical student next in line to get shot. He stands strong with a look of defiance on his face.

"That may be true, but that doesn't make you a better doctor. I think we need to revert to our old ways and tie it in to this new world of knowledge. However, to do this, we must cleanse the current world of medicine and start over. Next question, Dr. Wayne," Dr. Patel begins thumbing through a medical book. The words *Netter's Anatomy* are printed on the front cover. He stops at a page toward the back. "Superior mesenteric artery," he reads aloud.

Batman begins to pace back and forth in front of his targets mumbling to himself. He racks his brain trying to remember where the structure is located. Finally, he stops pacing, turns, and faces his next target. He's remembered.

"I've got it!" he exclaims. He cocks his gun, aims at the black student's abdomen, and fires. The student jumps out of the way.

"Who told you to move?" Dr. Wayne asks.

"Man, fuck that! You're just not going to shoot me like a crab in a barrel. You may pick them off one by one, but not me so easily," declares the medical student.

Frantically, he takes off running through the classroom jumping over tables to get away. You could have sworn a mouse entered the room the way he took off running. We all watch in amazement. He passes up Dr. Patel and continues to climb over tables toward the back of the room. I don't know where he's going. There's not even a back door to escape through. Without hesitation, as the young man passes him, Dr. Patel turns around and shoots him in the buttocks.

"You shot me in my ass!" he screams as he falls on top of the table he was crawling over.

"You're almost a full-fledged doctor now, Paul. It's time you start speaking like one," instructs Dr. Patel. "What you should have said was that I shot you in the posterior aspect of your gluteus maximus. The bullet traveled anteriorly and coursed through the other muscles in my pelvic area. These muscles most likely included the gluteus maximus and piriformis. Now, please return to the front of the room. We don't have all day. I have a flight to catch."

Paul limps to the front of the room and braces himself before he sits on the floor.

"Do I get credit for that one, Dr. Patel. You saw that I was aiming in the right place," Batman lifts up his shirt and begins pointing at his belly. "The superior mesenteric artery is located in the abdomen and comes from the abdominal aorta. It helps feed blood to the intestines. I know that for sure!"

"You are right Dr. Wayne. I will give you credit for that one. Great job! Now for the next structure," Dr. Patel picks up his book and begins thumbing through the pages again. A young brunette is shaking in fear as she is next in line to get shot. Tears stream down her cheek. I jump in front of her.

"I volunteer as tribute!" I cry aloud. I'm not sure if that statement fits into this scenario, but it sounds appropriate.

"Get out of the way, Daniel," instructs Batman with the gun pointed at me. I don't move. I've become numb to guns pointed at me today.

"No! She doesn't deserve this. She's innocent. Let her live. Let me take her place for the next question."

Batman begins to walk towards me and places the warm barrel of the gun on my forehead. I take a big, dry gulp. *Is this it? Is this the end? Am I really about to die now? I know I volunteered as tribute, but I didn't volunteer as a sacrificial lamb. Maybe just a sacrificial graze of a bullet. If he hesitates for one second, I'm going to take his gun and shoot him with it.*

"I admire you, Daniel. You've got heart stepping in front of her. But one thing I know you don't have is guts." Batman lowers his gun and punches me dead in my stomach. Instantly, I double over in pain and genuflect to the ground. Dr. Wayne leans toward me.

"Did the kids come by and get their brownies?" he whispers in my ear. I look at him confused and in anger. Mary gets up from her seat and bends down by my side.

"How cute," chides Batman. "Looks like someone has a little girlfriend. Such a loving couple. And is that a waffle house tattoo on your back? You must be crazy. Crazy for waffles. Or just crazy in general." He begins to laugh at his own joke.

I look up at Mary. Her look of concern about me morphs into a look of anger and then a look of restrained insanity. A big fraudulent smile comes across her face. She kisses me on the forehead and stands up. I flop to the ground and curl into a fetal position.

"Oh, you saw my little tattoo when I bent over. You know why I got this little tattoo, Batman?"

"No. Enlighten me. Enlighten us all here."

"Well, I had this handsome guy that I used to date a few years ago. Big, strong, and masculine guy with so much charm. I was madly in love with him and I thought he was madly in love with me. However, he would only call me to come over or visit me after he had a night full of partying and eating at Waffle House. He would never come see me during the week because he said he was *too busy*. But every weekend like clockwork, he would text me to see if I was still up when he left Waffle House. And like a fool, I would always answer, and he would come over for drunken sex. One day, I decided I couldn't take it anymore. So, I had a bright idea. I'd get a Waffle House tattoo!

"My goal was to try my own Pavlov's dog experiment. It kind of freaked him out the first time he saw it. I told him that you only come over after you leave Waffle House on the weekend. I figured that if you saw this during sex that it would make you think of me during the week when you saw Waffle House. Then, maybe you would come over during the week, as well. There are Waffle Houses everywhere, so I had high hopes that it would work. At first, he thought I was crazy, but it actually worked.

"The next week he called me and came over. He said he saw a Waffle House sign and kept thinking of me. We went to dinner and had a wonderful evening. The visits and calls increased in frequency from that point on. We were virtually in a relationship. I was happy and thought he was too. Then, he began to disappear. The Waffle House magic began to fade away. He became *too busy* again and one day I saw him out with another girl. Then, I knew why he was so busy. That was what ended it for me. I thought I could keep him around with good pussy and conversation. But in the end, I and my pussy failed."

"Well, we all know that crazy girls have good pussy. Sorry that you weren't able to keep him around with yours," says Batman.

Mary walks slowly in his direction. Her hips twist like a model on the catwalk. She ties her long black hair in a bun as she sashays toward Batman.

"Oh, you think I have good pussy. How sweet of you," Mary gently brushes up against Batman. "Well, I can't argue with you on that one, Dr. Wayne. But can the same thing be said for you? Do crazy men have good dick?"

"I'm not crazy," responds Batman in a confused voice.

"You're not crazy?" Mary sarcastically responds. "You're dressed in a Batman outfit, senselessly shooting people in some kind of medical spelling bee. If anyone should know crazy, it's me.

And this is the epitome of crazy right here." Mary gets even closer to him. I hope she doesn't grab his balls like she did Rip's.

"And I like it," Mary says in a sweet sexy voice. She wraps an arm tightly around his waist and strokes his mask with her other hand. I bet he can smell Mary's pheromones.

"How about you let me take that mask off and see the crazy person underneath it." Mary grabs his gun and places it on the table. She begins pushing the mask off his head. He reaches up and grabs her hand, but then lets it go. She continues taking off his mask and reveals the caped crusaders identity.

"That's not Bruce Wayne. That's mother fuckin Toddrick!" I yell. Toddrick rushes over and starts kicking me in my stomach while screaming.

"It's not Toddrick! It's Todd. Stop calling me Toddrick!" I attempt to protect myself, but it does little justice. He keeps kicking. "Where's my gun? I'm going to shoot him right now in his medulla oblongata. I know that structure."

"Oh, this gun right here?" Mary asks, now holding Toddrick's gun.

"Yeah, that one. Give it to me."

"Daniel. What was the one thing I warned Rip and everyone else earlier not to do."

"Don't call you crazy," I respond in anguish. Mary lifts Todd's gun and shoots him in the forehead. Blood spatters everywhere even on to Mary's face. He plops down on the ground with a thud. The whole room lets out a collective gasp. Mary runs towards Todd and straddles over his chest.

"No one calls me crazy!!! I am not crazy!!! I am totally sane like everyone else! Now, see what you made me do. Look what you made me do!" she screams in his face. Mary turns to look at me, her face bloody.

"I didn't want to do it, Daniel, but he made me do it. He was going to shoot you. I had to protect you. I had to protect us. I had to protect our future family. I love you!" Mary gets up and wipes the blood off her face with the bottom of her shirt.

"Thank you," I respond. My big mouth continues to get me in trouble. This time it got my ass kicked. I wish my sarcasm had an off button, but sadly it doesn't. Luckily, Mary stopped Todd before he could hurt anyone else. Including me. I thank her for that, even though her erratic behavior deeply concerns and confuses me.

Somehow, Mary has turned the interaction between her and me into an actual relationship. I don't know how I made this possible. You tell one girl in the psych ward who just tried to hang herself that you love her and look what happens. I have no one to blame, but myself. My actions continue to be to my detriment. I walked into the hospital with a wife and a normal life. However, somehow today I've picked up a girlfriend, two babies, and a lifetime of what-ifs. Once again, my black ass really should have just gone home.

Mary goes in my backpack and pulls out some pain pills and a bottled water. She hands them to me. I devour them instantly.

"Well, that was interesting," says Dr. Patel. He gets up from his chair and proceeds to the front of the room with his leather bag. "Thanks for taking care of that for me. Honestly, there is no letter in this envelope. There was no one letter that was just going to get

Todd into the program. There's an application, interview process, and other things that go into getting admitted. However, I sold him on the idea that I would be able to get him in. He was so gullible. People are so gullible when they want something."

"Why would you do that? Why did you lead him on," I question as I sit up.

"I actually tried to help Todd when I first met him. He is the son of one of the former hand surgeons at the Kleinert Kutz Hand Care Center, here in Louisville. His dad was at the forefront of hand transplant research and was known worldwide. He was the Derek Jeter of hand surgery. He was the best, and everyone loved him. No one would ever speak ill of Todd's dad. Sadly, he died in a botched robbery attempt along with Todd's mom and ever since, Todd has been trying to live up to his legacy.

He had a hard time getting into medical school, but his dad's friends pulled some strings and got him into one of the island medical schools. It was the best that they could do with the marks and test scores he earned in school. However, he was in. He fought his way through medical school. As he mentioned earlier, he wasn't the smartest or brightest, but he made it out. However, after graduating, he didn't have get a residency spot. He was so fixated on becoming a surgeon, but didn't get into any program. He had too many red flags, and no one accepted him.

"He wanted so desperately to get into a surgery program, so he could be like his dad. His dad was smart. His dad was handsome. His dad was charming. All of his life, Todd had to hear how much of an upstanding man his father was. He was a guy that everyone admired, including Todd. But, Todd's father never put any pressure on him to be a doctor. If anything, he wanted him to stay away from the medical field and do something different. Like be a lawyer or a world renowned chef. Nonetheless, Todd still felt that pressure on him. Either by his own doing or society's doing. That pressure to be a half the surgeon his father was. To be half the man his father was. To uphold his father's namesake and continue the family legacy.

"After not getting in residency he took a job as a transporter in this hospital. All he does is transport patients around the hospital for their various procedures. Transporting them to get X-rays and CT scans. Transporting the from the ER to the rooms upstairs. Transporting them to the cafeteria to get a hot meal. Transporting. Transporting. Transporting. Mind you, this guy has a fully accredited medical degree, and he is transporting people around the hospital. Todd is actually Dr. Todd. But he chose to humble himself and take one of the lowliest positions in the hospital.

"Todd just wanted to stay close to the world of medicine. To be around the doctors, nurses, and patients. To be around the beeping of the monitors. To be around the codes blaring through the PA system. He just wanted to stay ingrained in the culture until he figured out a way to permanently fit in. Would you do that? Would you humble yourself in order to reach your dream? Todd did.

"He hoped that he could network his way somehow into the surgery program here. They gave him two interviews as a courtesy to his late father, but he never got accepted. He had been working here for three years when I arrived and started mentoring him. I tried to steer him into a specialty that would be easier to get in to. Like family medicine or pediatrics. But he wasn't having it. He was dead set on becoming a surgeon. He would explain that his heart and manhood wouldn't allow him to do anything else.

"'I work in a hospital where my dad has a wing named after him and his face is plastered on the wall. That's what I'm striving for! That's the legacy I'm trying to uphold!' he would scream at me. I respected his grind, his hustle, and his determination to reach that goal. Not everyone has that in them to put for such effort to reach their dream. Do you?

"If I were in Todd's shoes, I would have given up a long time ago. I would have called it quits and chosen another profession. Maybe a teacher or researcher. But no, not Todd. Not him. He was going to find a way to become a surgeon. I would always find him talking to some surgeon or sneaking into some operating room to learn. He hoped his white privilege, charm, and boyish good looks would eventually get him in. However, he could never knock the door down and get in."

"How did he get to the point where he was shooting at us?" asks Jack.

"Well, that's an interesting story. One day we were having a conversation, and I jokingly asked him what was the craziest thing he would do to get in residency. I asked him would he eat a handful of live, crawling roaches. He said 'yes.' I asked would he walk barefoot across burning hot coals. He said 'yes.' I upped the ante a little and asked if he could change his test scores to get in would he do it. Just to test his integrity. He said if he didn't get caught and no one would ever know he would. Then, I asked flippantly 'would you kill someone?' He paused for a few seconds and thought to himself. I was shocked that he was really thinking about it because I was just joking. A normal person would say no immediately, but he was actually thinking about it.

"After thinking about it, he gave an eerie answer. 'With great success comes great sacrifice and I'm willing to sacrifice others for my greatness.' The tone in his voice was unnerving, and I believed him. At that moment, I knew that he was so enamored with his goal that he was reaching borderline insanity. A short time later, he would cross that line and become fully insane, partly by my own doing. I am both proud and ashamed to say that I played a role in creating that monster. I partly created that monster because of my own issues.

"Over the last few years, I have grown tired and weary to this new way of practicing medicine. My God, there is so much red tape that one has to go through to be a doctor and stay a doctor. Pass this test. Get this certification. Get this insurance. Then, the crazy workload on top of this. Review this. Review that. Sign this paper. Click this on the computer. Some days I feel more like a scribe than a real doctor.

"I miss the days of being a real doctor. I miss paper charts. I miss insurance companies not telling me what drugs I can prescribe. How the hell are you going to tell me what I can prescribe? I'm the doctor! This frustration with the health care industry and these young ungrateful doctors lead me to corrupting Todd.

"In Todd, I saw parts of myself that I missed. The things that made me fall in love with medicine. He was so bright eyed. He was so excited to be in the hospital. I, on the other hand, became so jaded with being in the hospital. I despised being around patients and their families. They pressed my buttons. I would often send in the residents to talk to them and give an update on their status. I would rarely talk to them, and if I did, I kept it short and straight to the point.

"One day at a local donut shop, I ran into Maestro. He saw me sitting with a frustrated look on my face doing work on my computer. He took an uninvited seat, asked me what was wrong and why I looked so upset. This conversation turned into a whole venting session about what's wrong with the health industry. He shared a lot of the same elements of my frustration. Some of the things he despised, I was guilty of, and he helped shed a light on the error of my ways. Then, he asked would I like to change things. I responded with an emphatic 'I'd love to.' So, we came up with this plan you see today. To get a random group of people with their own individual problems and give them this outlet to share their story. He was in charge of getting the crew of people to carry it out. I was in charge of getting the blueprints together of the hospital and sharing the best ways to take over the building. My side project was corrupting Todd.

"I wanted him to purge those I saw unfit to be doctors, those who didn't appreciate the opportunities they had before them. Those who took for granted the position that they were in. The position he wanted to be in. I knew that he would help with the cleansing. I saw the way he looked at you medical students with envy. And after a brief conversation he was much obliged to help me get rid of his competition for a spot in the program. Even though I knew I had no such power to grant him immediate acceptance."

"You're never going to get away with this you know," I inform him.

"Why, yes, I am. You don't think I have an escape plan?" says Dr. Patel. He pulls out a plane ticket from his brown leather bag. "I am going back home to Egypt. To practice medicine the way I want to practice medicine. To feel like a real actual doctor again. Free from all of the rules and regulations."

He takes the tip of his fingers and dips them in Todd's blood on the floor. He takes his bloody fingers and smears them on his white coat and face. "You guys aren't going to follow me. There's too many injured here and no one is going to leave the group to chase after me. Once I get outside they will just expect for me to have made it out alive and not be a part of this fiasco. By the time they figure it out, I'll be long gone and back in Egypt." Dr. Patel opens the manila envelope that Todd thought contained his letter. He pulls out a baton and rolls it on the ground toward me. The word *EFFORT* appears as it rotates toward me.

"What are you willing to put so much effort into that drives you crazy or makes people consider you crazy? Are you that determined to reach your goal? Are you willing to put that amount of effort in to complete your task and make it out of here, Daniel?" he asks me.

I stare at him blankly. I have put in so much effort already to make it out of here alive. *Do I have any effort left in the tank? I hope so.* Dr. Patel walks out of the door with a fake limp. He turns around and takes a final glance at all the pandemonium he caused in the classroom. He winks at me and walks out of sight. I presume I'll never see him again.

I stand up and look around the room. It's littered with dead, wounded, crying, and emotionally stricken people. I am one of the emotionally stricken. I don't know where to start. My mind hurts more than my body right now. I have tried to help a few people along my journey with little success. Now, I have a room full of people looking at me like I'm their savior. Mary stands by my side as though I'm her king seated on the iron throne. She has killed for me and professed her love for her king. Such loyalty. Such passion. However, she is not my queen. My queen is Sweet Cakes. Mary is a truly insane monster. *Did I create this monster like Dr. Patel did Todd, or was Mary already a monster when I met her? Maybe I should have left her hanging. But then would I still be alive?*

"I can't bring all of you with me. The two of you who are uninjured can better take care of those who are injured. Jack wrap your hand; you're coming with me. Enrique and Mary you're also coming with me," I instruct with kingly authority. "We will go get help for you all. Do the best you can to survive. Stay put until we come back or until the police arrive. Do you all understand." Everyone nods in agreement. We head back to the elevators.

"Enrique how many floors do we have left?" I ask as we get on.

"Two floors if you don't include the basement," he responds.

"Okay. We're going to make it out of here. Alive. All of us. I promise," I assure them. "However, on the next floor, I need to find a phone. I have to call my wife."

"You're married!?" asks Mary.

THE ROAD
TO
BECOMING
A
DOCTOR

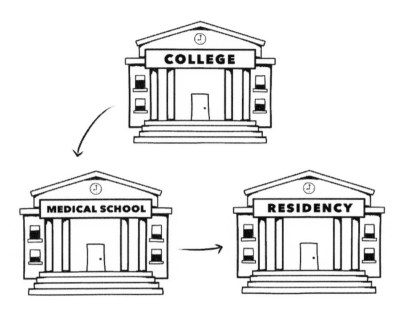

Most people know that it's not easy to become a physician. However, most people don't know what the process is to become one. The road is long, rough, and rugged. I'm going to break it down into 3 stages. These stages are what usually happens but can have some variation depending on people, schools, and other items.

Stage 1: First, you have to go to college and earn a bachelor's degree. You can get your degree in anything. Most people major in biology because it involves the study of life. Yet some people get a degree in other fields, including chemistry, engineering, music, and other majors. However, there are certain core classes that everyone must take before applying to medical school. These include certain biology, chemistry, physics, and math classes. Studying the trombone exclusively for four years won't get you into medical school. You must complete these core classes to have a good knowledge foundation for medical school. Most people apply to medical school and receive acceptance letters during their senior year in college, but some people apply later and get accepted later for different reasons.

Stage 2: Most medical schools have a four-year program. During the first two years of medical school, students generally only take classes. They take core classes in anatomy, pharmacology, physiology, and other classes. Medical students are rarely working in a hospital during their first two years. In years three and four, medical students learn different specialties in a hospital setting. These specialties include cardiology, surgery, pediatrics, and many more. The exposure to these specialties usually helps medical students decide their area of focus. During these four years of medical school, students take many tests. There are school-administered tests, as well as national tests that all students must take. The multitude of tests and retaining vast amount of information for these tests is one of the most difficult parts of medical school. The fourth year of medical school is when students apply to residency. Residency is essentially on-the-job training, because you can't go straight from the classroom to operating on people's brains. So, medical students apply to a residency program of interest. Sadly, like Todd, not everyone gets in.

Stage 3: Once a person finishes medical school and enters residency, they have the title of doctor. They also have the label of resident. This means that they are still in a training phase and aren't licensed in their specialty yet. Therefore, residents aren't "doctor rich." The length of time in residency can vary. For example, a family medicine residency is three years. General surgery residency is five years. So, let's do the math for a general surgeon. If a person graduates from high school at 18, then goes straight to college for four years, they will be 22 when they graduate college. Then, add an additional four years for medical school, which would put them 26 years old as a new resident. After five years in residency, that person will be 31 years old when they are finally finished with everything!

CHAPTER 10

LAST DYING WISH

Yes. I'm married. You didn't know?" I answer as we get off on the next floor.

"No! I didn't know. How was I supposed to know?! You never told me. I thought you loved me!"

"Whoa. Whoa. Whoa. Pump the brakes. I said I loved you in Christ. Not like for real loved you. Wait. I mean for real but, like, for real in Christ." In a fit of nervousness, I quickly make the sign of the cross on my chest. "I mean you cute and all, but I'm married. See," I hold up my hand to show my ring, but it's not there.

My ring finger is bare. Nothing is on my hand except the chronic ash between my ring finger and pinky. I forgot that I had taken my ring off before going into my CT scan. It's still in the pouch behind the wheelchair. No wonder Mary didn't know I was married. I haven't had my ring on this entire time.

"Oh, shoot. I don't have my ring on. I had to take it off before my CT. I'm sorry if my feelings were misconstrued, but I meant I loved you only in a Christian way. You are a beautiful woman with a wonderful personality and any man would be lucky to have you. However, I am not that man. I am a happily married man."

"I hate you, Daniel. I fuckin' hate you!" Mary shouts.

"I'm sorry that I forgot to tell you, but when was I supposed to tell you?" I ask bluntly. "Maybe I should have told you after I had a gun pulled on me? Maybe I should have told you after I was almost choked to death? No, wait. Maybe right after I saw a woman jump down an elevator shaft and plummet to her death. No, not then because you were just waking up after being knocked out when a freakin' bomb exploded on us! Or maybe I should have told you after you tried to hang yourself? Nope because once again you were passed out. Come to think of it, you've been passed out for almost half of this ordeal. Maybe if your *crazy* ass would stay awake I could have told you."

Oh, Lord. I called Mary crazy. I've done it now. My mouth relentlessly writes checks that my ass can't cash. I can literally see the rage building up in Mary. Her eyes have begun to bug out of their sockets. She clenches her empty fist tightly while clenching her pearly white teeth. Steam rises from her forehead as her anger begins to boil over. Her rage is similar to that in the horror movie *Carrie. She will probably use her power of telekinesis to throw something at my head. Surely, my life is about to end now.*

I've lived a good life. It was a good run while it lasted. However, there were so many things I wish I could have done. I never got to get a slice of strawberry cheesecake from Junior's in New York. I never got a chance to travel to France with Sweet Cakes and put a lock on the Pont des Arts bridge. I never got to go to Comic Con and dress up as black Captain America with a Confederate Flag Shield. Oh, I would have loved to see the looks on people's faces as they stare at the super hero oxymoron. Now I'll never get that great pleasure. All because of my big fat mouth. Well time to meet my maker. I close my eyes and prepare for my impending death.

"Really, Daniel?" Mary says with a cracking voice. I open my eyes. A single tear trickles down Mary's cheek to her finely chiseled chin. It hangs for a split second before falling to the floor. There's so much pain in that tear. Pain that I caused. I called her crazy, and I said I'd never do that, but I did. I can tell I have hurt her. If there was anyone she wasn't expecting to hurt her so far, it was me. We have been through so much together in our short time and she has been through so much on her own. Things that have broken her mentally and physically. And I have further added to her breakdown.

Sometimes the most hurtful feeling is being hurt by the person you don't expect to hurt you. The one you've put your trust in and shown your vulnerability. I've broken the trust we have developed in this short time. It will never be the same. Mary walks up to me and slaps me across my face. I turn red with embarrassment and shame.

"I deserved that," I respond remorsefully. Mary shoves Hope in my arms and takes off running through the doors labeled ICU. A hyphen and the word Maestro are painted in black to the bottom right of the label on the doors. I assume it means that he is watching this play out like a peeping Tom.

"Mary! Mary!" I halfheartedly yell in her direction. I hand Hope off to Jack, take off my backpack, and walk through the doors to find Mary. She has disappeared like a thief in the night. The entire hospital wing is pitch dark except for a dim light in the distance in one of the rooms. It is darker than the toast Sweet Cakes' made for breakfast. I can't even see my hands. I walk cautiously extending them in front of me to avoid crashing into anything.

"Mary. Mary. Where are you?" I whisper into the darkness. The darkness whispers nothing back. "Mary, I know you're in here."

"Fuck you, Daniel," whispers Mary in the shadows.

"Ah, come on, Mary. I said I'm sorry." I recapitulate. Suddenly, I run into a metal cart. It makes a thunderous sound. "Damn! Come on, Mary. Come on out. And turn the lights back on."

Silence once again fills the hallway. Unexpectedly, a sound whistles by my ear.

What was that? Another whistling sound passes my ear. *Is she throwing things at me? She really is Carrie!* All of a sudden, I am struck dead center on the bridge of my nose with a metal object. I grab my nose and drop to a knee. Spots of light begin to appear in my vision. *How can I see spots of light in a hallway full of darkness? She really hit the mess out of me. My black ass should have gone home.*

"What did you just hit me with?" I question with a muzzled voice.

"A bedpan. Since you're doing such a piss poor job leading us, I figured it would be fitting. You have some nerve talking to me like that. Calling me crazy. I'm not crazy," Mary responds in a calm soft voice. A calm voice Mary scares the crap out of me. I'd rather she yell.

"I'm sorry, Mary. I didn't mean it. I let my emotions get the best of me. I love you."

"Fuck you, Daniel, and your fake love." Another, item whizzes by my head and slams behind me. I guess Mary isn't feeling the love anymore. My southern charm isn't going to win her over now. It's time to develop a new strategy. I've got to get away from her and get to the lit room in the back.

Where is she throwing these items? I can't see her at all. If I can pinpoint her perch, I can find a way to throw something at her and get away. Glass shatters in the darkness. I crouch low like a soldier crawling through the trenches during wartime. *Sweet toddler Jesus, protect me from this mad woman.*

"You need to learn how to deal with your emotions better, Daniel. You can't just fly off the rails and react so emotionally. Why so sensitive?" Mary asks lightheartedly.

After all that Mary has done today she has the nerve to tell me not react so emotionally. Me! Murder Mary has been the epitome of an emotional firestorm. She has hanged herself. Forced me into a psychiatric fecal football game. Semi-castrated Rip.

And to top it off, killed Todd. K-I-L-L-E-D Todd! Now, she has the audacity to tell me to restrain my emotions. Me! How dare she? I would love to throw all of my emotions at her right now if I could. A whole heaping handful of dripping, oozing emotions right at her pretty face. That would surely serve her right. Then again, that will not help me out at all in this situation. My big mouth has gotten me in enough trouble today. I'll keep it shut, this time.

"You need to stop judging others and look in the mirror, Danny boy. How about you look in the mirror and judge yourself?"

Silence invokes again. I continue to stay low to the ground. Waiting. Anticipating the next item to be thrown at me. She better not throw any glass at me. Like clockwork a whirling sound travels through the darkness, heading in my direction. It crashes to my left and breaks into pieces. The shimmering pieces shine in the darkness. It's a piece of mirror. *How does she know where I am? Can she see me in this darkness?*

"Damn it, Mary, stop throwing things at me. You're going to hurt me. Let's just talk this out."

"I'm going to hurt you. Just like you hurt me. I want to give you that same judgmental medication you dispensed on me. Now, speaking of medicine where are some syringes?" she asks herself out loud. Mary slams open up a drawer. I hear a rustling sound as she digs angrily in search of a syringe. *How can she see in all of this darkness?* I pick up a piece of glass and hurl it in a direction opposite of me to distract her. Mary hurls various items in that direction. One of them sounds like a chair. I takeoff running a little bit down the hallway and stop. Mary halts throwing objects in my decoy area. She runs to the area and finds no one.

"Where are you, Daniel?" Mary says in her regular voice. "Bring your bitch-ass out here, for this ass whooping."

I cover my mouth to muffle the sound of my heavy breathing and my laughter. She's frustrated that she can't find me. Mary's shadowy figure paces back and forth in the darkness. I throw another object from the ground in another direction. Mary takes off running toward it. I run a few more steps toward the lit room.

"Who looks like the fool now, Mary?"

Mary lets out a frightening scream of frustration. Her feet stomp in the darkness. She turns on a light switch and it illuminates one solo light above her. An angry, red look of madness is on her face.

"Get out here and fight me like a man!" she demands while scanning for me in the hallway. I remain lying low, hidden behind a medical cart. Slowly, I open one of the drawers to find an item to throw at her. In the drawer, I see a small square plastic machine labeled AED. A small red button with a lightning bolt on it is labeled SHOCK. Mary is about to get the shock of her life. Literally. *But first, how do I work this thing?*

"Come out, right now!" Mary shouts as she unknowingly starts to walk in my direction. I have no time to figure out how to work this thing. If I spend my time trying to figure this machine out, Mary will undoubtedly find me. It's now or never. I stand up slowly in the dark and hurl the small machine at her face. It pops Mary dead center on her face.

"Bitch!" I yell in celebration before scampering off down the hallway. Mary wails in pain as I run down the hallway. Those cries are meaningless; my safety is more important. I really didn't want to hurt Mary anymore, but I had to get out of there. Hell, she's crazy. She may have actually killed me if she found me. I slide into the lit patient room, close the sliding door and lock it behind me. If only I had my Fitbit on to count all my steps today. I'm sure I've reached my goal.

Huffing and puffing, I take a moment to catch my breath. I turn around and see a man lying in the bed, sleeping comfortably. He's an older white man with an unkempt gray beard smothering his face, and even more unkempt hair covering his head. In his neck is a long plastic tube that is attached to a breathing apparatus. The air from the apparatus makes a low-pitched sound as it pushes through the tube to his neck. His chest rises slowly like dough baking in an oven, then deflates like a pierced balloon. He's looks thin, frail, and malnourished. His extremities appear to be wasting away. They resemble elongated toothpicks with hands and feet attached to one end and a torso connected to the other. He continues to sleep as I move cautiously through the room to find a phone to call Sweet Cakes.

I glance around the room searching for the seldom used landline phone. I find it plastered to the wall next to the porcelain sink. Finally, I get to call wife. My love. My heartbeat. My one and only. My hands start to shake as I nervously dial her number. I put the phone up to my ear as it begins to ring. *One ring. Two rings. Three rings. Four rings. Five rings. Where is she? Six rings. Click.*

"Hello!" says Sweet Cakes.

"Hey, babe."

"How are you doing? Are you okay? It's all over the news," she asks in a quivering voice.

"Yes, I'm okay. A little banged up but, I'm okay."

"What's going on in there? How are you banged up?"

"You wouldn't believe me if I told you all that has happened. The only thing you'd believe is that I really do have appendicitis."

"I told you so. You never think I know what I'm talking about. Where are you? Are you out of the hospital? They've delivered some of the patients that were there to my hospital."

"I'm still in the hospital. I'm in the ICU."

"What are you doing in there? Are you that sick? Why aren't you trying to get out of the hospital? I saw a video of some people getting thrown out of windows. You need to get out of there!"

"Don't you think I've tried to get out of here!" I yell.

"Well you need to try harder! I need you! I can't live without you. I love you," Sweet Cakes responds in a tearful loud voice followed by sniffles.

Her tearful voice has made me sad. I know that she's scared for me. Hell, I am also scared for me, too. She knows nothing of what I've seen or been through. If she knew a quarter of what I've been through she would freak out even more. She would probably jump in a car right now and crash it through the hospital to save me. Yet, I can't tell her anything. She doesn't need to carry my emotional baggage right now. I must be strong for the both of us and not show any weakness. I gather myself before responding.

"I'm sorry for yelling. I love you, too, Sweet Cakes. I know you're worried about me, but I'll be fine.'"

"Its my job to worry about you. I'm your wife."

"Understandable."

"Well do what you need to get out of there. Even if you have to kill someone."

"Kill someone?"

"Yes, kill someone. Sometimes you have to do what you have to do to survive. You need to survive," she instructs. Someone coughs in the background.

"OK. I babe I will. I heard someone cough over there. Who is over there? Am I on speaker phone?"

"No. No one is over here and you're not on speaker phone. You're hearing things. Now, I gotta go. You call me immediately when you get out over there. No, you better Facetime me. I need to see your face," Sweet Cakes demands.

"OK. I'll Facetime you. I gotta go. I think I hear someone coming."

"Tell me you love me!"

"I love you. Infinity times infinity plus one." I hang up the phone and wipe the tears from my face. I don't care what Sweet Cakes said I heard someone cough. Who is she over there with?

"That was sweet," says a robotic voice.

"Who said that? Who's in here?" I say in a shocked voice.

There is a long pause before a knock on the door. I turn to so see Enrique and Jack both holding a child. Jack has my backpack on. I unlock the door and they slide in.

"Wow, what happened to your nose, Daniel?" asks Jack.

"Mary threw something at my face. Did you guys see her out there? And what's wrong with my nose?" I walk to the mirror over the sink and take a look at myself. My nose is completely bent to the left. I taste dried blood on my lips that has fallen from my nose. "Oh, man! I didn't know it was that bad."

"No, we didn't see Mary when we walked in the hallway. We just saw a whole bunch of glass on the floor and two trails of blood. One of the trails led us to you," says Jack. He puts the backpack down and hands Sarah to Enrique. He walks over to me and grabs my nose between his index finger and thumb.

"OK, Daniel. On the count of three I'm going to twist your nose back to the right. One, two." Jack insidiously twists my nose with a forceful crank. The crunching sound reverberates through my ears. "Three."

"Damn it!" I yell in anguish.

"Ooops. I went too far. Let me yank it back some." Jack once again twists my nose, but back in the opposite direction of his first twist. "There we go. Now it's straight. First time doing that one."

I brace my hand on the wall to gather my bearings before responding. I begin to taste blood again, but this time it coats the back of my throat.

"Glad I could be your guinea pig." I respond in a nasally voice.

"Ha, ha," responds the odd robotic voice.

"Okay. Where is that voice coming from?" I ask again. "I know you guys heard that."

I look around for the source of the robotic voice. *Is there a speaker in here? Is it Maestro watching me and laughing through a speaker?* I bend down and look under a chair. No luck. I check to see if the TV is on. It's not. I check under the foot end of the bed for someone or something. Nothing. I get up and inadvertently make eye contact with the patient in the bed. He's now wide awake and staring at me with his bright eyes. His breathing rate has increased in his awake state. His eyes peer toward a computer screen that faces him. The screen is attached to an extension that locks onto the headboard of his bed.

"Hello, Daniel," says the robotic voice on the screen. I walk toward the top of the bed and look at the screen. On it are various words and letters. A cursor moves around the screen.

"I have been waiting on you all day. You woke me up when you started talking on the phone. My name is Andrew. Nice to finally meet you," he responds via the computer.

"How are you able to talk to me via the computer?" I ask.

"He's using something called eye tracking technology," answers Jack. He walks closer to the bed and points at the bottom of the screen. "As you can see here there is a camera attached to the bottom of the screen. It sends an infrared beam to his eyes and it reflects back to the screen. This allows him to select items on the screen and use his eyes like a mouse. He selects words and phrases with his eyes and the computer reads them aloud."

"Bingo," responds Andrew followed by a wink of his eye. "I have a prepared letter on my computer that the computer is going to read aloud. Let, me pull up the file," Andrew begins to open files on his computer using his eyes. Technology has come so far. I remember being mesmerized by a wireless mouse. And now we can select items on the screen using our eyes. The technology of George Jetson has come to fruition. Andrew begins to speak through the computer.

"My name is Andrew Luke Shoemaker. I am a 58-year-old man who lies here in a state that I couldn't have predicted a few years ago. Trapped in my own body. Three years ago, I was an active 55-year-old looking forward to retirement. I had a long career as a fireman. I loved being a fireman. It always provided me such an adrenaline rush. Running into burning buildings. Pulling people out of mangled cars. Doing CPR. Oh, the thrills of being a fireman were endless! However, as I got older those thrills began to wane and take a toll. Getting up at 3 a.m. to save lives is thrilling in your twenties, but not in your fifties. It gets old and tiresome. Hence, I was looking forward to retirement and settling down in five years. Little did I know, my life would be settling down in a different way.

"It all started with me arbitrarily tripping, for no reason. I would run to the firetruck and stumble like I had tripped over something. My co-workers would look at me crazy. 'Come on, Shoemaker,' they would say. 'Make you some new shoes since those don't seem to be working right.' Then, we would hop on the firetruck and have a good laugh. I didn't know why I was tripping so much. I just attributed it to getting old. I figured that I would eventually end up on one of those 'help, I've fallen and can't get up' commercials. Gradually, the tripping became more frequent. Frequent enough for me to worry that something serious was going on. Other changes began to develop, as well. Slowly, I noticed that I had trouble gripping the firetruck's steering wheel. I would grasp the wheel and it would slip out of my hand as if it had been greased with oil. Then, my legs began twitching erratically. At that point, I knew something was wrong. These ailments had been gradually accumulating for a little over a year before I sought help. I should have listened to my body sooner. I know me. I know my body.

"Finally, I went to the doctor. They did blood work, imaging, and a boatload of other tests. I was poked and prodded like a fat cow. After seeing a neurologist, she made a diagnosis. She told me I have ALS, also known as Lou Gehrig's disease. An incurable disease that affects the nerves of my muscles. She told me the disease would eventually affect all of movements, my breathing, and my speech. She gave me three to five years to live. Essentially, a death sentence. Every word she said after that went in one ear and out the other. My entire life flashed before my eyes."

Three to five years? Really?" A tear rolls down Andrew's cheek as the computer continues to read his story aloud.

"After the initial shock and denial, I came to grips with the diagnosis. I accepted my death sentence. There was nothing I could do to fight off the disease. I couldn't exercise or diet it off. I couldn't get it removed. I couldn't get chemo for it. All I could do was live the last years of my life, fight the good fight, and pray to the Lord above.

"There were good days and bad days. More bad than good. There were days that my grandchild would ask me to pick her up or play with her. 'Papa, pick me up! Papa, come push me on the swing! Papa, dance with me!' Sadly, I would have to tell her that Papa can't. The simple things a grandfather can do to bring joy to his grandchild, I couldn't do. Physically, I just couldn't do it. My body was too weak. My body was too tired.

"There were many days I argued with God. How could he do this to me? This can't be life. This can't be God's love. This can't be right. There's gotta be more. More time. More time to live with my family. More time to just relax and enjoy the fruits of my labor. To enjoy retirement. But, it wasn't meant to be. No more time for me. Luckily, I had my wife by my side the entire way.

"She would constantly preach to me Proverbs 3:5. 'Trust in the LORD with all your heart
and lean not on your own understanding.' At the onset of the disease, it was difficult to put this scripture into practice. The beginning of the scripture was easier to act out more than the latter portion. How can I not lean on my own understanding? It's in man's nature to lean on his own understanding. However, as a man of faith, how could I lean on my own understanding and trust in the Lord at the same time? The internal struggle of faithful and faithless thoughts ran rampant throughout my head daily.

"This disease has taken a toll on me. Over the past two years, this disease has totally crippled my body. It has affected everything, from the way I breathe to the way I move. I cannot move any of my limbs. They have just wasted away and, as a result, look like the long tree branches that you see here today. Earlier this year, I had this trach inserted because I was having difficulty breathing. It ultimately helped me to breathe better but came with the risk of developing frequent bouts of pneumonia, and I lost my voice as a result of its placement.

"It's inevitable that I'm going to die from complications of this disease. It may be from a bedsore, which I have now, or from pneumonia, but I'm going to die from something and soon. They won't find a cure in enough time to help me. Maybe someone else, but not me. I'm too far gone. I'm tired of suffering, and I don't want to die like this.

"I have accepted God's will that I have this disease. However, I do not accept that I have to lay here and suffer counting down the days until I die. My body may be dead, but my mind is alive and well. I feel all of my suffering. I don't know what would be worse, being trapped in my body or trapped in my mind. Sometimes, I feel like I'm trapped in both, but most of the time I feel imprisoned in my body. Now, I want you to set me free from this prison that I call my body and end my suffering.

"I don't want to suffer anymore. I don't want my family to see me suffer anymore. I want to go out on my own terms and not lay here withering away. I have considered physician-assisted suicide, but it is illegal in Kentucky. The government has decided that I have to lay, here trapped in my own body.

"Yet, the government isn't here today. I have the power today. I have the power to choose to end my suffering. I just need your help. I want you to end my life. Pull the plug from the breathing machine and set me free from the prison which is my body. Will you do that for me? Will you open the prison gates, and set me free? As my last dying wish, I beg of you, do this for me."

The prepared statement ends. Andrew looks at me with wide eyes. I turn and look at Enrique and Jack.

"Nope! Not doing it. You guys can do this, but I'm having no parts in killing someone. Even if they want to die. I will be of no assistance," I respond.

"I'll do it," volunteers Jack. He begins walking towards the ventilator. I step in between him and the machine to impede him.

"No, you're not going to do that," I inform Jack, as I place my hand firmly on his chest. He bats it away like it's an annoying fly.

"Get your hand off me. I'll do what I want and what he wants. And right now, we both want the same thing. Which is for him to not suffer anymore. He's suffering like many people unnecessarily do in this hospital every day. I want to help end his suffering like I've helped others in here."

"What?" a shocked Enrique and I respond in sync.

"Oh, shit. I said that out loud. Well, cats out of the bag now. Yes, I've helped a few patients like this end their suffering in the hospital."

"How many have you murdered?" I ask.

"Let's just say I'm still counting on my hands, but I'm almost on my toes. And don't say murder. It has such a negative connotation. I prefer to label it as a *compassion kill*."

"Compassion kill. Wow. Label it whatever you want so you can go to sleep with a clean conscious. It's still murder. But what I do know is there will be no compassionate kills today. I can promise you that." I respond with a deep authoritative voice, clapping my hands to punctuate each syllable. The tension in the room heightens. We lock eyes. Jack stares at me. I stare at Jack. Testosterone begins to reach peak levels. Jack breaks eye contact first. *I win, bitch.*

"It's obvious that neither one of us is going to budge. So, we'll let the janitor here decide," says Jack. He walks over to Enrique and reads his name tag. "Enrique. It's up to you. You make the choice."

"Me?" questions Enrique.

"Yes, you. The choice is yours and yours alone. You're the tie-breaker," Jack replies. "You agree, Daniel?" I nod in agreement.

Enrique begins to pace back and forth, holding both babies. They sleep quietly in his arms as he rocks them in the middle of pacing and pondering. The sheer irony of him holding babies in the midst of thinking about killing Andrew. Babies, the symbol of life, rest right in his arms. For sure, he will choose life with this obvious sign. *Come on, Enrique.*

"If the man wants to die, we should grant his wish," Enrique says. My head drops.

"Enrique!" screams Jack ecstatically. "Good choice. I knew I wasn't the only one to feel this way. Welcome to the compassion kill crew, mi amigo."

"I believe in honor. This man deserves an honorable death. He doesn't deserve to sit here and suffer any longer. If it is his wish to die, he should have that right. I have seen many people lie here and suffer. I have had thoughts of easing their suffering, but have not acted on them like Jack. Most of them pass on their own. Yet, Andrew has not passed, but wishes to. I believe a person should have a choice to decide if they want to live or die. He has made his choice. Let's give him his wish. I'll do it."

"But what gives you the right to kill him?" I question.

"What gives you the right to want to keep him alive? Someone people just want to die. Some people just need to die," Enrique answers.

As much as I hate to admit it Enrique may have a point. Andrew has physically suffered enough. His body is wasting away. He looks like a bag of bones. There's no cure for his disease and if they do find one it may be too late for him. Who knows how much all of this has toiled on him mentally. I'm sure the mental stress has contributed to the decision of him wanting to die. Hell, it may be the main factor. Well does that mean those who suffer mentally should also have the right to kill themselves?

They suffer too. Some of them may suffer more than others do physically. As deranged as Mary is, I'm sure she has suffered a lot mental trauma that has contributed to her suicidal actions. Should she have the right to want to hang herself? Should she be able to end her mental suffering? I want everyone to live, but is living right for everyone? I don't know. I really don't know. This is too much for one brain to figure out.

Jack takes the babies out of Enrique's arms, and Enrique walks toward the ventilator machine I stand in front of.

"You know you don't have to do this," I whisper to him as he walks past me. He ignores my plea and pulls black rosary beads out of his back pocket as he reaches the ventilator. He says a prayer to himself, then kisses his beads. He looks at Andrew.

"Thank you," Andrew says via the computer. He closes his eyes and prepares to meet his maker. Enrique reaches behind the machine to unplug it, but surprisingly pulls a baton from behind it. He hands it to me. It reads, **AUTONOMY**. I put it in my backpack and put it back on. I hold Andrew's hand as he prepares to meet his maker.

"From dust you came and to dust you shall return. May your pain resolve and your soul rest in peace," preaches Enrique. He unplugs the ventilator. Silence engulfs the room. Andrew reflexively gasps for air. I squeeze his hand as I kneel to rest my head on the bed and face the floor.

I don't want to see him die. I've seen enough death for one day. Even if it's a death he requested. His gasps become shorter and shorter. I hear him start to choke on his own saliva. I keep my face toward the ground. Finally, he stops choking. The heart monitor beeps. Andrew is dead. Wish granted. Slowly, I get up and wipe tears from my eyes.

"May I hold the babies?" I ask Jack and Enrique. "Only they can provide me solace right now."

"Sure. Makes no difference to me. They're heavy anyway," says Jack. He hands the babies to me. The loud beep of the monitor starts to wake them up.

"I'm going to take them out of the room. The beeping seems to be bothering them. Do you guys mind covering up Andrew? That's the least you guys can do."

"Sure," replies Enrique.

I walk out of the room and glance back at Enrique and Jack. They stare over Andrew's body before covering him with a blanket. The lights in the hallway are now on once again. I place Sarah and Hope on a countertop outside of the room. Hurriedly, I turn around and run back to the room slamming the glass door shut. I find an extension cord and wrap it around the outside door handle. They're locked inside the room now. Jack yanks at the door.

"What are you doing, Daniel?" questions Jack.

"Abra la puerta, amigo?" says Enrique.

"No!" I yell back angrily. "I can't trust either one of you. You killed him!"

"That's what he wanted!" Jack shouts back.

"But that wasn't what was right," I respond.

"Wasn't right? Who are you to say?" Jack questions. "Who are you to say who lives and who dies? What gives you that right?"

"What gave you that right to kill those patients? Did they have a right to choose? Did all of them say they wanted to die, or did you just end their suffering for them because you saw it fit?"

Jack says nothing.

"That's what I thought," I look at Enrique. He stares at me in sadness.

"I'm so disappointed in you, Enrique. If there was anyone that I thought I could trust, it was you. It was you, Enrique. But now, I know I can't trust anyone in here. Not even myself. I'm getting out of here. Me and these babies are going to get the heck out of here. You guys just sit in here and think about what you've done until the police arrive to get you out."

I pick up Hope and Sarah and walk away from the room. Jack continues to bang on the glass, screaming my name and demanding that I come back. I ignore his demands, just like Enrique ignored my request to not pull the plug on Andrew.

I'm continuing this journey solo with the two babies in hand. They have now fallen back asleep. I press them closer to my grief-stricken heart. *Am I doing this this to comfort them or myself?* I don't know. What I do know is that I'm getting out of here on my next floor. Some way. Somehow. I am getting out of this hospital on the next floor. Even if I must jump out of a window, I am getting out of this freaking hospital. I have milk to pick up. Sweet Cakes, I'm coming home!

AMYOTROPHIC LATERAL SCLEROSIS (ALS)

Definition: Amyotrophic Lateral Sclerosis (ALS), also known as Lou Gehrig's Disease, consists of a loss of motor neurons in the brain, brainstem, and spinal cord (3). In other words, nerves that help muscles function start to break down. As a result of this, the muscles can't function properly and begin to waste away. This disease is incurable and fatal. Most people survive an average of three years after they begin to feel symptoms of weakness. As many as 18,000 Americans may have ALS at any given time (13). The incidence of ALS is more frequent in men than women.

Cause: There has yet to be definitive cause of ALS. Genetics are thought to play a major factor in its development (3). However, scientists and doctors are still researching causes and a cure.

Symptoms: At the onset of ALS, gradual painless weakness develops in the face and limbs. The arms and legs can both be affected. People can have trouble walking or grasping things (13). Like Andrew, people can start stumbling for no reason. As weakness of the extremities progresses, people with ALS become unable to move their limbs at all. Their muscles then begin to deteriorate. The muscles that aid breathing can also waste away. This can lead to complications such as pneumonia and the need for a ventilator. Sensation remains intact, so those who suffer from ALS are still able to feel things. People with ALS also can develop many other symptoms, including limb stiffness and trouble with their voice (3).

Treatment: There is currently only one approved drug that shows efficacy in the treatment of ALS. However, on average it only extends a person's tracheostomy-free survival for 2-3 months. The rest of the treatments are geared toward alleviating the symptoms of ALS. These include muscle relaxers to help reduce stiffness of limbs and breathing apparatuses (ex. Ventilators) to assist with breathing (13). The television show VICE on HBO has a good episode detailing the struggle that people with this disease endure. You can find the episode on HBO or YouTube.

CHAPTER 11

WHAT'S IN THE BOX?

After making a makeshift baby carrier out of bedsheets I found on the last floor, I exit onto the next floor. I am on the ground level. Only now I realize what elevator I have been riding on. This back elevator is the same one that bought me upstairs for my surgery. I have come a long way since my initial ride on it. On my original ride, I was scared out of my mind, thinking about dying in surgery, and trying to block Charles from talking me to death. Now, hours later, I exit the elevator with two babies pressed against my chest in what I hope are clean sheets with the possibility of dying another way. *My, oh my. What a day today has been.*

Now that I'm on the ground floor I can get out of the building and to freedom. The CT room should be to the left down the hallway, and once I pass it, I should be back in the emergency department. Then, I can exit through the doors I came in. I take off running down the hallway. No time to waste. *I gotta get dee fuck outta here.* With a gazelle-like stride, I make my way down the hallway. My flat feet smack the floor loudly with each step. I pass the CT room with its doors now held with a chain woven between the handles and secured with a metal lock.

"Who's out there?" questions a voice as I pass the room. I halt in my tracks.

"Who is that? I hear you out there," questions the female voice again.

"Are you part of this? You're dressed like them. Please don't kill us. Are you going to kill us? If you're not part of this can you get us out of here?" questions another female voice. She pulls on the chained door. I stay silent and stare at the door.

Who's in there? Should I help them? Do I have time to help them? Is this a trap? Is this a setup for another test? Can I trust them? Who can I trust in here? Apparently, no one as I've learned.

"We can see you through the door crack," says the first voice.

"Why do you have those babies wrapped around you? Are those your babies? And why do you have a backpack on?" asks the other consistently inquisitive voice. I take two steps to the side to get out of their view.

"Can you see me now?" I ask.

"No," they respond in unison.

"Good!" I respond with the inflection of Verizon commercial in my voice. I begin to walk away from the door toward the emergency room.

"Don't you leave us here! You get back here!" demands voice number one.

"Why should I help you? If you've seen and been through the things I've been through you wouldn't help anyone in here."

Hope starts to cry. I try to soothe her by rubbing her head. It doesn't work.

"Looks like we both need help right now. We need help getting out of here and you need help with those babies. I can tell by the way you wrapped them around your chest that you don't know what you're doing with them. You're five seconds away from dropping both of them on the floor," says voice number one.

"Yeah, and they stink," says the high-pitched irritating second voice. "I can smell them all the way in here. When is the last time they've been changed? Have they eaten?"

"No. No, they haven't eaten. I've been busy trying to keep them safe and alive." Sarah follow suit with Hope and starts to cry.

"What's your name?" asks the first voice.

"Daniel," I respond over the screaming babies. I begin rocking them in my arms, but it only seems to make them cry louder. They need a woman's touch.

"I'm April, and the one who keeps pestering you with questions is Ally. We can help you with them. I know where we can get some diapers and formula from down here. Daniel, let us help you."

My eyes begin to well. I'm tired and emotional. They're right. I do need help. I am a total wreck right now. As much as I've tried to keep it together, I feel like I'm on the verge of a mental breakdown. *Confusion. Anger. Worry. Fear. Sorrow.* These are the thoughts and emotions that are circulating my brain. My stomach begins to hurt again. I use my hand to brace myself on the neutral-colored wall and grimace. Hope and Sarah cry even louder.

"I don't know what's wrong with you, but you don't appear to be well," says April.

"Yeah. You look all pale. And that's hard to tell on somebody black. Let us help you," Ally pleads.

"How can I get you guys out of there? The door is chained and locked," I ask.

"There's an axe in the glass case behind you. Use it to cut the chains," April says in an enthusiastic voice.

I take my backpack off and place it on the ground. Slowly, I swaddle the babies in the bedsheets and lay them on the floor. The swaddling does nothing to cease their incessant crying.

I open the glass door to the axe, which unexpectedly falls directly toward my naked feet. With cat like reflexes I jump out of the way to save my toes from amputation. The axe pierces the floor with a thunderous sound. Someone did not secure the axe properly.

"Watch out!" yells Ally with a late warning. I side-eye the door. After a few yanks of the wooden handle, I'm able to dislodge the axe from the floor. The axe has a long wooden handle at one end and a sharp metal blade on the other. The blade appears sharpened to perfection. It's as though it was made by Hattori Hanzō. With a few mighty swings of the Hattori Hanzō-made axe against the chains, I'm able to break them a loose. Out come the hidden figures behind the door.

"Thank you. I'm April," says the average height dark-haired Latina in royal blue scrubs. Ally runs from behind April toward Hope and Sarah. She's a young black woman with curly natural hair that bounces up and down like springs. The smell of the natural products she uses in her hair travel up my nose and tickle my senses as she runs by me.

"Give me those babies," she says as she rushes over to Hope and Sarah. "It's okay, I'll take care of you guys. *Ssshhh*." With a woman's touch she clutches them in her arms and silences their crying instantaneously. *What kind of voodoo feminine magic does she possess?*

"How long have you guys been in there?" I ask April.

"Basically, since this whole thing started. A group of what looked like at least 30-armed people stormed the emergency room and started shooting without warning. Ally and I ran in here to hide. One of the armed people searched the room, but they didn't see us. They chained the door and locked it after they left. We've been looking through the crack in the door for someone to help us, but no one came. We could see some of the doctors and nurses getting dragged down the hallway. I have no idea where they've been taking them. They just kept dragging them while they were kicking and screaming. We've heard gunshots and yells in the distance. It had been awhile since we saw someone come down the hallway, until we saw you. I hoped that you weren't one of the bad people. I figured that you weren't with the two babies wrapped around your chest."

"Yeah, I'm not. I was just trying to save them. We've got to get out of here. Right now," I respond while wiping my eyes.

"I agree," says April. "Let's cut through the emergency room. I'll grab some baby formula and then we'll sneak out the back door. It shouldn't take me two seconds to grab the formula."

April starts to lead us into the emergency department. I pick up my backpack and follow her. She's taken over as the new leader of the group. I'm happy to give up the reigns. My time as the decision-maker has become tiresome. I've lost all the adults who were with me, but I've managed to keep the babies. I've been a mediocre leader at best. We enter the emergency department. We're not alone.

"What in the hell?" says Ally upon entering.

The emergency room has been destroyed. Paper litters the floor. Gurneys lay overturned in the hallway. Motionless bodies lie next to the gurneys. The patient rooms' doors are chained like the CT room April and Ally were in. Some of the rooms are locked with patients still in them. While some of the other rooms are locked with staff in them. They stand up as we walk by. They stare at us in a daze through the glass doors. They all have a distraught look on their faces. April recognizes someone she knows in one of the rooms. She runs to the door.

"Jessica!" she yells at the person inside the room. "Are you okay?" Jessica nods her head slowly.

"Who is that?" I ask Ally.

"That's her sister. They both work as nurses here," answers Ally.

"I'm going to get the axe to break you out," April says to Jessica. April runs back to get the axe. Jessica pounds on the glass. April stops and turns around. Jessica shushes her and points for her to continue going down the hallway in the opposite direction.

"You want us to go down the hallway?" April asks. Jessica nods her head again.

"Let me get you out of here first," pleads April. Jessica shakes her head no.

"No. Why?" she asks. Jessica once again points down the hallway reaffirming that we should continue walking.

"I think she wants us to go that way," I say.

"I will be back to get you. Stay strong," April says to Jessica. Jessica nods in agreement.

We forge ahead and maneuver through the dismay. We reach the center of the room and are greeted by Maestro sitting on top of the counter swinging his feet while staring at his iPad. He has on a white medical coat with Dr. Morrison's name on it. He has changed his appearance. His beard is now shaven, and he has dyed his hair dirty blonde. Next, to him is someone who is strapped to a chair with clear plastic tape and facing away from us. Bo stands tall next to the person strapped in the chair. His leash is off and he looks ready to pounce on me.

"Took you long enough to get here, Daniel," says Maestro as he lifts his gaze from the iPad.

"Sorry. I had to make a couple of stops."

"I see you still have the babies. Where is the rest of your crew?"

"I couldn't trust them, and they slowed me down. So, I had to let them go. I have all that matters to me."

"What matters to you, Daniel?" he asks.

"Well, right now, getting out of here alive with Hope and Sarah and seeing my wife."

"Hmph. We'll see what matters to you in a second." Maestro rotates the office chair and reveals who is tethered to it with packing tape. It's Richard, the doctor who checked me into the emergency room. His hands and arms taped to the arms rests. His torso bound to the seat. A piece of tape is plastered over his mouth. His right eye is blackened and swollen shut.

"Honey!" screams April. She runs toward him.

"Honey?" Maestro and I respond in unison.

"Yes! This is my fiancé," April informs us before whipping the tape off Richard's mouth.

"Wow. Wasn't expecting that. Well, this will be very interesting," mumbles Maestro under his breath. I wonder what he means.

"Baby what are you doing down here?" April asks while caressing his brown hair.

"I'm working in the emergency room this month. Remember?"

"Are you okay?" April asks while caressing his gelled hair.

"Yeah. Just a few aches. My eye kind of hurts." April stands up and turns to Maestro.

"Get him out of the chair now!" she demands.

"In due time," he replies, now staring back at his iPad. It looks like he's perusing Facebook. *Who could do such a thing in a time like this?*

"Daniel, I think it is fate that you and I met today," Maestro says. He sits his tablet down, jumps off the table, and paces while he talks. "I had no idea of how this day would unfold, but I truly believe that you were meant for this mission. And if you so choose, this mission could be over right now."

"I would very much like for that to happen," I respond eagerly.

Maestro reaches in the office drawer next to him and pulls out a small plastic box. He hops off the counter and places the box on the countertop next to me. Maestro pulls a cigar from his pocket and lights it. He takes a puff, then starts talking again.

"To your left, my right, is an exit door. You can freely walk out of that door. The police are located approximately 50 yards from the door. I've fired off a few warning shots outside of the door to keep them at bay. I've been talking to them on the phone. I informed that I'd be releasing people within the next 10 minutes and that could be you."

"Me and the babies," I firmly state.

"Hey! Um, me too," interjects Ally, pointing at herself.

"Yeah. Her too. April and Richard as well." I state.

"Deal," Maestro answers.

"What's the catch?" I ask.

"No catch at all. Just head out of the door. However, just know that this box right here is for you," Maestro taps the top of the plastic box. "This floor is for you, Daniel. You are the lesson."

"What's the lesson? What's in the box?" I question.

"You'll have to open it up to see, but if you leave you don't get to see what's in the box. You can walk out of here scot-free. You and the rest of your new group, but you won't get to see what's in the box."

"I vote let's get out of here," says Ally with her hand raised. "Any other takers on this offer? Anyone?"

"What's in the box?" I ask again.

"I can't tell you," he says.

"Well riddle me this, Maestro. Would you look in the box if you were me?"

"Can't really answer that honestly because I know what's in there. So, my opinion would already be skewed knowing what I know is in the box. What's in there is life altering but you can walk away without it altering your life any more than it has already been altered today."

What could be in such a small box? Money? Someone's cut off finger? Mary?

"I wanna see what's in the box," I boldly respond. I don't know what lies inside, but I am curious. Maestro hands me the box.

April walks over from Richard and grabs my wrist. "Daniel, don't open the box. Let's just get out of here. He said we could all leave. All of us. The babies, too. Think about the babies," she pleads.

"Yeah. Don't open that box. Let's just go," Ally agrees.

"I have to April. I need to know what's inside," I respond and pull my wrist away. I lift the latch on the box and take a deep sigh before opening it. Inside the box, I see a picture of Sweet Cakes and me on our wedding day. I break into a huge smile. Teeth showing.

"It's amazing the things you can find online," says Maestro. "Just Google a person's name, and pictures of them pop up in the blink of an eye. That's you and your wife. Correct?" asks Maestro.

"Yes. That's Sweet Cakes and me."

"You guys look so happy together. You look happy, and she does too."

"It was the happiest day of our lives. I remember just like it was yesterday. Where did you find this picture?"

"On Facebook. You should really change your privacy settings," he informs me. "I was able to see all your pictures and posts without being your friend. How was that cinnamon scone you had the other day?"

"A little crunchy, but I still ate it," I respond honestly. I look down in the box and see another picture of us. I pick it up. It's a picture of us eating at Proof on Main Street in Louisville, celebrating our anniversary. Sweet Cakes is feeding me pink cotton candy during a candlelight dinner. I begrudgingly agreed to take the cheesy picture at the behest of her.

"You guys are cheesy," says Ally looking nosily over my shoulder at the pictures.

"When it is appropriate," I retort.

"What's the next picture?" she asks. I look back down and pick up the next picture. It's a picture of Sweet Cakes and Richard sitting in what looks like a cafeteria eating lunch. She has a big grin on her face. The same grin she has when she's eating with me.

"What's going on here?" I ask. I hand the picture to April.

"Yeah. What's going on here?" she asks Richard while thrusting the picture in his face. "You rarely eat lunch with me when you're here. Why are you eating with her?"

"Nothing's going on, April. We're just eating lunch. I can't eat lunch with a coworker at work? Now get me out of this chair," Richard says.

"For a married woman, your wife sure spends a lot of time with another man," says Maestro.

"What do you mean?" I ask. Maestro gestures for me to continue looking in the box.

I look in the box and see another picture of my wife and Richard. This time they are standing talking to each other in the emergency room. It looks like they're having a jolly good old time, yucking it up. Richard's hand is on Sweet Cake's elbow as they laugh. *Why is he touching my wife?* No man should touch another man's wife in that manner. That's my wife. That's my woman. *What else has he been touching?* I look at Maestro with worrisome eyes and he looks at me with a subliminal answer in his. I look in the box and see a final picture. I fall to the floor and stare at the pic.

"What is it?" April asks. I continue to sit and stare at the picture with a blank face. "What is it?" she asks again. I toss the picture and it lands face down. I plop my head down. Down like my heart. Down like my emotions. Down like my soul. In the picture a woman is leading Richard into a closet in the hospital. That woman is my wife. I can see Richard's face, but I can't see my wife's. However, I make out my wife's silhouette. I know the back of her head. I know her curves. I know my wife. She walks ahead of him holding his hand leading him into a closet. April picks up the picture off the floor.

"What the fuck is this? What is this, Richard?!" she yells as spit flies out of her mouth like a rabid dog. He turns his head to the side. No answer.

"At first, I thought that they were married when I saw them interact with each other. The sweet eyes they gave each other. The subtle touches between the two of them. The way she laughed loudly whenever he would say something. But there was one thing I couldn't get past," says Maestro.

"What was that?" I ask as I pick my head up with tears rolling down my face.

"Why does she have a wedding ring and he doesn't? That just baffled me. But then one day through the grapevine I found out that they were just messing around with each other."

"It was fairly evident that they liked each other. Everyone assumed that they were screwing around," agreed Ally.

"You knew!" exclaimed April.

"Kind of. It was just hospital gossip. You know how it goes. I didn't know how to tell you nor did I want to tell you. I just wanted to stay out of it. I figured you'd eventually find out whether it were true or not, but not like this," explains Ally.

"No. No. No. This isn't happening. We've ordered wedding invitations. I've named our kids already. This can't be real," April says to herself pacing back and forth with her hands on her head.

"How long has this been going on?" I ask Richard.

"I don't know. A few months," he slowly responds while looking away.

"Why?" I ask.

"I don't know."

I get up and rush toward him in anger. Maestro restrains me from proceeding further.

"Whoa now, lover boy," he says sarcastically.

"What do you mean you don't know," I yell angrily, restrained by Maestro's arms.

"It just happened. I'm sorry. We didn't mean for it to happen. We just got a little *too comfortable* around each other, and one thing lead to another."

"Too comfortable? How about I get comfortable with my hands around your neck?" I'm heated. I toss Maestro to the side like a child and charge toward Richard who is still strapped in the chair. He squirms to get a loose, but there's nothing he can do. I brush past April; she doesn't stop me. I kick over Richard's chair and he lands face first on his injured eye. He moans.

"Did you fuck my wife?" I question him. He doesn't respond. He only groans more.

"Oh, don't get quiet on me now." I kick him in the stomach. He groans in pain. Toddrick would be proud of my kicks.

"You heard me. Did you have sex with my wife?"

"Yes!" he answers loudly.

And there's the answer. The answer to the question for which I already knew the answer. My wife. My soulmate. My Sweet Cakes has cheated on me. I can't believe it after all that we've been through. I really can't believe it. My heart is empty. My soul is empty. After all I've done for her. I put my heart and soul into this marriage. We entered into a covenant before God with each other. To not be individuals anymore, but to be one. One body. One mind. One spirit. And this is what I get. This is the return on my investment. Man, fuck Sweet Cakes and Richard, too. I turn Richard over and straddle on top of him. I wrap my fingers around his throat.

"'Got too comfortable.' Is this comfortable?" I ask Richard, but he doesn't respond. He only gasps for air.

"Are you as comfortable as you were in my wife?" I squeeze harder. He gasps harder.

"That's enough, Daniel!" April yells. She rushes over and jumps on my back. She tries to pull me off him. I take one hand off Richard and toss her to the side like a rag doll. She flies into a wall and winces worse than LeBron after a hard foul. I firmly place my hand back on Richard's neck and recommence the choking. Richard continues to struggle to breathe.

"We told you not to open that box," says Ally.

I take my attention off Richard and look at her. "What did you say?"

"I said, we told you not to open the box. Now, look at you," she says.

I turn my head and see my reflection in the glass door of one of the patient's rooms. I look behind Ally and see the staff locked in rooms staring at me in shock through the glass doors. Bo looks at me confused. Ally's right. *Look at me. What am I doing? What have I become? I look like a monster. This isn't me. This isn't who I am.*

Am I really mad at Richard or am I just funneling my anger at my wife through Richard? I don't know. I'm so confused. However, what I do know is I'm not a killer. Unlike Mary, I won't kill for love. I release Richard from the clutches of my hands and stand up. April slides across the floor over to Richard.

"Baby, are you okay? Breathe. Just breathe," she instructs him. Richard struggles for air as if he has just come from underwater. "Someone help me get him out of this chair. He can't breathe."

Maestro pulls a medium-size knife out of his pocket, and with a snail's pace, walks over to Richard and starts to cut him out of the chair. The tape snaps with each cut as Maestro releases Richard from the chair. I pace back and forth, breathing deeply in and out of my mouth with my hands on my head. I need to calm down. I almost killed Richard.

"How could she!" I state aloud in a high-pitched voice. My voice always goes up an octave when I'm mad. I could probably break a champagne glass with my tone right now. Maestro picks Richard up from the ground and wraps one of Richard's arms around his shoulder.

"Just breathe. Breathe, Richard. In and out. That's it. You're all right. You're all right," Maestro comforts him while holding him up. April stands in front of Richard holding her hand on his chest. It rises with each rapid breath he takes. He begins to settle down.

"I thought you had it in you. I really thought you had it in you to kill him," a disappointed Maestro says.

"That's not me. I'm not a killer. I'm better than that."

"You're better than me. I surely would have killed him if he'd slept with my wife, but he didn't sleep with my wife. He just killed mine." Maestro takes the same knife he used, to untape Richard from the chair and smoothly pierces Richard's side with it. Richard doesn't scream. He just looks down with his good eye at the knife in shock. Maestro removes Richard's arm from around him. Richard topples over onto April. She screams along with the staff trapped in the rooms.

"I wish you would have done it for me, Daniel. I was hoping you would do it for me, so the blood didn't have to be on my hands. But you couldn't. So, I had to do it myself."

I run over to Richard and flip him off April. He's bleeding from his abdomen. I apply firm pressure. The blood soaks my hand. April continues to shriek as she shakes on the ground. She has Richard's blood all on her. Maestro kneels beside me as I continue to apply pressure.

"I'm going downstairs to the basement floor, Daniel," Maestro informs in a calm voice. "You have two choices. Choice number one: You can stay and help poor Richard. The back exit is open. There are no traps or bombs. As I said previously, the police and everyone else are about 50 yards away. Choice number two: You can follow me and complete your mission. You'll get all the answers you've been waiting on." Maestro gives me a pat on the back like a proud dad to his son, and then he stands up. He whistles for Bo, and they walk out of the emergency room. Trapped staff members beat on the glass doors as he walks by. He ignores them with ease.

What just happened? Did Maestro really just stab Richard and then ask me to go with him? What do I do? Do I stay here and help Richard, the man who slept with my wife? Or should I follow the psychotic Maestro. Or should I just leave everyone here. I should do that. I should just leave, and head to safety. The cops can sort all of this out. It's not my job to save everybody.

But, then I would be left with so many unanswered questions. *Did Richard really kill Maestro's wife? What is the true meaning of today's chaos? How did he get those pictures of Richard and Sweet Cakes? Wait she doesn't deserve to be called Sweet Cakes anymore. She's deserves to be called by government name now, Lisa. She's just Lisa now.*

"April. I need your help. I need you to calm down and help me out over here," I say in a peaceful, soothing tone. April ceases her relentless yelling and rolls herself over to help Richard.

"Am I dying?" Richard asks softly.

"Not if I can help it," I respond. April is too shaken up to be the leader anymore. I retake the reins. "April, I need you to place pressure right here. That's the only way he's going to make it. You got it?" April nods her head in understanding. I stand up and walk toward Ally. She's been quiet and just taking in the whole situation since the quick turn of events.

"I told you not to open that box," she repeats as I walk up to her.

"Yeah, I don't need your lip right now. What I need for you to do is give her to me," I say, looking at Hope. "And go to the back door to wave for help."

"Why do you want her?" she asks with a confused look on her face.

"Because I said so. Now, you can give me her or I can take her from you. Your choice," I tell her firmly. Ally looks me up and down with a wrinkled brow. She hands me Hope.

"Thank you. You take care of Sarah. Now, go out of the back door and wave for help." Ally starts walking to the back door.

"April, keep applying pressure. Richard, you doing okay?"

"Just getting cold," he responds, shivering.

"I'm going to go get the axe April, so I can break some of the staff out of the rooms in here. So, they can help us out."

"Hurry, Daniel!" she encourages.

I run out of the room toward the place where I left the axe. Hope is in my hands and my backpack is on my back. I make it into the hallway. The axe lies in the same place I left it. At the end of the hallway Maestro stands in the elevator with the doors open. He pets Bo's head.

"You coming?" he yells from a distance. I look at the axe and then back at him then back at the axe. I start walking toward him.

"I thought you were going to stay and save him," he says as I get on the elevator.

"Man, fuck him. I need answers," I respond coldly. I guess I've lived long enough to see myself become the villain.

"And you will get them," he responds. He presses the button for basement. The final floor on my journey.

CHAPTER 12

WHAT WOULD LOVE MAKE YOU DO?

"I've been in this hospital multiple times before today, Daniel. As a patient, a family member, and observant. I observed Richard and your wife interact inappropriately on multiple occasions. After I found out they weren't married to each other, I decided to take a few pictures of their interactions. Those are the pictures that you saw in the box. I didn't know what I'd do with them, but I took them anyway. I printed them in the emergency room while I waited for you." The doors of the elevator open and we walk out.

"You hungry, Daniel?"

"Man, I don't know what I am."

"Cheer up. Let's head into the cafeteria. There's always time for food. I'm sure the baby could use some food as well," Maestro leads me to the cafeteria. Bo tags along by his side. He continues his monologue.

"It took me a long time to concoct what you see here today. It was formed out of a mix of emotions over time. Anger. Loneliness. Depression. Stress. I could go on for days with emotions, but mostly today's event was bred out of love. Like you, I also have a wife. I have a kid, too. You got any kids?"

"No, but we've been trying."

"Good. Good for you guys. I hope you two are successful. Everyone isn't able to have kids. Just make sure the kid's yours. You know?"

"Um yeah. You said you have a wife? I thought you said Richard killed your wife." Maestro stops in his tracks and faces me.

"Yes, he did. But does that mean she isn't my wife anymore? If you lose something so arbitrary as your wallet isn't it still your wallet? If your wallet is found fifty years from now, you will say 'that's my wallet.' It is still yours. The same thing is true with my wife.

"Even though I lost her, she still is and always will be my wife. Death won't separate the love we have for each other. I love her even more in death, than I did when she was alive. I appreciate her more because she's gone. I love her more because I realize no one can compare to her. No one can replace her. So, don't get caught in the verb tense of whether I have or had a wife. I will always have a wife." We continue walking side by side to the cafeteria.

"What's your definition of love, Daniel?"

"I thought I knew, but then I opened that box. Now, I don't know what love is. Now, I'm like 'fuck love.'"

"That's understandable. Right now, your heart is hurt. Well, what was your definition of love before?"

"Please, stop with the love questions."

"Why?"

"Because every time you say love, I think of her!" I yell. "I think of the feeling I felt inside when I met her, when she spilled chicken on me. I think of when I first kissed her soft lips. I think of the butterflies I had inside as she walked down the aisle at our wedding. I think of the big smile I flash whenever she makes a corny joke. And I don't want to feel that right now."

"Why not?"

"Because I'm hurt. She's hurt me. Love isn't supposed to hurt me like that. Love doesn't do that. Man! I've wasted so much on her. I've wasted time on her. I've wasted energy on her. I'm content with wasting that. That's part of relationships and life. However, one thing I'm not ok with wasting on her is love. I can't get the love I put into her back. Ain't nothing worse than wasting love on someone that doesn't deserve it. So, I don't want to think of her. Even though all I can do right now is think of her."

"Love will make you do that. Love is a force that does whatever it wants. A force that can't be contained. Love will have you thinking of a person even when you don't want to think of that person. It's like telling yourself to not concentrate on breathing. Next thing you know you're focusing even more on breathing," says Maestro.

"Yeah. It is kind of like that."

"I've been there. Love is hard."

We enter the cafeteria. Bo starts walking around on his own.

The cafeteria is huge. There are different stations for different cuisines with signs labeling the selections. One sign reads "Asian Cuisine." Another reads "American Cuisine." Tucked away in the back, right corner is a pizza station. There's also a soul food area that I'm sure that is full of tasty yet unhealthy grub. In the center is a salad bar with various leafy greens, toppings, and salad dressings. All of the food in each section has been laid out for lunch, but is still covered with saran wrap. I presume today's events started in the middle of lunch prep. A long metal curtain separates the cafeteria from what I assume is the seating area behind it. Maestro walks over to the drink station.

"They always keep some formula down here in the mini fridge for unruly babies," Maestro informs me. He finds a can of formula behind some Sprite cans in the mini fridge, next to the soda machine. He shakes it up, opens it, and pours it into an empty bottle that was also in the fridge. He hands me the bottle. I hold it to Hope's mouth. She sucks on the bottle intensely.

"You sure know where everything is in here." I comment.

"Like I said. I've been in here many times. I first came here as a patient. Almost drank myself to death and ended up in the drunk tank area in the emergency room. That happened to me more than once," says Maestro. "I'm hungry. I haven't eaten all day. I've used an exorbitant amount of energy today. I'm going to make me an egg sandwich."

Maestro walks towards the American food cooking area. He turns on the large metal grill and then opens the large doors to the refrigerator next to it. He looks into the freezer first. He takes out a large brown bag labeled curly fries. Ice flakes fall off the bag as he brings it to the grease traps. He pours a hefty amount of curly fries into a metal basket and then dips them into the hot grease.

He returns to the refrigerator and grabs a carton full of eggs and a slice of cheese. He grabs the liquid butter and sprays the grill with it. It's hot now and pops loudly with each spray. He grabs an egg out of the carton and turns around to me. He holds it up in the air.

"There are many different paths that this egg could have taken. It could have hatched and become a layer, a chicken that lives at a hatchery and produces eggs. Or it could have been hatched and become a broiler, a chicken raised to be slaughtered and end up on someone's Thanksgiving table. However, it didn't. It ended up here in this carton, ready for consumption. Now, how it ended up here and not on one of those other routes, I don't know. I think it's just fate that makes some things go down one route and not the other. I think that it was fate that bought you and I here together. You could have ended up anywhere in the world, but you're here with me. After I looked you up online and found out who you were, I knew it was fate, not happenstance. Your route bought you here, with me. On this day." Maestro uses the grill to break open the egg, then he fries it.

"Despite what you may have been told, I planned most of this by myself. I gather by now Enrique and Dr. Patel have informed you of their roles in today's matter. I must say that I manipulated them very well to get what I wanted. It's amazing the number of things one can accomplish, using the power of words. The right person, using the right words, can manipulate anyone and put fear into any person's mind. This can be seen throughout history. From slave owners to Hitler to street pimps. Slave owners could use their words to mentally shackle a slave. Pimps can make a woman believe that her value is centered around her body and that she is nothing without him. Hitler used his words to manipulate millions of soldiers, some of them children, to perform mass genocide. These people often used violence or the threat of violence to back up their words. I've mastered this art in a sinister way with just a hint of fear. Take you for example." Maestro takes a loaf of bread off the top of the refrigerator. He skips the first few slices and pulls out three slices of bread. He lathers two of them with the butter roller and throws them on the grill next to his egg. He whistles for Bo who has been in the distance, sniffing something near the pizza area. Bo rushes over happily. Maestro tosses him the other piece of bread. Bo catches it in his mouth and begins smacking. Maestro turns back to face the grill. His back is toward me.

"What about me?"

"You are still walking around with that stupid backpack on. You have collected batons on each floor and kept them in that backpack. I put a few words into your head, backed them up with a little fear, and look what happened to you. You followed my words to a tee. Did I tell you that you had an ultimatum, if you didn't follow them?"

"Not really," I respond. He's right. He didn't. I am still carrying around this backpack. I guess sometimes we carry around baggage that we don't need. Afraid to let it go. Maestro scrapes his egg off the grill and flips it over.

"No. No, I did not. No threat of death or punishment from me. Didn't even lay a finger on you. I just gave you your assignment and sent you on your way. I instructed you to go to each floor, learn a lesson, and collect the batons. I never stated that you would die if you didn't do that. However, I knew what I had done. I had instilled fear in you by using a choice few words, having others project fear onto you, and injure others in front of you. Seeing death can put fear in anyone. I know this first hand from serving in Iraq as a physician.

"I saw a lot of death and mutilation there. I was able to save some people, but not everyone. While there, I came face to face with death many times. As a soldier and as a physician treating soldiers. Personally, facing death was the worse. I faced death when an IED exploded on my platoon as we traveled from one part of town to another. I still have tinnitus in my ears from that explosion.

After it exploded some of the terrorists captured me and some of my crew. They did unspeakable things to us." Maestro walks over to the grease traps removes the now-golden curly fries.

"What did they do to you?"

"Indescribable horrors that I dare not reach into my brain to bring back up. It was there during the torture that I learned about fear. Daily, I was threatened with death. I was tortured and watched others get tortured. I was sleep-deprived and separated from the others. They kept us isolated so we never knew whether someone was alive or dead until we saw or heard them getting tortured. Five of us were captured and only three of us made it out alive. We were saved by special ops forces." Maestro dumps the fries from the metal basket into two paper food baskets. He slides one to me across the counter.

"Eat up. You've had a long day."

"Thanks," I respond. I reach for the ketchup on the counter. Maestro pushes it away and returns to cooking on the grill.

"I had PTSD when I returned home. Drove myself to drinking. Drinking a lot. Sometimes to the point of blacking out. I was trying to mask the pain with alcohol. I knew what I was doing, but I didn't care. I was so selfish then. My family began to crumble. My wife was scared to be around me. I often had flashbacks. They would come with any loud sound. I also had trouble sleeping. I had frequent nightmares. I often was afraid to go to sleep because I knew that I would relive those moments. Those moments of torture.

"My wife eventually reached a breaking point one stormy night. There was a tremendous thunderstorm. Lightning and thunder rocked our house. Our son Jaxon walked into our room because he was scared and couldn't sleep. I had difficulty sleeping myself. Jaxon tapped on my shoulder, trying to wake me up because he was scared. Big mistake. Him tapping me along with the thunderstorm triggered a flashback. I attacked him." Maestro takes his bread off the grill and places the slices on a paper plate. He puts a square of cheese on one slice. He takes his fried egg off the grill and places it on the other slice. He combines the two pieces to make a sandwich. He cuts it diagonally.

"Did you hurt him?" I ask.

Maestro eats while talking. "No. Lucky for him, I didn't. My wife pulled me off him in the nick of time. Then, she went apeshit on me. Kicking and punching me. That was the last straw. I put our son in danger. She gave me an ultimatum. Go to counseling or leave the house. So, I left the house. I left my family and continued my drinking. An inner battle brewed inside me. On one hand, as a physician, I knew I needed psychological help. I knew that I needed to lie down on a couch and share my thoughts with a professional. I had already diagnosed myself with post-traumatic stress disorder and depression. I had all the typical signs. Trouble sleeping. Decreased appetite and energy. Problems concentrating. Suicidal thoughts. Substance abuse. I was a textbook case. However, I didn't want help.

"The man in me was too stubborn to seek help. I didn't want to sit and open up to someone. Opening yourself up is scary. I hate being vulnerable like that. The way you felt when I had you undress in front of everyone is how I would feel opening myself to a therapist. I would feel psychologically naked. And I don't like that feeling. Not one bit. So, I continued to wallow and drink daily after my wife kicked me out."

"Where did you stay?" I question.

"Sometimes in my car. Sometimes on the street. Sometimes in a shelter. I met Ron, who you met initially on your journey through his friend Mac who was with him. Ron helped me one night after I passed out on the street. He stuck with me until I woke up and made sure I was okay. I drank way too much. I ended up here in the hospital on a few occasions when I was drunk or suicidal. That's how I met Mary. We ended up getting to know each other in the psych ward. That girl's a character."

"Man, tell me about it," I respond.

"Yeah. I know. One time I saw someone call her crazy. Let's just say he never did that again."

"Yeah, I saw that, too. She killed one person, Todd."

"I didn't know Todd, but Dr. Patel informed me about him. I let Dr. Patel do whatever he wanted to do on that floor. I had to give him a little taste of power to make him feel as if he was a part of the planning of this, but he wasn't. This entire thing today was originally constructed as a ruse."

"A ruse for what?"

"To get revenge for my wife's death. My wife," Maestro reflects. "She was my first and only love. She was the first woman I told 'I love you' and actually meant it. I couldn't have asked for a better spouse. She cooked. She made me laugh. She loved me for me. Most importantly, she took care of our family when I was away, and when I was at home physically but not mentally. She held the fort down when I couldn't. I couldn't have asked for a better spouse, but she could have asked for a better husband. I didn't take care of her like I should. My issues took physical and emotional toll on her.

"She tried her best to never let it show, but every now and then a part of her frustration would slip out. A deep breath here. A shaking of her leg there. A rare outburst. But for the most part, she did her best to not let her emotions show. Especially, in front of Jaxon. He never knew what was going on. She would lie and tell him I was gone for work when I wasn't around. She never changed his routine. He always went to school and got his Saturday morning donuts. When I was sober, she would let me take him to get them. A little father-and-son time. When I was drunk or feeling down, she would take him. The latter happened more times than not.

"One fine morning, while waiting for donuts, a woman accidentally drove into the donut shop and hit my wife and child as they stood at the counter. Jaxon only had a few minor scratches. However, my wife, Rachel, was banged up pretty badly. She had to go the hospital and get some tests done. When they scanned her abdomen, they incidentally found cancer. A big mass in her colon. When I went to visit her in the hospital, she told me that she had been having stomach pain for a few months. However, she just chose to pay it no mind. She figured it would eventually go away. She didn't have time to get it checked out. She was too busy trying to provide for the family and keep it together. Something I should have been doing, but wasn't.

"She could have possibly been saved with surgery and chemotherapy. It hadn't spread yet. There was hope! The days leading up to her surgery we discussed how we would rebuild our family. I promised to go to rehab and seek counseling. I wanted to do whatever it took to make it work. I apologized a thousand times and she forgave me a thousand and one. Rachel said that she was willing to give me a second chance because she loved me and loved having our little family together. She wanted us to be whole again. I guess that's what love's about. The night before her surgery, we laughed and cried together about the good and bad times. We went to sleep in each other's arms, as we lay in the hospital bed. Like the movie, *The Notebook*.

"The next morning, she had her surgery to remove the mass. The surgery team told me that a resident and an attending would be performing Rachel's surgery. I understood that this was a teaching hospital and there was a possibility that residents would be involved in her care. Hell, I was a resident once. So, I know the ropes. Residents have to learn, and attendings have to teach. However, I made my wishes known that I wanted the attending to do most of the surgery. I wanted a more seasoned doctor performing most of the work. I wanted to make sure my wife received the best care and had someone who knew what they were doing. However, this did not occur. The surgery was botched."

"How so?" I ask, listening intently and devouring my curly fries.

"At first, I didn't know how. I sat in the waiting room eagerly awaiting an update as the surgery was being done. It was nerve-wracking. I paced back and forth in the room and outside the room. I tried to sit down and watch TV, but not even *The Price is Right* could distract me. The screams of a woman playing Plinko echoed in the background as Richard came in to tell me the unfortunate news. He stated that there were 'complications' and that they were unable to save her. I asked, 'what kind of complications?' He said that she kept bleeding during the surgery and that they couldn't stop it. They couldn't find the main source of the bleeding. They tried to save her for twenty-two minutes, but unfortunately weren't able to. That's why I gave everyone twenty-two minutes to exit the building. I gave everyone the same amount of time they devoted to doing CPR on my wife. After I put you to sleep after shooting Dr. Holloway, I woke you up a few moments later by giving you some oxygen. I figured you didn't deserve to die in your sleep like my wife. You, like her, deserved better than that. You started to breathe on your own again. I looked at your name on your chart before I left the room. I figured you'd eventually fully wake up on your own and you did. After Richard told me of my wife's death, I sat for a few minutes in silence and soaked in the news.

"My wife of ten years was dead. The love of my life. We had just reconciled. Made plans together. Hugged each other. Kissed each other goodbye. Not knowing that the last kiss was goodbye forever. And now in a short moment in time, she's dead.

"I asked to speak to the attending physician, Dr. Morrison, but Richard said that he was busy helping with another surgery already. He said that he was sent to tell me the unfortunate news. He said that Dr. Morrison wanted him to get practice telling people bad news. Isn't that crazy? We, people in medicine, have to get practice in telling people bad news. 'Ma'am you have a breast mass.' 'Sir your test came back positive for HIV.' You eventually develop a numbness to it. But let me tell you, it's totally the opposite when you're on the other side, hearing the news. I didn't feel numb, I felt everything. Every. Single. Bit.

"I went outside the hospital to gather myself and cry in my car. A man isn't supposed to cry in public. I couldn't let anyone see me break down. However, I did break down just as I exited the hospital. I dropped to a knee and began weeping like a little baby. I just couldn't contain my emotions. They bubbled over and there was nothing I could do to stop them. I just had to let them flow.

While kneeling and bawling my eyes out I lifted my head and watched Dr. Morrison walk right by me. The hem of his white coat brushed my shoulder as he passed by. He didn't say anything. Just walked right by. I don't even know if he saw me. Sometimes we are so blind to things that we do and don't want to see. He might not have wanted to see me at that moment.

"I don't know whether Richard lied to me or Dr. Morrison lied to him. Nevertheless, it was fairly evident that he wasn't helping with another surgery. He just got in his car and took off. So, I got in my car and followed him. Like you today, I wanted answers. So, I trailed behind him as he drove across town. He drove to a local pub called Molly Malone's Irish Pub. He sat by himself at the bar and I watched him from a table in the back. He ordered a few drinks. Five total. I, at the time, assumed that he was drinking because of the guilt of losing my wife. We all have our vices to let off some steam. Mine is smoking.

"I thought about approaching him. I ran through what I would say or do to him. Would I push him? Drag him off his stool, into the streets and give him a good pummeling? Would I yell at him? If so, what would I yell? 'What happened? Why did you kill my wife? Did you really do all that you could to save her? Why didn't you come talk to me? Are you sorry? Do you even care?' But I didn't do any of that. I decided not to approach him. I just sat and observed from a distance, like a lion watching its prey, waiting for the right time to pounce. This wasn't the right time.

"After his fifth drink, the bar cut him off. He became slightly irate and was asked by name to leave. It was apparent that he was a frequent patron at this establishment. I shadowed behind Dr. Morrison as he staggered to his Mercedes and sloppily slid into his car. He drove drunk all the way home to his gated community in the suburbs. Surprisingly, one couldn't tell that he was drunk by the way he drove. He stayed in his lanes. Used his signals and came to complete stops at every stop sign. It was amazing and frightening at the same time. A man is driving drunk and no one knows, but me. I can't imagine how many people get on the road driving drunk without anyone knowing. I know it happens, but it's even scarier watching it happen.

"After witnessing that whole scenario play out, I decided to start following him more often to learn more about him. Some would call it stalking. I would call it observing from a distance.

"I've been observing Dr. Morrison intermittently for the last five years. That incident wasn't the first time he's drank like that. It turns out, Dr. Morrison has a drinking problem. He's a creature of habit. He goes to the same pub every few days. He gets the same few drinks and flirts with the same bartender. He drinks like that frequently. He fluctuates between being on and off the wagon. He's gone to work drunk sometimes after drunkenly sleeping in his car. I followed him a lot. Therefore, I knew when he was off the wagon. He was off the wagon and drunk when he performed my wife's surgery."

"How do you know he was drunk that day?" I question.

"Enrique told me. Let me tell you how I met him. I often came down to the cafeteria while my wife was in the hospital. I would grab a few snacks, a meal, or just something to drink. Just to get away and give myself a mental break. We all need mental breaks. One day, I sat down and struck up a random conversation with Enrique while he was on his lunch break. We sat in the seating area behind the curtain over there." Maestro points at the metal curtain behind me. It blocks the view of the seating area. "We hit it off. He was my sounding board and I was his. We would talk randomly throughout the day on various topics, from things going on in the hospital to sports or world news. I even helped him improve his English. When my wife died, I came back and talked to him. I asked him to find out what really happened in my wife's surgery. I even slipped a few dollars in his pocket. I knew that he could find out. No one keeps their mouth shut around this hospital. No one keeps their mouth closed at any job. There's always gossip. You just have to find the right messy person to talk to."

"Well, did he find out?"

"Of course, he did. It took him a little bit longer than I thought it would, but he got the information. He got the story from various sources, but I was able to put it together for the most part. The surgery started an hour late because Dr. Morrison was nowhere to be found. They paged him. They called him. They emailed him. But there was no response. Then, mysteriously he popped up and acted like nothing was wrong. No one questioned him. He was the main doctor, so everyone was just glad he showed up. The surgery started and initially went well. They cut Rachel open, found the cancerous mass, and started to cut it out. Then, all of a sudden, Dr. Morrison fell on top of Rachel while Richard was making an incision. He literally fell on top of her. Enrique heard two stories about how he fell. One was that he accidentally slipped. Another was that he fell asleep."

"What do you think happened?" I question eagerly.

"I think he was drunk and passed out. When he fell, he landed on top of Richard's hand while he was holding the scalpel. That made him accidentally puncture one of the major arteries in her abdomen. The aorta. Rachel began to bleed profusely. They tried to suture the artery to stop the bleeding, but they couldn't stop it. She coded. Richard did CPR while Dr. Morrison continued to try to stop the bleeding. Dr. Holloway was slow in getting the medicine they needed to save her while they did CPR. They tried for twenty-two minutes to get her back, but their efforts were futile."

"Damn," I respond.

"'Damn' is right. I can see why Dr. Morrison didn't want to come out and talk to me afterwards. He murdered my wife. If he were to come talk to me after the surgery, he would either have to blatantly lie to me or admit to murder. Therefore, to avoid doing either one of those things he sent Richard to deliver the news. Such a coward. As a man and a physician. He didn't take ownership of his mistakes at all. Just passed the buck on to someone else. How dare he do that?

"Consequently, I wanted to make sure he paid for what he did. All of them who were involved. They would all pay. One man's actions would affect them all. Just like you today."

"Why did they have to suffer? It was Dr. Morrison's fault."

"They all played a role in her death, therefore, they all should suffer. Richard should have been watching Dr. Morrison. I'm sure he was probably showing signs of being drunk before he fell. You have to pay attention to your surroundings and who you're working with it. A good surgeon should have a heightened sense of awareness. However, Richard was a young resident surgeon and inexperienced. Maybe he just didn't know any better. Therefore, I was on the fence about doing anything to him. I mean, does his lack of experience excuse him from the situation? I was torn. However, yesterday I was pushed over the edge and decided that he had to learn a lesson."

"What happened yesterday?" I asked.

"Yesterday, I did a final walk through of the hospital to make sure everything was lined up perfectly for today. Like I said earlier, this was a ruse. One big distraction to help me get revenge. I couldn't just murder or beat up these people in broad daylight. I would probably get caught. On the other hand, I could have just as easily snuck up on them randomly and administered justice. But that would have been too easy. I needed something more theatrical, a method people might not agree with, but could understand the reason behind it. Also, I needed a diversion to help cover my tracks.

"Amid all this chaos you could essentially murder anyone and get away with it if there aren't any witnesses. And if there were any, it would take them forever to get an accurate description from all the witnesses. You could walk out of the hospital as if you were one of the hostages and no one would know. Like Dr. Patel. Hence why you've seen me with multiple different looks today. Only the people who helped me with this know what I really look like. And they wouldn't dare betray me.

"So, I came up with what you see here today. Like a maestro, I conducted this beautiful fiasco. I devised a plan to organize a group people with their own gripes against the health care system and society an outlet to express their frustrations. I allowed the ones I knew most closely to have their own floor and do with it as they pleased. While they did those things, my goal was to exact revenge on Dr. Morrison and the rest of the staff who killed my wife. I would search the hospital to find them while someone of my choosing would learn something." Maestro points at me.

"You helped to distract them from what I was doing. They stayed put waiting for you to make it to their floor. I contacted them via text to let them know you were on your way. I've been watching you via the hospital cameras I hacked. You gave those people on each floor something to look forward to. A way to get their message out. They followed my orders well and didn't move until you made it there. Once again, the power of words used by one in power. I used my military training to train them.

"I trained them daily for the last year for today. They were trained in weapons, hand to hand combat, and how to work as a team. They lived and slept at the compound where we trained. During the day, they would go about their own individual activities, but they would return afterward for training. They shared their own individual stories with each other and learned why the other person was there.

"As they told their individual stories I learned so much about the health care and how messed up it is. I thought I knew everything, but I was so wrong. I was wrong. I learned how people are mistreated. I learned how people are overlooked. I learned how people are allowed to suffer. And as they shared other stories, I learned how evil and cruel people in the world can be. I now realize why my grandmother constantly played gospel music throughout the house. She was trying to keep the devil at bay. He's always lurking outside trying to a find a way to get in.

"In them I saw pieces of me. Things that had happened to me. Things that I knew that happened to others. And sadly, the things I had done to others as a physician. Hearing their stories added fuel to the fire that burned inside of me. I became less selfish and narrow minded in my purpose for today. The vengeance for wife's death continued to burn brightly. However, their stories added more flames to the fire. I wanted to shed a light on My quest for revenge equaled my wanting to display for the world what's wrong with health care and people in general.

"I trained them well. They are a very cohesive group and began to think as one unit, with the training I gave them. They did their job well today as my little foot soldiers. My job as their captain was to train them and plan everything accordingly, which started with scouting the hospital.

"It's amazing the amount of freedom I got around the hospital by walking around with a long white coat, cheap stethoscope, and dingy glasses on. I came to this hospital two to three times a month and learned the inner workings of it. I did this for the past two years. No one ever questioned me or asked who I was. I've worked in hospitals before, so I knew how to blend in and act like I actually belonged. Yesterday, I did my final walk through of how things would go, making sure I knew everything. How we would get in. Where the security was located. How many staff were in certain areas. Which stairs to take and which ones to avoid. That type of stuff. While doing that yesterday, I saw Richard for the first time since he told me of my wife's untimely death. I saw him walking down the hallway. Immediately, I got nervous thinking he'd recognize me. I hadn't seen him since she passed. I started fumbling papers around in my hand and ended up dropping them. They scattered all over the floor. They had all my notes for the inner workings of the hospital scribbled on them.

"Richard stopped on his way down the corridor and helped me pick up the papers. Do you know he didn't even recognize me?

He looked me straight in my eyes after helping me pick up the papers and said 'Have a nice day. Don't let these patients get to you,' followed by a chuckle. He didn't even recognize the man who he'd told his wife died! The man whose wife he killed!" Maestro says while banging on the table. "At that moment I knew he had to pay in some fashion for what he had done. He didn't recognize who I was today until I stabbed him."

"Do you know how deranged you sound?" I ask.

"Oh, I am fully aware of how I sound. I am aware of all of my words and actions. I may be bordering on insanity right now. Hell, I may have crossed over the insanity line already. It's too late to go back now. Love and death will drive you insane. I'm totally content with being insane right now. Insane for love." The metal curtain behind us opens. In walks Big Mac from the first floor I visited on my mission.

"We found Enrique like you asked. He was trapped in one of the rooms like you said," says Big Mac.

"Yeah, I trapped him. He needed to be in time out. He killed someone."

"Didn't he want to die?" asks Maestro.

"Yeah, he did. But ..." I respond.

"But what? That was his choice. He wanted to move on in life. Have you not learned anything?"

"Oh, I've learned a lot. Trust me."

"Well, walk with me. Tell me and a few others what you've learned." Maestro has completed his meal and I have completed my

fries. Maestro whistles for Bo who is over sniffing something by the pizza area again. He makes his way to Maestro.

Maestro, Big Mac, I, and a well-fed Hope walk toward the curtain. Big Mac opens the curtain. Maestro walks in first, and I follow with Hope in my arms. As I walk in, I am in utter shock. In the seating area of the cafeteria is every doctor and nurse unaccounted for in the hospital. Almost one hundred people. Some are standing and some are seated. Some bloodied. Some unbothered. Some unconscious on the floor surrounded by others. Surrounding the staff are a group of men and women armed with guns. About fifty people dressed like me. Black shirt and blue scrub pants. The doctors and nurses stare at me curiously as I walk in. On the opposite wall beyond the curtain are glass windows 25 feet high. I can clearly see outside. On the opposite side of the glass windows are S.W.A.T. policeman with guns aimed at the glass windows, ready to fire. *Sigh. Is it too late for my black ass to go home?*

CANCER

Cancer is a malignant tumor of potentially unlimited growth that expands locally by invasion and systemically by metastasis (14). A tumor is an abnormal mass of tissue whose growth exceeds and is uncoordinated with that of the normal tissue (3). A tumor may continue to grow after cessation of the stimuli which caused it to grow. Wow, that's a mouth full. Don't worry. I'll break it down.

Take a look at the picture above. The collections of kids represent an organ. Let's say it's the stomach. Each kid represents a cell in that organ. Initially, all the kids are good. They behave. They say "yes ma'am" and "no ma'am." They share toys and are the perfect little children. Then, one of the kids starts acting up. He curses. He doesn't go to bed on time and cries for no reason. Let's call him Bad Ass Billy. Billy is a handful. Now, imagine Billy replicating himself. There are two Bad Ass Billies now. Oh, Lord. Then, the first Billy replicates himself again. Now, there are three bad ass Billies, and so on. They're causing ruckus. They're throwing things. Smashing plates and sticking metal into sockets.

That's essentially what happens with cancer. Cells aka Billies keep replicating and causing chaos. In some cancers, cells replicate fast and in other cancers the process is slower. What causes them to replicate? It's very complicated, but to keep it simple, it involves a problem with the cell's DNA.

Now, let's return to the word "metastasis" used in the first sentence of this section. It is the process by which tumor cells spread to distant parts of the body (1). All tumors don't necessarily metastasize. Let's say that the Billies stay in the stomach. If so, this tumor is not considered to have metastasized. However, if one of these Billies leaves the stomach and ends up in the brain, that would mean the cancer has metastasized. Now, Billy has left his house and is causing a problem in someone else's house. Bad Billy.

Cancer is a difficult topic to cover. There are multiple different types of cancer. Ranging from skin cancer to colon cancer to breast cancer. There are also many different treatments, from surgery to remove the cancer to chemotherapy or radiation therapy. It would take many more pages to cover all of these items. This synopsis serves as a brief summary for those who may not know the basics.

CHAPTER 13

WHAT

DID

YOU LEARN?

*W*hy am I still here? I shouldn't have opened that stupid box. I could have gone home. Maestro gave me the option to walk out of here freely and I didn't. Now, look where I've ended up. At the end of the rabbit hole about to die. *Stupid. Stupid. Stupid mistake!* Maestro walks with me on the outer edge of the circle with Bo walking ahead of us. We walk on the outside of the gunmen. They have their backs to us and are facing the hostages.

"What's going on here?" I ask in confusion.

"What's going on is that you're going to attest to all of the things that you learned here today."

"To whom?"

"To everyone here. Every single person in this room." As we continue around the circle I begin to see familiar faces.

Standing in the center of doctors and nurses is Alex, who took my vital signs in the emergency room. She sits in a chair with her hand on her chin looking down at the ground. She's here physically, but mentally she's somewhere else. Next, I see Ann, the nurse who took my blood. She stands with her hands on her wide hips looking at me as I walk around the circle. Her facial expression reads, *this some ol' bullshit*. I agree with her, this is some ol' bullshit. Lying on a table is Charles, the resident who wheeled me up to the surgery floor. It looks like he's been shot. A nurse applies firm pressure to his arm. He appears to be in a fair amount of pain. Probably needs a simple surgery. *They'll cut him there, there, and there. Then, take his arm off. Easy peasy.*

On the outside circle of armed individuals are more recognizable faces. Sitting in a wheelchair with a gun resting on his lap is Ron. Ron snacks on a graham cracker while facing the hostages. Crumbs fall from his mouth as he chews with his mouth wide open. I hate that. *Close your mouth. Have some manners for Christ's sake.* Flanking him are his two flunkies Barry and Cam, aka Beebop and Rocksteady, who were gathering things for Ron on his floor. Big Mac has returned to the line, standing next to Rocksteady. A few unfamiliar faces separate them from the next faces I recognize which are those of Amy and Tina. Tina gives me a casual wave as I approach her. I don't wave back. She steps out of line.

"I'll hold Hope for you," she offers.

"No. I've got her. I've protected her all day," I inform her.

"Daniel, give her Hope," Maestro instructs. I look at him and then look down at Hope. She sleeps quietly. It amazes me how much she's been able to stay quiet through most of this. If I hadn't seen this baby be born I would have sworn that she wasn't real. No baby ever manages to stay quiet for this long. I reluctantly hand her to Tina.

"I'll take care of her. Trust me," Tina says. *Trust her. Trust the woman who threw a baby down the trash.* Today I have a new outlook on the word "trust." I don't trust her one bit. I don't trust anyone. Maestro and I continue walking.

I keep looking for more familiar faces. Will I see, Tundé? Will I see Hope's mom? Will I see Andrew risen from the dead? Will I see Mary? Oh, God, I hope I don't see Mary again. She will kill me for sure. But I don't see them. I don't see anyone else I recognize.

There's just a smorgasbord of armed strangers. Men. Women. Short. Tall. Round. Petite. Black. White. Middle Eastern. Asian. Bald. Long-haired. Dreads. Natural hair. Wigs. It's almost as though every section of the world population is represented in this circle. Now, I see there are easily more than fifty-armed people. Way more. They keep their eyes on the hostages as I walk past them.

"Who are all these people?" I question Maestro.

"These are all the people I mentioned earlier. Those who have had their own ups and downs with the health care or people in general. Each person has their own personal reasons for being here. As you can tell, they are very diverse in their background. Some have lost family members like me. Some have gripes concerning health insurance. Others have been discriminated against based upon race, sexual orientation, or gender," Maestro explains. We walk up on a young African-American man. Maestro pulls him out of line.

"This is Michael. Michael was at Thunder Over Louisville a few years ago. He accidentally jaywalked across the street when police told him not to walk. He was just texting and walking. Something a lot of people do. The police proceeded to run him down and tackle him just for jaywalking.

"When they tackled him, they broke his jaw. He ended up needing surgery. Had to have his mouth wired shut. Do you know that the hospital sent him a bill for that? The police refused to pay the bill because they said he was running away from them and they had to apprehend them. If he wouldn't have 'run away' he wouldn't have needed to be tackled. Therefore, it was his fault and he would have to pay the bill," says Maestro.

"Run away? Man, I was just walking and texting," Michael justifies. Maestro eases him back in to line. We continue walking. Maestro pulls another person out of line.

"This is Emily. Emily, this is Daniel," Maestro introduces.

"Hello, Daniel. Nice to meet you," says the fraudulent female voice. Emily firmly shakes my hand. Her hand is huge and overlaps my entire hand. Her fingers almost touch my elbow. Emily is well over six feet tall with broad shoulders. Her makeup is done to the tee on her white skin. The slight 5 o'clock shadow is a clue that Emily may truly be Edward.

"Emily use to be Tyler. She's been gradually transitioning from a man to a woman. A while back, Emily had to get admitted into this hospital for pneumonia. Tell Daniel what happened when you were in the hospital."

"At first, my stay was pleasant. I was in one of the shared rooms. I had a female roommate in the same room as me. We were very nice and cordial to each other. We laughed and joked a lot. Even shared snacks. However, after she found out I was transgender her entire demeanor changed. She talked less. Stayed to herself more and often put the curtain divider in between us. It hurt a little bit at first, but I understood. She was older, and some people aren't accustomed to us yet.

"One day I was mysteriously moved to another room by myself. They said it was to give me 'more privacy'. Later in the day, I found out why. I heard two of the nurses talking to each other. I can still hear those two nurses, April and Ally, cackling loudly, like it was yesterday. 'I'm about to go give It its medicine.' 'Girl, who is It?' 'Girl, you know who It is. That he-she down the hallway. It has its own room now. Mrs. Smith complained to the nurse manager and they put him in another room. Now, It can do whatever It wants. Stand up and pee. Sit down and pee. Lay down and pee. Twirl and pee. Whatever It wants.'

"They referred to me as 'It.' Like I am a freaking inanimate object or monster. I can understand being confused about whether to refer to me as mister or miss. For the layperson, it can be confusing. The simplest thing to do would be to just ask me. However, them calling me 'It,' was very hurtful. I cried as I walked back to my room and gathered my belongings. I left the hospital. Walked straight out and crawled into the gutter as the 'It' monster that I am." Emily's eyes begin to well. Maestro guides her back to her position in the circle. We continue walking passing other individuals. It isn't until now that I realize that they each have a baton sticking out of their back pocket.

"Each one of these people has a story. Just like you, Daniel," says Maestro. "They have their own personal reason for being here. Tucked inside their batons is a hand-written note detailing why they took part in this. They all were well aware of the potential that they may not make it out of here alive. Consequently, they wrote those letters to make sure their message got out if they didn't. Some of those letters have damning information about some of the people in this very room. I'd be very worried if I were them. They could go to jail." Maestro looks toward the glass window where all the officers stand with their guns ready to fire.

"Unfortunately, we don't have time to give everyone a platform to express themselves. Time is of the essence," he states. We reach the point on the circle where we originally started walking. Maestro breaks the circle and enters the crowded area of the doctors and nurses. They'd been eyeballing us the entire time we were walking around them. Their eyes pierce us even harder as we walk through them. Maestro leads me to the center. On the way to the core, I see more injured and bloodied people. I step over bodies. Some alive and injured. Some dead. We reach the center where I am surprised to see Jack and Enrique.

"Why did you lock us in the room?" Jack asks.

"Yes, amigo. Why did you lock us in there?" says Enrique.

"Man, y'all know why. Because you killed someone!" I exclaim. The nurses and doctors gasps upon hearing the charge.

"You killed someone, Jack?" asks a tall black man in a long doctor's coat.

"Yes. Yes, he did," I answer before Jack responds. I jump on top of a long plastic table and peruse the crowd. They all stare at me attentively, looking to see what I may say. Looking to see what I may do.

"My name is Daniel James! I'm Dr. Lisa James's husband, and despite how it may look or what you may think, I did not have anything to do with today's events. Yet, I'm somehow becoming an unwilling, integral part of today's events. Like you all, I have been through and seen a lot today. As Charles over there can attest, I was supposed to have a simple surgery on my appendix and then go home. Yet, this did not occur. My black ass got dragged into some kind of moral scavenger hunt. I have learned and seen a lot on this hunt." I point at Ron in his wheelchair.

"That guy over there, in the wheelchair. I watched him beat a woman with a crutch. All because he didn't get the support he needed from your staff in his time of need. He said no one helped him when he was down on his luck. I wonder would you all do the same thing. Do you help people when they are down, or do you find some excuse not to help them? I know I help some people, but I know I can do so much more. I pick and choose who I help. Knowing that I can help so many more people in their time of need. Whether that be financially, time wise, or just by being someone who will listen to them.

"Some people just need an ear to vent to. Not someone to judge them or give them unsolicited advice. Just an ear. Today, I watched a woman hang herself. Literally, hang herself here in this very hospital. Luckily, I was able to revive her by doing CPR. But just to think, she hanged herself all because she felt like no one listens to her. Not even some of you doctors. She just wanted to be heard. Wanted someone to listen to her.

"Do you know how much it costs to listen to someone? Nothing. It's free! When your children say that they need to talk to you, do you stop what you're doing and give them your undivided attention? Or do you tell them give me a minute and eventually forget that they needed to talk? When your friends call you to vent do you listen to them? Or do you pass judgement on them and discuss their issues with mutual friends behind their back? You know it's okay to keep people's personal business to yourself, right? You don't have to share everything with everyone. And you doctors. You pretentious doctors. Do you listen to your patients or do you talk over them and act like you know everything, treating them like trash? You marinate on that. And speaking of trash. One of your fellow colleagues over there Dr. Tina threw a baby in the trash." The staff gasps again.

"He picked the baby," Tina yells, implicating me. Everyone looks at her, then back at me for a response.

"Technically, yes, I did pick the baby, but it was by circumstance and not by choice," I respond in defense.

"What circumstance would make you choose a baby to throw away?" asks the tall black man in the white coat.

"I was being choked and another baby was being held at gunpoint," I respond angrily.

"You still didn't have to choose. You're really team Slytherin and not team Gryffindor," Ann responds with a look of disappointment.

"Man, fuck you, Ann! You, Mudblood! You weren't there. None of you were there except for Enrique. So, don't judge me and the choice that I made. Who knows what any one of you would have done if you were in my shoes. There may have been two dead babies if I didn't make a choice. So, I made a choice. A choice that ended up saving one baby. A baby whose mom gave birth to her and left. I named the baby Hope. She's the baby Dr. Tina is holding. Her mom was strung out on drugs and left after we helped her deliver. I have kept her alive after all I've been through! Being threatened with guns pointed at me. Being choked. Being kicked. Having a bomb explode on me. Cradling a dead person who I was trying to save. And on top of all that, I still have appendicitis! So, don't you guys pass judgment on me.

"Y'all haven't even said one word to the one who actually threw the baby away. All because she misses her dead child who can't be replaced. I've learned that the pain parents feel after losing a child never goes away. I pray that I don't ever have to experience that pain. No child can be replaced. Each child is special. No matter how old or how young. No parent's child can ever be replaced. Even if you have another, and some people can't have another. Some families can't even have one. I saw a couple run off with someone else's baby because they couldn't have one on their own.

"They took a baby and sprinted off through the hallway and went down the elevator. I presume they made it out of the hospital alive with the child. Don't ask me why I didn't try to save that baby because I did. I tried in the midst of one of my newfound friends dying. The child's mother died, too! She tried so hard that she accidentally killed herself. In that baby-snatching scenario, I saw two different extremes. On one, the lengths someone will go to have a child. And the other, how far a parent will go to protect their child.

"I am an adopted child. So, trust me I know the lengths people will go to have a child. I saw my mom have the failed infertility treatments. So, trust me, I know. Some people want someone who is of their own flesh and blood. However, that doesn't mean you have to go and steal someone else's flesh and blood. People will go to great extremes to protect their flesh and blood.

"That stolen child's mother pried open a closed elevator and jumped down the elevator shaft to save her child. Even though she had a bunch of other kids she was going to save her kid at all costs. Sadly, she didn't and plummeted to her death. I was able to save her other child. The stolen child's twin sister. She's in good hands with one of your nurses. I hope you guys in here who are fortunate enough to have children will cherish and love them as she did hers.

"I know you guys work hard and long hours. Probably don't even feel like talking to your kids or anyone when you get home. But don't be like that. Cherish them. Love them. Care for them.

Because there are plenty of people in this crazy world who would love to be bothered or cherished by their own kids, no matter how busy they are. I know it may take some sacrifice and personal time, but do it. They will love you for it. I know, to everyone else you're a doctor or nurse, but to them, you're just mom and dad. I know it's hard to take off that medical super hero cape. I know it took a lot for you all to get to that position in life.

You've probably studied for more hours than I've been alive. Worked your asses off to get to this position. Not everyone is able to reach your status. Some people would kill to be in your shoes. You guys probably think that comment is a figure of speech. No, I mean that factually. There are people out there who would kill for your spots as doctors and nurses. How do I know? Because I saw it today for myself. There was a guy upstairs shooting people for a spot in the residency program here. Just for a spot. He reached a point of insanity trying to achieve his dream job.

"So, while you complain about your job — the many notes you have to write, the early hours you have to go in, the daily stress, the lack of appreciation you get for your hard work — just know that there is someone somewhere who would gladly take those burdens. They would take those burdens and be thankful to have them. So, don't take your jobs or this life you live for granted. Especially, your life. Life, as you know, is always in flux. You can be the picture of perfect health one day, and be paralyzed the next. Then, what would you do?

"What would you do if some of the basic liberties of life were taken from you? If you couldn't walk down the same hallways you complained in? If you had a stroke and couldn't talk with the same mouth that you cursed others with? If you lost your hearing and were no longer able to hear the loud monitor beeps in the hospital. What would you do?

"I know you guys see stuff like this all the time. Healthy one day, and at death's doorstep the next day. You see how people suffer. You see them at their lowest points, and you see what it takes for them to recover. If they recover at all. Y'all have probably gotten numb to it. However, if the tables were turned and that was you with the condition how would you feel? Probably worse than normal people feel because you are more informed and know what it takes for you to get back to normal. A lot of you would probably get depressed. Probably would want to kill yourself. If I'm not mistaken, you health care people have a high rate of suicide. Cracking under pressure.

"But seriously, what would you guys do? Think about it. What would you do if it were you suffering with a disease that you knew you were going to die from. Would you continue on, living out the last few days of your life, knocking out all your bucket list items before you die? Or would you just want to end it all and die right then? Would you choose to not go through any suffering and just end it all by taking your own life? I learned today that some people just want to die. They want to die on their own terms and go out with some sort of dignity. Like the guy who Enrique and Jack killed. The man wanted to die. He just didn't have the physical capability to kill himself. So, they did it for him and pulled the plug. Some people just want the autonomy to choose whether they live or die. I don't know how I feel about that.

"On one hand, I empathize with people's suffering. I don't want anyone to suffer. No one should have to suffer. So, I can see how someone would want to end their own life to relieve the suffering. Its logical. On the other hand, I do recognize that suffering is a part of life and I would want someone to fight. Fight for life. Fight until the very end! But who am I? Who am I to decide who lives or dies? I'm not Jack who has killed other patients in what he deems compassion kills. No, I'm not him. I'm just me a lowly electrical engineer. It's not up to me. It's up to you and politicians to decide who lives, who dies, and how people live their lives. Not me. You are the ones with people's lives in your hands.

"And one of your very doctors here doesn't give a damn about that responsibility. Did you guys know that you have an alcoholic doctor working here? Well, let me be clearer because I'm sure there are other low-key alcoholics in here. But this is an alcoholic doctor who shows up drunk. He killed this man's wife in surgery." I point at Maestro. Everyone looks at him in shock.

"His wife was killed here by one of your drunken doctors, Dr. Morrison. Now this man seeks vengeance against any and everyone who has some tie to her death. And shed a light on what's wrong with health care. I'm sure if we played six degrees of separation, he could tie all of you here to her death. Therefore, you're all at risk of dying. Due to one physician's actions. Everyone's actions no matter how big or small have some negative or positive effects on others. I have definitely learned that today. Mostly, via my actions. But I am content with all of my actions today.

"All of my actions were done out of instinct, some curiosity, and out of love. Love to get back to my spouse. It's crazy some of the things we do for love. I did so much today for a person who doesn't even love me. As some of you may know my wife has been unfaithful to me. I didn't find out until today, and I must admit that I am broken. After all that I have witnessed, heard, and felt this has hit me the hardest. I haven't had time to soak it in and feel all the emotions. And honestly, I don't have time to feel because I'm still trapped in this fucking hospital, with appendicitis, and trying make it out of here. Alive!

"So, as I step down off my proverbial soapbox, I hope you have learned something from what I shared and that you will share it with others. I know I shared a lot. I've talked for way more than I thought I would, but I had to get all of this off my chest. Hopefully, what I shared will make you change your thought process on a lot of things. May you all go look in the mirror and reflect on the actions and decisions you've made in your own life and the impact it has on others and yourself. If you make it out of here alive." I hop off the table and everyone's staring at me. Each face has a different emotion painted on it. Maestro starts a slow clap.

"Wow. That was one heck of a speech," he says standing next to Enrique. "I hope you all got that. I could have not said anything better myself. You fully captured everything I envisioned. After a speech like that, I gotta let you go. Just one last thing."

"Now what?" I respond with a combination of anger and exhaustion.

"Kill Enrique," he says calmly.

"What?" Enrique and I respond simultaneously.

"You heard me. Kill Enrique," Maestro repeats. He reaches from behind his shirt and pulls out a handgun. Then, hits Enrique with the butt of the gun on the back of his head. Enrique hits the floor.

"Enrique where is Dr. Morrison? Dónde está Dr. Morrison?" Maestro asks.

"I don't know!" Enrique responds in pain. The back of his head is bleeding.

"I've been searching this damn hospital for hours and have had no luck finding him. Why is that? You text me that you saw him upstairs in one of the operating rooms?"

"I thought I saw him, mi amigo."

"Oh, don't 'mi amigo' me now. Did you see him?"

"I thought I did, but it was someone else. When I realized it, you were already upstairs shooting people on the surgery floor. I was too scared to tell you that. I was afraid you would shoot me. I didn't know you were bringing guns. That's not what we talked about."

"You're damn right, I would have shot you. Is there a Dr. Baker in here? Where is Dr. Baker? Raise your hand."

"I'm Dr. Baker," says the tall black man in the white coat who commented earlier.

"I went through some papers upstairs in the surgery office. I was able to find your work schedule. Did you switch work days with Dr. Morrison?"

"Yes. Yes, I did. He's off today," he answers. Maestro looks back at Enrique.

"Did you check the schedule like I asked Enrique?"

"Sí. I checked it last week," he responds.

"We changed that schedule a month ago. It says that I work today and Dr. Morrison is off," says Dr. Baker. It's obvious that Enrique has lied. Maestro stares back at Enrique.

"So, you're just going to lie to me? Right to my face?" Maestro questions. Enrique doesn't respond. He just keeps his head down in angst. "Well, now you gotta die." Maestro grabs Enrique by the back of his collar and yanks him to my feet. He places the gun in my hand.

"You kill him. I let you go. You don't kill him, I kill you. Then, I kill him," Maestro says loudly.

"Why do I have to kill him?" I say in an awkwardly high-pitched voice.

"Because I said so. Like you said, six degrees of separation for everyone and you and Enrique share a connection."

"You are the one who connected us!"

"Yeah, you're right. Tough break. You should have gone home instead of coming here."

"I've been telling myself that shit all day!"

"Everyone move back. Spread the circle. I don't want anyone in front of the window. I want the cops to see this clearly," Maestro instructs. Everyone begins to move slowly. Maestro pulls a gun from his waistband and shoots it in the air. "I said move!"

The doctors and nurses pick up the pace as instructed. Everyone is now standing as Maestro instructed. Outside the glass window, to the right of me, the armed cops continue to peer in. They appear more attentive due to the hurried movements of the group. Twenty feet away from them, I stand with a gun in my hand, a bloody Enrique at my feet, and motionless bodies scattered around me. I look as if I have shot them. To the left of me stands the collection of doctors and nurses held hostage. Maestro deceptively blends in with him. Behind them are Maestro's armed foot soldiers with their guns pointed at the hostage's backside. I'm in a literal gun sandwich.

"Here's the scenario, Daniel. The cops have been looking through the windows for the last couple of hours. By now they probably have figured out who is friend and who is foe. Right now, you are dressed as a foe and I am standing with those they see as friend. Consequently, that is why you have that red laser dot on your chest and not me."

I look down at my chest. A bright red dot is at the center of it. The cops have me in their sight.

"I estimate that you have twenty seconds before they shoot you. However, you have ten seconds before I shoot you. Shoot him, and I'll grab you before they get a chance to shoot you. Don't shoot him, and I'll shoot both of you. Then, for the rest of the staff. The countdown begins now. Ten, nine," Maestro counts aloud.

I stand with my head down, looking at Enrique. He sits on the ground, staring at me in fear. *Have all my actions today really lead me to here? Here, in front of the man I started this whole journey with?* Despite the mistakes I perceive that he has made, he has somehow become my friend. He even saved my life by pulling me away from all that bomb smoke. I owe him. I won't shoot him. Not just because he saved me, but because he is my friend.

"Maestro!" I yell at the top of my lungs. "You said this whole thing for you was done out of love. So, I'm going to do this out of love. I'm not going to shoot Enrique. John 15:13 says 'there is no greater love than to lay down one's life for one's friend.' And I'm going to express my love and lay down my life for my friend, Enrique. I won't shoot him."

"Four. Three. Two. One. Times up. Your wish to express your love is granted." Maestro aims his gun at me and shoots. I dive out of the way and the glass window behind me shatters. I aim and fire at Maestro with the gun he gave me. The bullet strikes him in the left shoulder. He clutches his wound with his hand and takes off running into the crowd. The crowd disperses in a frenzy.

Maestro's soldiers begin shooting. Bodies hit the floor. The glass shatters behind me. The police rush in. They fire their weapons. Screaming ensues. I start to feel a burning sensation in the back of my shoulder. I reach around to touch it and then look at my fingers. They're covered with blood. I've been shot. Well, it was only a matter of time. I close my eyes, fall face forward to the ground, and brace for my impending death. I guess I finally get to go home. To glory.

CHAPTER 14

BACK, FRONT

AND BACK

AND SIDE TO SIDE

lie face down and watch the blood spill from my shoulder and cover the ground. The blood moves closer to my face. I can't move. I'm in shock. Not physically, but mentally. I've been shot! Shot by the police! Not Maestro or his flunkies, but by the police. The people I hoped would have saved me and got me out of this situation. They shot me after all the people I've saved. Hope. Sarah. Enrique. Those medical students. Maybe Richard. They shot me, the good guy. Out of my peripheral, I see Enrique sliding towards me as the bullets continue to fly above us.

"Are you okay?" he yells.

"Yeah. I'm okay. Just been shot. No biggie," I respond optimistically.

"Thank you for not killing me."

"No problem. I'm going to go ahead and die now. It's been a long day," I close my eyes.

"No. You can't die, Daniel!" Enrique says as he places his hand between my backpack and shoulder on my wound. He applies firm pressure to help stop the bleeding.

"Thank you, Enrique."

"No problem, my friend."

I feel additional firm pressure. But this time it's not on my shoulder, but on the center of my back. The full weight of someone is on top of me. I open my eyes and turn my head around to the right. Kneeling on my mid-spine is a S.W.A.T. officer. He's in full tactical gear. All black everything. Black hat. Black mask. Black goggles. Black shirt. Black gloves. Black assault rifle. He's virtually an armed shadow. He quickly pans his gun around the room to make sure the room is secured. He keeps a finger firmly on the trigger. The shooting has ceased. A few screams echo in the distance.

"Do you mind getting off my back?" I ask. "You're hurting me. I'm one of the good guys."

"Don't move!" he yells at me. I roll my eyes.

"It's fairly obvious I'm not moving. You have your knee in my back and I've been shot. So, it's kind of hard for me to move."

"Don't move and keep quiet, asshole!" he yells again.

"Why I gotta be an asshole? I just asked you a simple question." The officer gets off my back. I breathe a sigh of relief. Finally, my simple wish is granted. I take a few deep breaths in and out of my mouth. Suddenly, my right wrist is grabbed, then my left. My hands are cuffed tightly together behind my back.

"Am I being arrested?" I ask, confused.

"Yes. You're in custody." The officer picks me up by my left arm and sits me on my butt. I moan in anguish. My shirt is cold and bloodied. I now sit in a pool of my own blood. I swear that stuff was supposed to stay inside of me. I'm not the only one in handcuffs. Around the room officers are tying up all of Maestro's armed soldiers.

"For what!?" I question loudly.

"You know why. We saw you shoot that doctor."

"Wait, wait. What? No, I didn't. The person I shot wasn't a doctor. Well technically he is a doctor, but not one of the good ones. He is the one who put this whole thing together. I shot him to save everyone!"

"Yes, he's right," agrees Enrique.

"Whatever, man," says the cop. The officer kicks the gun I shot Maestro with away from me. Another officer in the middle of the room begins to yell.

"Officers are all of the suspects secured?"

"Yes," says all of the officers in union. Even the officer who is adjacent to me.

Wow. I'm a secured suspect now. How's that for ironic alliteration? I walked into this hospital a patient, and now I may walk out a secured suspect. *Ain't this about a bitch? This can't be happening. I must be dreaming. Wake up, Daniel. Wake up!*

I rock wildly side to side, trying to tip over and hit my head and wake myself up from this horrid dream. Finally, I tip over and smack my head on the ground. I open my eyes and see that I'm still in the same place, just now with a headache. *Damn it.* This isn't a dream. The lead officer begins talking again.

"All of the staff members who are able to get up and walk, on my command, I need you to stand up with your hands in the air. Raise them toward the sky. Then, walk slowly to the cafeteria area."

One of the officers opens the curtain area between the dining room and the cafeteria.

"Everyone stand up and walk slowly," the officer commands. Enrique gets up slowly and looks back at me with a look of concern, not knowing what will happen to me. I look at him with a look of worry.

With a sideways view on the ground I watch all of the people I helped to save migrate in to the safe zone. They walk as instructed and begin to hug each other in comfort as they make it to the cafeteria. The lead officer speaks again.

"Officers, stand up all the secured suspects who are able to walk. Take them to the wall on the right and sit them down." The officer next to me picks me up with a firm grasp of my left arm. He escorts me to the wall with the other suspects, as instructed. While walking, I am able to survey the damage done in the shootout. There are vastly more injured people on the floor than previously. Some of the injured are staff and some of them are Maestro's soldiers. I step over them as I'm shepherded to the wall. Alive and dead alike, I recognize some faces.

Ron is in his wheelchair dead with a gunshot wound to his chest. His injured leg with the metal pins is still propped up in the air. Beebop and Rocksteady lay motionless on the side of him. Presumably they're dead, as well. I look to my right to see Big Mac being escorted by an officer half his size. He's has been shot in the leg but is still able to walk with a slight limp. I look to my left and see Amy being pulled toward the wall. She squirms in the officers' grasp. She's not going down without a fight. I stumble on something and almost fall. The officer grabs me before I hit the ground and yanks me back up to my feet. I look down to see what I stumbled on. It's Tina. She's dead.

"Keep it moving!" demands the officer.

"Where's Hope?" I say out loud.

"Keep it moving!" he instructs again.

I look at Amy and yell. "Where's Hope?"

"I don't know! Let me go, you pig!" she shouts at the officer. Amy continues to squirm in her handcuffs. She resembles a child being forced into timeout. Mac, Amy, and I simultaneously reach our appointed area and are placed firmly on the ground. Amy sits on my left and Mac on my right. We face the open seating area. We're sitting with our legs crossed and hands handcuffed behind our back. The rest of Maestro's soldiers who are still alive are escorted over to our area by other officers. One by one, they are dragged over and dropped on the ground.

I frantically scan the room for Hope. My heart beats rapidly in my chest. *Where is Hope? Where is she?* I look to the left. I look to the right. I look close. I look far. *Is she alive? Is she injured? Did she get trampled on? Did she get shot? Is she still here?* I don't even hear her crying. *Lord, please don't let my baby be dead. I keep scanning the room. Finally, I find her in the cafeteria.*

Ann is clutching her in her arms as she rocks her side to side. A calm feeling rushes over me, from my head to my toes. I don't know what I would do if I were to lose Hope. Not now. I am nothing without Hope. She's been my rock since I landed on her floor. Hope is the last person here that hasn't betrayed me. The only one who has been faithful. I need her. Just as much as she needs me. How do I get back to her? Officers continue to drop people off in our line.

"Can I get some medical attention? I've been shot," I tell the officer who drops off a sobbing Emily. The officer walks over to me and doesn't utter a word. He just eyeballs me from head to toe with his dark goggles and mask on. He stares at me long and hard. I stare back at him just as hard.

He's a small officer of below-average height. His frame is scrawny and resembles that of a prepubescent teenager. The gun that he totes is almost bigger than he is. His S.W.A.T. uniform fits loosely. I guess that they don't come in junior sizes. If there's anyone who I can overtake and steal a gun from to get out of here, its him.

Finally, the staring contest stops, and he walks toward me. Slowly he squats down in front of my face and stares at me again as to intimidate me. I return the stare with a mean mug on my face and peer deep into his mask hoping to see the weak man underneath. However, I can't see inside of his dark goggles. I wonder what he sees as he looks at me. Sadly, probably a criminal.

I watch curiously as he begins removing the glove from his boney right hand. He takes his white ungloved index finger and sticks it deeply inside my bullet wound in the front of my shoulder. My flesh makes a squishy sound as he rotates his finger, penetrating further into my shoulder. I squeeze my eyes closed and moan in anguish while gritting my teeth. Finally, he takes his finger out of me. I open my eyes and begin panting. His finger is covered in blood from the knuckle to the tip. It drips blood, my blood, on the ground. With the same bloody finger, he places it on his metal helmet and marks it with blood. Two eyes and a smile. A bloody red smile now stares at me from the helmet.

"You'll live," he responds in a deep voice. He then pushes me in the forehead with his bloody finger before getting up to walk away, leaving what I presume is a bloody dot on my forehead.

"Are you okay?" asks Mac.

"No. I'm not. I'm shot, and my stomach is hurting again. This time worse than before. If I don't get some medical attention, I feel like I might die," I honestly respond.

"Hey, get this guy some help!" yells Mac at the officer as he continues to walk away. He doesn't turn around. He just puts his glove back on and returns to the group of officers. I, along with approximately twenty other suspects, watch as the cops separate the injured. They separate them into two groups. Hospital staff and suspects. EMS personnel begin to rush in from the broken windows where the cops entered. They come in two by two, carrying heavy medical bags and pushing in squeaky gurneys. Their footsteps pop as they stomp on pieces of shattered glass. The hospital staff is triaged first. There are about twenty injured staff.

Some are checked out in the cafeteria. Others are loaded onto gurneys and are quickly whisked away. The injured suspects are put in a separate corner. There's about fifteen of them. Some are laid on tables and handcuffed. While others are handcuffed and placed forcibly in chairs. I wish I was over there. Maybe I would have gotten help faster.

I look back over to the cafeteria area to check on Hope. Ann is feeding her now. I'm glad she's within the safe arms of Ann. She will protect her just as much I as I have. Dr. Baker is talking to the lead officer. They both look over in my direction. Dr. Baker points at me. The officer turns and looks. They continue to talk. Dr. Baker uses an assortment of hand gestures as he explains to the officer. The officer continues to look back and forth at me with a look of confusion. Finally, he gestures for one of the officers to come and get me. *Am I being saved?*

The officer who stuck his finger in me picks me up by my injured arm and escorts me over to the other officer and Dr. Baker. I walk, hunched over, to the lead officer. I'm in tremendous pain now. Not just in my arm, but in my stomach again. It churns like a washing machine. There's definitely a heavy load of colors in my stomach. The lead officer takes off his mask. He's a white man approximately in his early forties. He has a dingy goatee and shaggy brown hair.

"Hello, son. I'm S.W.A.T. Commander Freeman," he says in his southern twang. "This doctor here tells me that you're an innocent man and you need some medical attention. Is this true?"

"Yes, sir. Yes, it is."

"Well, how did you end up over there in the suspect area. You're dressed like one of the bad guys."

"I wish I could tell you, sir."

"Well, you better start explaining something if you want to get out of those cuffs and get out of here."

I want to explain, but where do I begin. There are so many emotions running through my mind. I don't have the strength or energy to explain anything. I. Am. Beat. *How can I sum up everything that I've been through in a few words? Can I even do that? Can I say enough that will convince him to make me a free man like his last name?* I open my mouth.

"He was kidnapped!" yells a familiar voice in the background. Out from the crowd comes Enrique. "He was kidnapped and forced and to do crazy things."

"Yeah, they made him choose a baby to kill," says a female staff member. "I don't know what I would have done if that were me."

"Me neither. I probably wouldn't have chosen," says a male staff member to her.

"Then, there may have been two dead babies," she responds.

"Well is that my fault if I didn't choose? I didn't kill them," he answers. They continue to argue back and forth.

"He saved a child," says one man.

"But he also killed a man," says another man.

"No, he didn't. That was Jack," says a woman.

"Who is Jack?" says the man. The entire staff begins to argue amongst themselves. They argue in pairs. They argue in groups. The commotion gets louder and louder. I'm not sure if all these arguments hurt or help me get out of this. At least I've started a discussion. However, no one has said for him to let me go.

"Hush! Everyone hush!" Ann yells. She commands the attention of everyone. They cease arguing.

"Commander Freeman. My name is Ann and let me tell you that my nephew here has done no wrong."

"Sir, is this your aunt?" asks Commander Freeman. I look at Ann, and she looks back at me with wide eyes. We both know that this is lie, but in order for me to get out of here, I must roll with whatever plan she has up her sleeve.

"Yes. That's my Auntie Ann. Every summer I would go to her house and she would fix me the best cinnamon pretzels."

"Okay. So, I'm assuming you want me to let him go."

"Yes. Not just because he's my nephew, but because he helped to save all our lives. There's a mad man in here that was going to kill us all. It looks like he may have escaped with all the commotion you and your men caused. He's the real bad guy. If it weren't for Daniel, there would be even more fatalities. He deserves to be celebrated as a hero and not treated as a criminal."

"I concur," says Dr. Baker.

"What do you all say? Do you all agree? If so, raise your hand," instructs Commander Freeman. Slowly, one by one, they each raise their hand. *One hand. Two hands. Five hands. Ten hands.* A sea of supportive hands is now raised in the air for me to be let go. Thank God.

"Well I don't know what you did here Daniel, but it looks like you have a lot of support here. I will make a note of that and we'll have to take down everyone's statement. However, until we do our investigation we have to keep you in custody. Now, what do you need medical attention for?"

"Well, as you can tell, I've been shot and I ..." my sentence cuts short as I begin to vomit on the commander. His shirt is covered with the undigested remnants from the Chipotle chicken bowl I consumed last night. They barely gave me a respectable scoop of meat and now it's all gone to waste.

"Oh, God!" says the commander.

"I'm sorry. I've got appendicitis. I'm not feeling too well."

The officer begins to wipe the vomit stains off of his clothes. The more he wipes the more it spreads over his uniform.

"Let's get him out of here before he throws up on me again. Officer take him outside and get him in an ambulance out of here. You ride with him to the hospital."

"I'm coming with him, too," says Ann.

"Ma'am you can't go with him," the commander tells her. Ann steps in front of him and me.

"I said I'm going with him, and the baby is coming, too. I have to make sure she is evaluated at the hospital as well for injuries," she repeats with sass. She locks eyes with him. Commander Freeman gives up and lets out a long sigh.

"Okay. You can go with your nephew, but you have stay with this officer. He will go with you wherever you go. You'll be transferred to Louisville General Hospital. That's where we've been transferring everyone."

Oh, shit! That's the hospital Lisa is at.

"Take him out the entrance we just came through, and put him in one of the empty ambulances. Now, get him out of here before he throws up on me again!"

The nameless officer grabs my arm again and escorts me out through the shattered window where the cops entered. There's a back door that we can easily walk through, but the officer makes sure my bare feet walk over the shattered glass. He's determined to make me suffer. Shards of glass penetrate the bottom of my feet. I grimace with each step. Finally, I go through the metal window frame and enter the outside world. We're in the courtyard dining area.

I look back as we walk at a hurried pace. My trail of bloody footprints covers the pavement. Ann follows, coddling Hope. *Protect her Ann. Protect her as if she's yours. I'm too injured and emotionally drained to protect her now.* Before I'm led up the outside stairs of the courtyard, I look back at Maestro's soldiers. I give them a head nod and they nod back in unison. The officer jerks my arm as he leads me to the street level. Bo runs by me and brushes against my leg. He's made it out alive. As I climb farther and farther up the stairs, the commotion above gets louder and louder. *What's going on up there?* Finally, I reach the top, and it's a sight to see.

It's dusk now. I've been trapped in the hospital almost all damn day. There are cop cars as far as the eye can see. Regular cop cars, as well as armored vehicles. Their blue and red lights flash wildly as the sirens blare. Helicopters fly loudly above. Cops and EMS personnel run around in a frenzy providing aid and escorting patients and staff out of the building.

To my right, I see Kenasauras plopped in a wheelchair parked on the sidewalk. He sips from an apple juice box and forces a few graham crackers into his mouth. I guess someone found a wheelchair for him. To my left, further ahead, is the group of the parents I saw in the nursery. They are huddled, talking to some officers. A few of the moms appear to be crying. I know it's been a long emotional day for them. I hope their babies are okay.

In the distance I see a few of the injured medical students being transported on gurneys toward an ambulance. I'm suddenly bumped by an object from behind. I turn to see Richard on a spine board being carried by two paramedics. He's still alive, but barely. April follows behind him with a look of concern. They pass us by. She doesn't even notice me. I'm invisible to her.

Each officer gives me a look of disgust as I pass by them in my handcuffs. I put my head down, not because of being ashamed or feeling guilty, but because I'm in an absurd amount of pain. I don't know what's going on in my stomach now, but it's not right. I need help. Finally, we reach the location of the EMS vehicles. There are approximately thirty of them. Paramedics load injured and sick people into each vehicle.

An ambulance with its doors wide open is tucked off in the corner. We head toward it. About thirty yards away from us, held back by large barricades, is the press. They flash cameras and record video. They yell inaudible questions. I'm fairly sure that as a young black man in handcuffs I will be portrayed incorrectly on the nightly news. *I'm famous now, Fat Steve.*

"I'm innocent!" I yell at them from a distance. They yell back even louder with microphones pointing at me. The officer opens the back doors. I step on the silver metal bumper and crouch my head before entering. I flop down on the gurney and lie all the way back. The batons in my backpack poke me on my backside as I lie back. Officer A-hole gets in behind me and shuts the doors of the ambulance. He sits beside me in the small leather chair. Forcibly, he pushes my upper back forward and reaches down toward my handcuffs. He uncuffs my hands.

"Thank you! Finally, some respect around here. I'm tired of being treated like a criminal." The officer pulls up the rail on the side of the gurney and handcuffs my right hand to it.

"I just can't win. I just can't fuckin' win today," I say in frustration. At least I have my left hand free. I wish I could use it to slap the shit out of this cop. I fake scratching my shoulder to test out my range of motion. I don't have enough range to slap him. He's too far. But if I did. *Slap slap!*

"Hey, you guys going to the hospital?" says the ambulance driver. I turn around to check him out. All I see is the back of his head and side of his face. He's a young white man with red hair sticking through the back of his baseball hat. I turn back around as Ann hop-s in the passenger seat next to him.

"Yeah. Let's get this thing moving," she says as she slams the door shut.

"Yes, ma'am! To Louisville General we go. I'm Chad by the way."

"No, time for introductions, Chad. Let's get out of here. We've got a sick patient in the back," Ann says while beating on the dashboard.

Chad hurriedly snaps in his seatbelt and throws the ambulance into reverse. He quickly shifts into drive and peels off. I jerk around on the gurney. Chad turns on the siren as we bail out of the parking lot through the back exit. I stare out the back window. Cameras continue to flash at us as we skirt away. I flop my head back and relax.

I'm finally getting out of here. After all this, I'm still alive. I can't believe it! My heart is still beating in my chest. My brain is still working. Yeah, I've been choked, kicked, and even shot, but I'm still alive! Who would have thought? I should be dead. Something or someone should have killed me by now, either the appendicitis,

Todd, Maestro, or Mary's crazy ass. They all had their chance, but didn't succeed. I must be built Ford tough.

"Aaaahhhhh," I groan aloud in agony as my stomach starts to hurt once again. I fold over and rub on my stomach. The pain is a ten out of ten now.

"You okay back there, sugar?" asks Ann. I vomit on myself. The officer sitting silently next to me looks down at me then returns to staring at the back doors.

"No!" I respond as vomit continues to spew from my mouth. Hope starts crying.

"Come on, Chad! Get us to the hospital," Ann demands. We merge onto the highway.

"Okay. Okay. I'm trying, but the roads are slippery. There's still ice on them. Let me turn on some music to calm everyone down." A long pause follows as Chad searches for something to play on his phone. Suddenly, a bass guitar plays through the vehicle's cheap speakers. It's a familiar song. One of my favorite songs. UGK's "One Day."

Well, well, well, well | Hello baby | For one day you're here and then you're gone. The intro sings. Hope stops crying. I guess she loves the song, as well. I lie back and begin laughing uncontrollably.

"What are you laughing at?" asks Chad.

"You're a white boy, playing UGK. That was not what I expected you to put on."

"Man, these guys are my favorite group of all time. Don't judge me just because I'm white. What am I supposed to be playing 'Boot Scootin' Boogie'?"

"Touché, Chad. Touché."

"Thank you. And I see the baby likes it, too," Chad speaks to Hope with in a baby voice. "Do you like UGK? Huh, do you? Are you trill? Are you a trill little baby?" Suddenly, the ambulance starts to skid. The officer reflexively grabs my handcuffed hand while we skid. Chad regains control of the vehicle.

"Quit talking and focus on the road, fool!" Ann tells Chad.

I look down at my hand now connected to the officer's hand. *Why is he holding my hand? The fear of being in a potential accident has ceased. He can let me go.*

"Um, you can let me go now," I inform him. He doesn't let me go. I attempt to pull my hand, but he squeezes it harder.

"When you hit me in the head with that object, Daniel that shit hurt. It hurt me inside and outside. I was like how could he do that? How could the man who loves me do that to me? I didn't know what to do. I didn't know how to react. So, I just ran away crying," says the familiar female voice under the mask.

"I bawled my eyes out in one of the empty patient rooms. By that point I had been through enough. I was ready to get out of the hospital. I had reached my peak. I was tired of getting picked on and being told that I was crazy. I know I'm not crazy. So, I planned my escape." She let's go of my hand and takes off her helmet, masks, and gloves. It's Mary. The asshole officer is Mary. She shakes her long hair and then puts it in her customary bun. She does a few stretches of her arms. I guess it's been hard staying in character.

"Mary! But how?" I question with a look of shock.

"After you assaulted me, I went back downstairs to where the bomb explosion occurred. I was hoping that the entrance would be partially open, but it wasn't. The entire ceiling was caved in. There was debris everywhere. There were a couple of dead cops on the ground. I took the uniform off of one of them who was missing a hand. I took his gun too. My plan was to act like I was a S.W.A.T. officer. I'd go to the ER, find some people who needed help and casually sneak out while helping evacuate them. So, I went to the ER. I heard a whole bunch of noise as I approached. I peaked in through a crack in one of the side doors. I saw you choking some guy. So, I turned around. Plan number one ruined.

"So, I devised another plan. I'd sneak out through the cafeteria. I knew that there was a back-patio entrance. I used to smoke back there sometimes when I was here. So, I went down to the cafeteria. I got there and the whole damn hospital was there. I forgot Maestro was bringing people down there. Plan number two ruined. As I was about to walkout, I heard Maestro and you about to walk in. Just like you, I couldn't win either. I hurried up and hid in the pizza area. Bo kept coming over there and licking me. He's such a friendly dog. He wouldn't dare hurt a soul. He just wants to play with everyone. I heard you guys entire conversation while I hid. Very interesting. Maestro's story was very interesting.

"After you all left and went into the sitting area, I watched and observed some more. There was a partial separation in the metal curtain and I could see and hear everything clearly. Your little speech was cute. You learned a lot. When the cops came in I saw that as the perfect opportunity to sneak in. I could blend in with the other officers inconspicuously as they rushed in. Surprisingly, it worked. I mixed in with them perfectly. No one even noticed."

"But, but your voice. You sounded like a man when you talked to me," I stutter.

"You'll live," says Mary repeating the statement in the same manly voice she'd used earlier after she stuck her finger into the wound in my shoulder. It's scary how easily she's able to switch from her sweet girly voice to a baritone manly voice. "Those acting and voice lessons I took as a child are finally starting to pay off. Mom would be proud. Daniel, what C word did I tell you not to call me?" Mary begins cracking her knuckles. I look at her with a look of terror with vomit residue on my shirt. This is a rhetorical question. I know the answer.

"Chinese?" I respond sarcastically.

Mary jumps on top of my lap and straddles my torso. She puts her small hands around my neck and starts choking me. I try to fight her off with my uncuffed hand, but I'm unable to. It's hard to fight her off with my non-dominant hand. I begin to struggle for air.

"You guys okay back there?" asks Chad.

"Yea. We're good. Just enjoying the music," Mary responds in her manly voice.

"That's what I like to hear," responds Chad.

Mary squeezes harder on my neck. I continue to try and push her off, but it's useless. My vision starts to get blurry. I'm feeling weak from my head to my toes. Unexpectedly, we hit a large pothole and the vehicle bounces up and down. Mary's grasps loosen. I take a big gasp of fresh air then punch her in the nose with all my might. Immediately, she lets me loose and grabs her nose.

"She's trying to kill me!" I yell in a raspy voice.

"What!?" yells Chad in response.

"This bitch is trying to kill me!" I repeat.

"Oh, hell no!" says Ann as she unbuckles her seatbelt. Mary picks up her gun from off the floor and shoots Chad in his back. The ambulance skids from left to right. Suddenly, we flip over. I'm pulled every which way. *To the back I go. To the front I go. To the back I go again. Then, side to side. Oh Lord, my black ass is about to die.*

The back doors of the ambulance open in the midst of us flipping. Mary tumbles toward the open back doors. I reach out to grab her before she sails out, but I'm unsuccessful. My hand barely grazes her fingertips as she is sucked out the back door like a vacuum. We continue to topple over and over on the icy road. Out goes Ann through the windshield. Somehow Hope flies back in my direction and stays in the cabin of the vehicle. We slowly stop rotating. The vehicle is now upside down. I smell smoke. My uninjured arm is pinned underneath the gurney. I can't move at all. I start to hear loud popping sounds. The ambulance is on fire.

I guess I spoke too soon that I was going to live. The end has come. I'm going to die in a burning ambulance, listening to UGK. This is not how I saw my life ending. I thought I would at least make it to 65. Have a couple of kids and then die from a heart attack in my sleep or something. But no. I'm going to die, burned alive along with a motherless child. What a way to die. Smoke begins to engulf the ambulance. I start coughing.

"Hey, is anyone in there?" a voice yell from outside.

"Is anyone in there?"

"Yes! I'm alive!" I respond with every last bit of energy I have left.

"Hey! Someone is still alive in here. Leave her alone. She's dead. Come help me pull him out."

All of a sudden, I hear the shuffling sound of someone crawling through the ambulance. The gurney is flipped off of me. My guardian angel grabs me by my backpack straps and drags me. My hand is still cuffed to the rail. However, during the chaos of the accident, the rail has detached from the gurney. I'm somewhat free.

I am finally pulled outside of the ambulance. I open my eyes and see a white figure dragging me to safety. *Is this really an angel or are my eyes tripping?* I get farther away from the burning vehicle. The figure stops dragging me.

"There's a baby in there," I whisper to the white figure.

"What did you say?" the man asks, leaning closer to me.

"There's a baby in there," I whisper in his ear. I am gassed. I have no energy left in me.

"Oh, God. You, come over here," he commands someone. "I told you she's dead. Look at her. I'm a doctor. Dr. Morrison. So, trust me. I know when someone is dead. Now, you watch him. He said there's a baby in the ambulance. I'm going to see if I find it." He takes off running. Another shadowy figure comes to my side and stares over me.

Did I hear that right? Did he just say Dr. Morrison? The doctor that Maestro has been looking for all day? He just saved my life, but it may be a life that's too late to save. I don't know what it feels like to die, but I feel like I'm doing it right now. I can feel my essence leaving my body. I'm losing the fight to keep my eyes open. They close. I pray to God I will open them again.

References

1. Mosby. *Mosby's Dictionary of Medicine, Nursing, & Healthy.* 7th. Philadelphia : Mosby Elsevier, 2006.

2. [Online] https://www.merriam-webster.com/dictionary/inflammation?src=search-dict-box.

3. Kumar, MBBS, MD, FRCPath, Vinay, et al. *Robbins and Cotran Pathologic Basis of Disease.* 8th. Philadelphia : Saunders Elsevier, 2010.

4. Jenkins, MD, Brian, et al. *Step-UP to USMLE Step 2 CK.* 3rd. s.l. : Lippincott Williams & Wilkins, 2014.

5. [Online] http://www.diabetes.org/diabetes-basics/statistics/.

6. [Online] www.afsp.org/about-suicide/suicide-statistics/.

7. [Online] www.cdc.gov/media/releases/2018/p0607-suicide-prevention.html.

8. *Neurotoxicology and Teratology.* Day, N. L., et al. 2, 1994, Vol. 16, pp. 169-175.

9. *Postnatal consequences of prenatal cocaine exposure and myocardial apoptosis: Does cocaine in utero imperil the adult heart?* Feng, Qingping. April 2005, British Journal of Pharmacology, pp. 887-888.

10. *Fetal Alcohol Syndrome and Fetal Alcohol Spectrum Disorders.* Denny, MD, Leeanne, Coles, MD, Sarah and Blitz, MD, Robin. Oct 2017, American Family Physician Journal, pp. 515-522A.

11. [Online] www.americanpregnancy.org/pregnancy-health/illegal-drugs-during-pregnancy/ .

12. *American Family Physician.* Lindsay, MD, Tammy and Vitrikas, MD, Kirsten. 5, March 2015, Evaluation and Treatment of Infertility, Vol. 91, pp. 308-314.

13. [Online] www.emedicine.medscape.com/article/1170097-overview?src=refgatesrc1#a5.

14. [Online] www.merriam-webster.com/dictionary/cancer.

BOOK CHECKLIST

LAUGHED	☐
CRIED/ GOT EMOTIONAL	☐
LEARNED SOMETHING	☐
RELATED TO A CHARACTER OR SITUATION	☐
PURCHASED MERCHANDISE	☐
MET THE AUTHOR	☐

PLACE A CHECK MARK IN THE EMPTY BOX REGARDING EACH ITEM. THEN, WRITE SOMETHING IN REGARD TO THE TOPIC IN THE SPACE ALLOTED. I HOPE THAT YOU ARE ABLE TO MEET ME. I WILL CHECK THE LAST BOX FOR YOU! SHARE YOUR COMPLETED BOXES ON SOCIAL MEDIA AND TAG ME AND USE THE HASHTAG #APPENDICITISTHENOVEL!

58902682R00214

Made in the USA
Columbia, SC
28 May 2019